PRAISE FOR

JOHNNY BOY

"From the first few pages of this fantastic book, I felt I understood the main character's personality and the dynamics of this family. Every character has been created with the utmost care. The dialogue is especially strong and the narrative is extremely visual. I was swept into the 1950s and '60s Italian/American New York. This is an exceptional story about complex family relationships and the battle for authority. This novel truly evoked strong emotions as I read it. I was sad to finish this book. I wanted to know about the next chapter in Johnny's life. I hope the author writes a sequel. An exceptional story from a very talented author."
— 5 Stars, Readers' Favorite

"Califano's prose delivers the realism of a memoir ... the author's descriptions bring a feeling of immediacy to each scene. The emotions behind (Johnny's) relationship with his parents, which range from love and admiration to fear and disgust, are heartbreakingly authentic. Keen writing illuminates a collection of striking memories."
— Kirkus Review

"Fiction can serve many storytelling purposes. But it is notably impressive when it manages to uncannily replicate real life in ways that are powerfully resonant with how people actually talk, act, feel and live. And author John Califano does just that with impressive success in JOHNNY BOY."
— IndieReader

JOHNNY BOY is truly outstanding—that exceedingly rare kind of book so gorgeously written, powerful and authentic in its details, it flies high above most fiction and hits right at the core of what it's like to be a sensitive kid growing up in a chaotic place—in this case, Brooklyn, NY, circa the '60s. I have never been to Brooklyn, but since reading John Califano's semi-autobiographical novel, I feel I know the area intimately. This vivid realism extends into Califano's superbly crafted characters as well, including minor characters, who each manage to show a sense of who they are and linger long after the story ends. Reading Johnny Boy is to step into a time machine and the mind of intelligent Johnny Caruso as he comes of age in his unique yet quintessentially Italian American family, along with the beautiful highs and crushing lows his journey into adulthood brings—and Califano ensures we feel deeply each peak and trough. It's an exquisite experience. This is literary fiction at the highest level.
— Philip Elliott, Editor-In-Chief, Into the Void

"JOHNNY BOY is an engrossing, tightly written fictional account that reads like a fantastic (albeit heartbreaking at times) memoir. The characters are exceptionally well developed and we're given an immediate sense of who they are even through the eyes of a three-year-old. Califano writes with a realism that is not so easy to find these days, and the dynamic of the family comes to life through dialogue that you can actually hear being played out in front of you. For all the damage they cause each other and their own children, Bellisario and Marie feel the most like flesh and blood, and it's hard not to feel sorry for them also—victims themselves of their time and circumstances. I genuinely loved this book and think it's an excellent read for anyone in the mood for a taste of mid-century Brooklyn through the window of an Italian family."
— 5 Stars, Readers' Favorite

"Califano conjures (characters) with the skill of a master storyteller. He has an ear for voices and dialects that add a layer of realism to these imagined characters. Not a word is out of place in the mouths of each Caruso kid as their hopes, fears, and frustrations are released in every argument and conversation. Each encounter propels the story forward as Johnny careens in and out of potential destructive pathways.
The family conflict leaves the fate of Johnny uncertain as he moves through junior high into high school and compels the reader to keep turning pages."
— U.S. Review of Books (Rating: Recommended)

"A compelling work of fiction bearing the authentic voice of a memoir, JOHNNY BOY by John Califano is a visceral slice of life from a skilled, but subtle pen. Narrating through the eyes and mindset of a young boy can often come across as overly sentimental, but Califano artfully captures the innocence of childhood—and the savage loss of it. This vulnerable account of growing up makes for excellent, heartfelt reading, and Califano shows abundant skill in this debut novel."

— 4 Stars, Self-Publishing Review

"JOHNNY BOY is a quick read. The author creates vivid childhood scenes that are gripping. I loved the depth of character and followed the development of the protagonist with keen interest. The prose is beautiful and highly descriptive and the narrative remains real and gripping. It is a story with powerful lessons, well told, and with scenes that will resonate with many readers."

— 5 Stars, Readers' Favorite

JOHNNY BOY

John Califano

Verve House Books

JOHNNY BOY
Copyright © 2021 by John Califano

For information visit:
http://www.johncalifano.com

ISBN: 978-1-7372961-0-2
First Edition: 2021
10 9 8 7 6 5 4 3 2 1

Cover design: Verve House Books & Evan Stein

To my older siblings Vivian and Jesse

"It is not our parents' loins, so much as our parents' lives, that enthralls and blinds us."
—Thomas Traherne, c. 1672

"The supreme law [of life] is this: the sense of worth of the self shall not be allowed to be diminished."
—Alfred Adler, 1946

alone
in my mother's womb
piglet with no siblings
I still
in the dark of my room
can toss
and turn
and hear
her moan

New York City, Spring 2021

ONE

WE LIVED IN the depths of Brooklyn on the top floor of a two-family house not far from Coney Island. There were five of us in the Caruso family: my father Bellisario, my mother Maria, my older siblings Frank and Connie, and me. Frank was nine years older than I was, and Connie six years older. It seemed like whenever Connie and I were together, we held hands.

"Take your brother to the store with you," my mother would say, "and make sure you *hold his hand.*"

When I was around three, Connie and I sat huddled on a wooden chair in our pajamas, watching Frank trying to light a match in front of a clunky old stove in an attempt to bring some warmth into the kitchen.

"Frankie, be careful," Connie said.

"Will you please *shut up?*"

My brother looked determined. A clump of brown hair swayed in front of his eyes as he tried to ignite the match. After several attempts, the matchstick snapped. He tossed it into the sink and reached inside the box for another.

"Remember what Daddy said about playing with the stove," Connie said.

"I don't care what Daddy said. It's freezing in here. The whole apartment is freezing."

"I'm cold," I said.

My sister slid me onto her lap, where I sat with my legs wrapped around her waist and my nose pressed against her plump cheek. It felt good to be so close to her. Her skin smelled sweet, and her eyes sparkled beneath the dark bangs that fell halfway down her forehead.

"Uh-oh." Connie wrinkled her nose and sniffed a few times. "I think I smell something."

Frank ignored her. After a few more attempts, the match head flared into an orange flame.

"Okay, here we go," he said, leaning over, carefully extending the match toward the oven. "Now we can get some heat in this place."

The instant Frank's hand came near the stove there was a loud *boom* and a massive purple blaze burst out of the oven. Several pots that lined the shelf above the stove toppled onto the floor.

Connie screamed, and I began to cry. I wrapped my arms around Connie's neck, drawing her closer.

"*Shit.*" Frank rubbed his eyes with his palms.

"Frankie!" Connie shouted. "Are you okay?"

"Dammit! My eyebrows!"

"Daddy's gonna kill us," Connie said.

"*Shit. Shit. Shit.*" Frank shook his head.

My parents rushed into the room. "What the hell happened?" my father said, tying the belt of his bathrobe.

"I was trying to get some heat going," said Frank, unfazed.

"What? What heat?"

"From the oven. This place is like an icebox. We're freezing our asses off."

"What are you, *stupid?*" My father slapped the back of Frank's head. "Wha'd I tell ya, huh? Wha'd I tell ya?"

"Bill, *stop*," my mother said. "You're gonna hurt him."

"Hurt him? I'll hurt him. I'll knock his *block off.*"

I felt a twinge in my belly, and warm pee trickled down my leg.

My father checked the knobs on the stove, turning them in different directions. "Didn't I tell you not to play with the oven? You're lucky you didn't blow up the whole goddamn house. The last thing I need is to get evicted because you have your head up your ass."

Someone pounded on the back door adjacent to the kitchen.

"*Shit.* The landlord—just what the hell I need." My father glared at Frank.

My mother opened the door, and a bald, heavyset man rushed into the kitchen. "What the hell are you people doin' up here?"

"I'm sorry, Mr. Kempt," my father said, "but as you can see, we, ahh ... we had a little accident."

"*Accident?* What kind of accident? My wife thought a bomb went off. She and the dog are scared to death."

"I'm sorry about that. It seems my son here was having a little trouble with the stove. He went to light the oven and didn't realize—"

"What, *again* with the stove? First he clogged the toilet with newspaper, then he left the pot on the burner and almost set the place on fire, and now *this*. Listen, Caruso, if you can't control your kids, I'm gonna have to ask you people to leave."

"I know, Mr. Kempt, I know." My father wrung his

hands. "Again, I'm very sorry. I promise it won't happen again."

Mr. Kempt marched to the stove and examined the inside of the oven. He surveyed the mess of pots and lids scattered on the floor, shaking his head. "Jesus Christ," he said. "I should have my head examined." After Mr. Kempt left, my father continued to berate Frank.

"You happy now? The son of a bitch is ready to throw us out of here."

"All right, Bill, go easy, will ya?" my mother said. "He didn't mean it. For Chrissakes, he's just a kid."

"I'm not a kid," Frank said.

"He's just a kid, just a kid," my father said, mimicking my mother. "He's old enough to know better! He's gotta learn some responsibility. And he can't do it when he's got you protecting him all the time. Right?" He faced Frank. "What are you, a mamma's boy? You need your mamma to protect you?"

Frank gazed at the floor, rubbing his head.

My father slammed the oven door shut with his foot. "*Vafangoooool.* Get the hell out of my sight." He nodded toward the door. As Frank passed, my father whacked his head again. "*Stunad.*"

My mother stopped Frank and examined his face. "Look, Bill. His eyebrows are singed."

"That's what he gets for being stupid."

"Let me put something on that." My mother touched Frank's forehead.

"Hey, mamma's boy, your mamma's calling you."

Frank leaned away from my mother. "Leave me alone."

"What are you, a sissy?" my father said.

"Go put some cold water on it, honey."

"Ma, I don't need anything. Would you leave me *alone*?" Frank stormed out of the room.

"How's Janoots? Is he okay?" My mother reached over and lifted me into her arms. Sharp lines creased her forehead, her hands tensed against my body. "Aw, shoot. Look at this. He's all wet. Why didn't you tell me?" she asked Connie.

"*Me*? What did I do?"

"I told you to keep an eye on your brother. I swear"—turning to my father—"you can't leave them alone for two seconds."

"I didn't do *anything*!" Connie cried.

"All right, go to your room!" My mother's face twisted with disgust.

"Oh boy." Connie stomped out of the kitchen. "I get blamed for *everything* around here."

"Look at you," my mother said, eyeing my wet pajamas.

I stretched my arms in the direction of my brother and sister, wanting to be with them. I didn't understand why my parents were so angry, but I thought it was because of something I had done.

My father bought a used, streamlined, four-door Hudson that my five-year-old brain saw as a big turtle with headlights. The car constantly gave him trouble; every other time he turned the key, the thing wouldn't start. It wheezed and sputtered, and we'd all sit in silence, wondering if the car had finally dropped dead.

"Well, I guess you got what you paid for," my mother once commented in her *I told you so* voice.

"C'mon, honey," my father said, repeatedly turning the key while pumping the gas pedal. "*Talk* to me. *Talk* to me." When he finally got the car started, he leaned toward my mother and gave her a flurry of loud kisses inches from her face. "Ya see?" He smiled. "It's not what'cha say. It's *how* ya say it."

Some weekends my father would take me for a ride, always on the spur of the moment. "Okay, buddy." He'd clap his hands with excitement. "Let's go—just me and you."

Part of the fun was that I never knew where we were going. I'd hop in the car, and we'd drive around Brooklyn, each time visiting different places—Coney Island, Prospect Park, Sheepshead Bay. Once we took the ferry from Brooklyn to Staten Island. From there, we caught another ferry to lower Manhattan, where we ate in Chinatown and he read my fortunes. That was the most fun. I cracked open a few cookies with my fist and handed the small slips of paper to my father. He read the inscriptions on each of them in a deep, mysterious voice. "*A journey of a thousand miles begins with the first step.*" "*All good things come to those who wait.*"

I handed him the last fortune, and his face darkened. "Oh boy," he said, "this one doesn't look too good."

"What's it say?"

"You sure you wanna know?"

I hesitated, then nodded.

My father put his arm around me. "It say you *very ticklish!*" He tossed the fortune over his shoulder and wiggled his fingers, tickling my stomach and underarms. I couldn't stop laughing.

Later that afternoon we drove over the Manhattan Bridge on our way home; the hum of the tires against the cement filled my ears. We rode around Brooklyn for about ten minutes and wound up on a bleak cobblestone street not far from the cluster of dreary warehouses that surrounded the Brooklyn Navy Yard. My father drove slowly, glancing at the row of brown-brick tenements that lined the block. He stopped in front of a run-down, three-story apartment house.

"Son of a bitch. I can't believe it's still here."

On one side of the building was an abandoned diner, on the other an empty lot littered with mounds of garbage and a burnt-out car. My father rolled down his window. "See that building? That's where Daddy lived when my family came to America. We lived right up there on the second floor," he said, pointing. "I shared the small room on the right with four of my brothers."

I was excited to learn this. I climbed over my father's leg for a better look at the three dust-covered windows on the second floor. "Where did you come from?"

"We came from Italy. When I was around your age, my family moved to America. There were twelve of us, and we crossed the ocean on a big ship." He dipped his hand in a wavelike motion.

"How come?"

"How come what?"

"How come you moved from Italy?"

"My papa was looking for a better life. He worked hard, sometimes eighteen hours a day. He saved his money so he could come to New York."

As my father spoke, his eyes widened and his voice had a childlike innocence. Listening to him was almost like listening to another kid.

"Your grandpa owned a grocery store called Caruso's Italian-American Market." He framed his hands in front of him as if around an invisible sign. "It was one of the biggest Italian stores in Brooklyn."

"Can we go see it?"

"It's long gone." He smiled sadly. "It closed many years ago."

My father rarely discussed his childhood. I later learned that my grandfather had managed the store poorly. A few years after opening, Caruso's Italian-American Market went bankrupt, leaving the family near penniless on the cusp of the Great Depression. At one point the situation became untenable. Grandpa Giovanni could no longer feed his family, and the Children's Aid Society intervened.

Two of my father's sisters died of pneumonia, and the remaining Caruso siblings were farmed out to different homes out of state. My father and his brothers and sisters were away for nearly three years before they returned home. The episode created much division and mistrust in the family; all the Caruso brothers and sisters had felt abandoned. Grandpa Giovanni, the hardworking entrepreneur who had once shepherded his family across a vast ocean to the land of hopes and dreams, was no longer the strong, unshakeable *padrone* managing the family's affairs.

When the Caruso children returned to Brooklyn, most were in their early and late teens. My father and his brothers worked long hours in factories to help support the family and put food on the table, a necessity that fueled lasting resentment among the siblings—half of them moved away from New York when they were old enough to live on their own.

"We used to call ourselves the twelve apostles," my father said, chuckling. "We were always together, having fun. We all got along and loved each other."

"Where is Grandpa now? Is he in Italy?"

"No." My father forced a sad expression. "He died before you were born. You would have loved him. He was a good man. That's why I named you after him, so you'll always remember him."

"Was he smart?"

"Oooh." My father leaned away, as if overwhelmed by the notion. "He was *very* smart. Papa knew about everything. He was a mechanic, a farmer; he knew about cows and horses; he made his own wine; he made his own cheese; he was a businessman, a carpenter who knew how to build houses and barns. He taught me everything he knew, and I'll teach you someday, so you can be smart just like him."

I thought about all the things my father had learned, but I couldn't picture him making his own cheese or working with horses and cows, let alone building a house or a barn.

"Yeah, Papa taught all of us." My father nodded. "He taught us everything … everything." His voice had changed, and his eyes grew distant. He was looking right at me, but his face glazed over with a frozen, angry stare.

"Where are they?" I said.

"Huh?"

"Your other brothers and sisters."

"They're around. They just don't live nearby."

"How come we never see them?"

"Whaddaya, writin' a book?" he said, ending the conversation.

As we drove away, I caught a last glimpse of my father's childhood dwelling. I was thinking that the building held secrets my father wasn't telling me. An elderly woman wearing a black headscarf appeared and popped her head out of the doorway. As if to check for rain, she looked up at the sky and extended her hand into the warm spring air, then disappeared back into the shadows.

TWO

MY FATHER WAS meticulous about his appearance and always left for work wearing a pressed suit and a starched white shirt, his tie knotted perfectly. He carried a leather briefcase filled with technical books, mechanical pencils, a slide rule, and differently shaped drawing angles. He told me he was a scientist and often brought home glossy photographs of rockets and jet fighters. "See those babies?" he'd say. "Your daddy designed that whole wing system."

In his twenties, my father had worked with his older brother Joseph ("Big Joe") as a machinist in a tool-and-die shop. After a few years of working a drill press, he decided to go into business for himself. With meager savings and money borrowed from his brothers, he bought a warehouse shipment of bumper jacks that he planned to sell to local gas stations and body shops. He convinced everyone that the jacks were a sure thing and that he and his brothers would make a killing once the business got rolling. It all sounded great, except for one unanticipated glitch: the jacks—as it turned out—were defective, and my father lost everything and wound up selling pots and pans door to door. While working odd jobs, he managed to take some night courses in engineering at Cooper Union. One of my mother's cousins taught him mechanical drawing and helped him get work as a draftsman, mainly for aircraft companies. Most of his jobs were out of town: he'd sign on for six-to-eight-week assignments in places like Binghamton and Poughkeepsie.

When he left for work on Sunday evenings, I was mostly happy to see him leave, taking with him all the tension that filled the house when he was home. But when he returned on Friday evenings, all would be forgotten and I'd be happy to see him, mostly because he'd greet me with open arms and a big smile, as if we hadn't seen each other in months. Even if I wasn't happy to see him, I would pretend I was, because I knew that was what he expected of me.

Sometimes his homecomings weren't so jubilant. On a number of weekends, he walked through the door exhausted and pissed, ranting to my mother about what a jackass his boss was or how *he* knew what he was talking about but other people weren't listening to him. "I know, Daddy, I know," my mother would say, trying to calm him.

When he was in one of these moods, he'd wash his hands and head straight for the liquor cabinet. He'd put away three or four scotch highballs and start knocking things around. ("Look at this house. It's *a mess!*")

One Friday night, my father came home in an unusually good mood. "Where's my little Janoots?" he said. "I got something special for him."

His eyes were glassy, and his breath reeked of alcohol. I cautiously followed him into his bedroom, where he handed me a cardboard tube, the kind that held his blueprints.

"What is it?"

"Well, let's take a look." He slipped a roll of paper from the tube.

"Wow!"

It was a treasure map, hand-drawn and filled with sketches and illustrations in various colors, all surrounded by a detailed border with fancy swoops and curlicues like a carved picture frame.

"See what that says?" He indicated the Old English lettering at the top of the map. "It says 'Treasure Map to Success.'"

Below that was a group of kidney-shaped islands connected by dotted lines, surrounded by a blue ocean that he'd labeled the Sea of Success. In the upper right-hand corner, he'd drawn an elaborate black-and-red compass with arrows pointing in the cardinal directions. At the bottom he'd sketched a skull and crossbones with dark holes for eyes.

"Wanna go on a treasure hunt?" he said, rubbing the back of his hand across his mouth.

"Yeah!"

We started at the bottom of the map where two swords with thick, shiny blades crisscrossed under the words *Start Here*. Near that, a pirate ship with three wind-filled sails followed a dotted line to the first island, marked "Elementary School." There was a small red schoolhouse on the island, with a bunch of musical notes drifting out of the window along with some numbers and letters.

"Ya see? This is where you learn your ABCs. Do you know your ABCs yet?"

"A B C G D B E ..."

"Boy, are you smart. Lemme see now. How old are you?"

"I'm almost six."

"*Six*? Wow. How'd you get to be so smart?"

"I don't know."

"You must take after your old man." He patted the top of my head. His touch felt heavy, and I leaned away to avoid getting thumped again with the back of his ring.

"Okay, *matey!*" he bellowed, turning back to the map. "Let's see what's on yonder horizon." He placed his finger on another pirate ship that looked just like the first. It followed another dotted line across the sea to the next island, marked "Junior High School." This island was bigger than the last and displayed a picture of a boy writing at a desk.

"What's he writing?" I asked.

"He's studying his English. Very, very important." He tapped the side of his head with his finger. "English and math, those are your two most important subjects." He paused for a moment, nodding and blinking as if reminding himself. "I betcha didn't know, but when Daddy came to this country, he didn't speak English."

"Wha'ja speak?"

"We spoke Italian. I wanted to go to school to learn English and math so I could get ahead, but most of the time I hadda work in my father's store, slicing cheese and mopping floors. But I knew ... knew I was too smart for that. When I was in school, I kept my mouth shut and my ears open and listened to my teachers. Don't ever forget." He shook a finger. "English and math. When you got those under your belt, you can go anywhere."

"What's next?" I turned back to the map.

My father continued tracing the dotted line to the next, even larger island, named "High School." In the middle of the island, he'd drawn an imposing brick building with half a dozen rectangular windows. A winding path led to two oversized front doors. An American flag hung on a pole above the building, waving proudly in the wind.

"Okay," my father said, and belched. "Now we made it to high school." He placed a finger on the pathway leading to the front doors. "This is where you need to study hard so you can go to college. A lot of wise guys think they can get to the buried treasure without finishing high school. Then they end up breaking their backs instead of using their brains, like your Uncle Joe and Uncle Sally Boy."

"Did Uncle Joe and Uncle Sally Boy finish high school?"

"Forget them." He smirked. "You don't wanna be like them. You listen to me."

My father often had negative things to say about his brothers. Rather than close relatives, I got the feeling that he thought of them as outsiders. He sometimes referred to them as *cafones*: uncultured, old-country peasants who hadn't quite adapted to America as he had. For me, this was both confusing and unsettling. In my eyes, Big Joe and Sally Boy were hardworking, down-to-earth guys who had always been nice to me. Hearing my father talk about his brothers like they were inferior made me think I shouldn't like them.

"Okay, skipper," my father called out, cupping a hand around the side of his mouth. "Batten down the hatches; I sees me some rough weather ahead!"

He moved his finger along the dotted line, following the course of a fourth ship through the rough waves that he'd sketched in the Sea of Success. As he did this, he made a noise that sounded like howling wind. "Thar she blows!" he hollered, his finger approaching the next island. On it was a picture of a graduation cap and a diploma neatly rolled up and tied with a ribbon. Just above that, the word *College* was printed in big letters.

"College," my father said. "*Bingo. We made it.*"

"We *made it!*" I blurted. I was swept up in my father's excitement but had no idea what college was outside of a destination on the map.

"College is the place you go after you finish high school," my father said, pointing to the diploma. "If you don't go to college, you can't get to the buried treasure."

"Did you go to college?"

"Yeah, but I had to go at night. During the day I worked two or three jobs to help support the family. I had to study long, long hours in the library just so I could keep up. Reading, reading, always reading." He snapped his fingers. "I read anything I could get my hands on. Sometimes I'd be reading and studying so hard, I'd fall asleep right there in the library. A coupla times the guard had to wake me up. 'Excuse me, Mr. Caruso,'" he said, lowering his voice to a respectful tone, "'but the library is closing now.'"

As I listened, I imagined my father sitting at a big desk stacked with books, grabbing them one by one and reading them as fast as he could. Then I pictured myself doing the same thing, only I was *devouring* the books, reading them twice as fast, flinging them over my shoulder after I finished each volume.

I looked up and caught my father smiling at me. "Am I gonna go to college?" I asked.

"Don't you want to get the buried treasure?"

"Yeah, but how do you get it?" I fidgeted with the bottom of my T-shirt.

"Well, you gotta get a career." My father put his finger back on the dotted line and followed the fifth ship to

"Career Island," the last island on the map. "Ya see?"

On this island a man peered into a microscope, his head surrounded by a halo of red stars and green dollar signs. In the middle of the island a small door, made of graph paper and bearing a thick black *X*, was taped to the drawing.

"What's a career?"

"A career is what you do after college. You become a doctor, lawyer, scientist … anything you want. That's when you find the buried treasure." He tapped the *X* with the tips of his fingers.

I reached over and pulled back the little paper door, exposing a small magazine photo of a treasure chest overflowing with diamonds, pearls, and gold coins. Just above that a small pocket contained a five-dollar bill, folded up and neatly tucked inside.

"Holy cow!" My eyes widened. "The *buried treasure!*" I plucked the bill from the pocket and waved it in the air.

"You found it," my father said, pinching my cheek.

Five dollars—it was all the money in the world. I could go out and buy gum, candy, and a million baseball cards.

"Lemme see whatcha got there." My father held out his hand and flapped his fingers, motioning for me to give him the money.

"Can't I keep it?"

"Yeah, but … not now." He pulled the bill from my hand and stuffed it in his shirt pocket. "Daddy's gonna save it for you for when you get older."

"But why can't I keep it? I found it. I found the buried treasure."

My father didn't answer, he just stood staring at me

with a strange, sad look on his face. I felt cheated. The bond of trust I had for him had suddenly been swallowed up and washed away as if I were hit by a tidal wave. I turned back to the map. All the lines and pictures were a blur. I imagined I was on the ship, fighting the waves to find the buried treasure. I reached out and gently passed my fingertips over the picture of the treasure chest. From behind, my father wrapped his arms around me. He squeezed my body tight and kissed my face. His breath was warm and heavy, and my nostrils filled with the smell of tobacco and alcohol.

"Do you love me?" His voice cracked with sadness, as if he were asking for forgiveness.

I hesitated, then nodded.

"Huh?" He sniffled, squeezing me tighter. The stubble on his chin pressed hard into my cheek. "Do you love Daddy?" Tears dripped from his face onto the back of my neck.

I nodded again.

"Say it for me. Tell Daddy you love him."

His breathing became heavier. I tried to move away, but he pinned my arms to my sides. His body shuddered as another tear hit my neck, and panic swelled inside me. Seeing and hearing my father cry scared me. I wasn't sure what he wanted from me and was terrified of giving him the wrong answer. "I love you, Daddy," I said.

"Oh God …" he moaned, kissing me again and again.

I swallowed and stood still, letting my body relax in his grip. Part of my face was squished against his chest, but out of the corner of one eye I could see the map and the Sea of Success. My eye followed the dotted line from island to island, all the way to the buried treasure.

THREE

SUNDAYS WERE ALL-DAY productions. In the morning my father took Frank, Connie, and me to the nine o'clock Mass at Saint Fingar while my mother stayed home and prepared the dinner she always started on Saturday nights when she "put up" the tomato sauce, which everyone referred to as "the gravy."

One Sunday was my grandmother Angelina's birthday. My father had been talking about it all week. "This is Grandma's seventy-fifth, and I want to make it real special for her. I ordered a nice big Zuppa Inglese, with candles and everything."

Grandma Angelina arrived with Uncle Joe and sat on the beige, high-backed couch in the living room. The couch was positioned between two matching end tables that supported matching lamps with huge decorative shades. An oil painting of Napoleon hung on the wall behind the couch, one of my father's prized possessions. Napoleon was standing in the foreground near a shoreline, one foot resting on a beached log, one hand tucked inside his dress coat, decked out with ribbons and medals. In the background, the sun peeked through gray clouds, shining down on an armada of war ships with wind-filled sails on a dark-blue sea. On either side of the painting, two porcelain plates hung on the wall, one a mask of comedy, the other tragedy, each with flowing ribbons attached to their sides.

"Bellisario! Bellisario!" Grandma called out for my father in a rickety voice as he entered the room to greet her. Arms stretched, she leaned forward and held his head in her hands, kissing his cheeks one after the other. My father did the same, both of them making cooing sounds and speaking in Italian after each kiss, a ritual they performed every time she came to visit. Rather than greeting each other, they seemed to be saying goodbye forever.

After a moment or two she caught my eye. "*Janoots! Janoots!*" she called to me, waving her arms and wiggling her fingers to beckon me closer. "*Veniqua! Veniqua!*"

"Did you say hello to Grandma and kiss her happy birthday?" my father asked, nudging me from behind.

Grandma Angelina was a short, wide, hard-faced woman with wrinkled cheeks and breasts that hung halfway to her stomach. Her head was sparsely covered with brittle, silver-gray hair, and dark eyes glittered under her tangled brows.

I hated when she came to visit; she always treated me to the same creepy reception. The second I was within reach, she pulled me close and smothered me in her arms, kissing and slobbering my face and neck like an old bulldog in heat.

"Nice-a-boy ... nice-a-boy," she said, sticking her hand down the back of my pants, affectionately rubbing my bare ass as if it were a magic lantern. Her warm body gave off a musty odor, and I couldn't wait to get free of her clutches. I quickly planted a kiss on her damp forehead and pried myself from her arms.

"Did you say happy birthday?" my father asked.

"Happy birthday, Grandma," I said, and skipped away.

"Janoots! Veniqua!"

Near the dining room, I ran into Uncle Joe; it was like running into an oak tree. Tall and husky, Joe had a huge head and a pockmarked face. He wore a gigantic gold pinky ring and always had a toothpick in his mouth, which he frequently shifted from side to side with his tongue.

"How's my little Johnny Boy?" He crouched down, catching me in his arms. A lit cigarette hung from his lips, opposite the toothpick.

Joe worked as a machinist in a factory. Sometimes he'd pick me up and carry me on his shoulders or whirl me around by my arms. He often brought me gifts. Once he gave me a set of shiny, marble-size ball bearings that he'd made at work. Another time he brought me some foreign coins and told me that the writing on the back of them was a secret message.

"Awright—let's see whatcha got," he said, holding both hands out in front of him, his palms facing me like two punching bags.

I whacked his hands as hard as I could. They felt like rocks.

"Attaboy," he said, squinting from the smoke trailing up into his face. "Now jab. Jab."

I loved sparring with Uncle Joe. I felt like Rocky Marciano. I took a few more swings, and every so often he curled his huge, banana-like fingers into fists and gently tapped my chin. "Okay now—watch ya guard ... watch ya guard." He lifted my arm, positioning it in front of my face.

"Whaddaya teaching the kid?" a voice said from

behind me. It was Aunt Rose, the wife of Uncle "Sally Boy," my father's youngest brother. I could smell her from a mile away; she always doused herself with the same heavy perfume.

"Kid's got some wallop," Uncle Joe said.

"Hey, Johnny Boy," said Uncle Sally Boy, patting my face. His hands were rough from years of pulling ropes and lifting crates at the Brooklyn Navy Yard. "This guy givin' you trouble?"

"Wanna see my jab?" I poked Big Joe's palms a few more times, and he slowly rose to his feet.

"Awright, champ," he said, brushing ashes from his pants. "No more boxing for today."

Uncle Sally Boy moved in closer to his brother. He looked agitated. "We gotta talk," he said in a lowered voice.

"Che succede?"

"Nothin' ..." He shrugged. "It's just that, you know ... we gotta talk."

Joe took a long crackling drag from his cigarette. "Awright." He spit a piece of tobacco from his lips, his nostrils exhaling long streams of white smoke. "Talk. I'm right here."

There was an awkward silence. Uncle Sally Boy glanced down at me and then looked back at Uncle Joe. He started speaking Italian. I couldn't understand a word, but I could tell he was pissed. Every so often he would gesture, flicking the tips of his fingers off the bottom of his chin. I craned my head all the way back, checking out his face. Sally Boy was lean, with angular cheeks and watchful eyes. He didn't look anything like Joe or my father, who were both heavyset and broad-chested.

"I mean, that ain't right," Aunt Rose interrupted, adjusting the charm bracelet dangling around her wrist. "Like what a' we, all a buncha *idiots*?"

I always thought of Aunt Rose as stylish. Unlike my mother, who was comfortable in a plain housedress with little or no makeup, Aunt Rose wore colorful blouses and tight skirts that made her nylons rub together with a loud shushing sound whenever she walked or shifted her weight. She had fiery eyes and jet-black hair pulled tight around the sides of her head and knotted in the back, where it fanned out into a bushy ponytail. Once I overheard my mother talking about Aunt Rose on the phone. "Well," she said, "I guess we know who cracks the whip in *that* family."

"Naw, I'm sorry … I'm sorry," Uncle Sally Boy said, shaking his head. "This is bullshit. And we're suppose ta be *family* here?"

Big Joe cupped the bottom of my chin and drew me closer. "Awright," he said. "We'll talk later."

I wasn't sure what they'd been talking about, but I had a feeling it was my father. Sometimes when they came to visit with Uncle Rocco, my father's other brother, who lived in the Bronx, they would all argue about the care of Grandma Angelina. Whenever my father and his brothers locked horns about their mother, my father would press a hand against his chest and ask, "And what do you want from *my* life?"

ൿ

Later on, my grandmother watched fervently as my father sang and played his violin, something he liked to do on special occasions. He belted out his favorite song, "Darktown

Strutters' Ball": "*I'll be down to get'cha in a wheelbarrow,
honey. Pick you up 'bout half past eight. Now, honey, don't
be late. I wanna be there when the band starts playin'…*"

He sang one verse in English and the next in Italian.
As he crooned, my grandmother wiped tears from her eyes
with a small lace handkerchief that she kept tucked between
her breasts.

"Why is she crying?" I asked Aunt Rose.

"I don't know. I think she's just happy."

"How come? I don't cry when I'm happy."

"What can I tell ya?" Aunt Rose shrugged, wiping
excess lipstick from the corners of her mouth with a tissue.
"Everybody's different."

My father sang a few songs in Italian, swaying his
body in time with the music as he played. The tunes were
upbeat, and his violin had a distinct high-pitched, almost
scratchy tone. Occasionally he leaned forward, dipping the
violin close to his mother's body. Every time he did that, she
reached for him, then clasped her hands together, shaking
and pressing them to her chest. "Bellisario! Bellisario!" she
said, as if they were the only two people in the room.

"Okay. We're ready to eat in a few minutes," my
mother announced, wiping her hands on a kitchen towel.
"Who's hungry?"

"Me! Me!" I said, raising my hand.

"Go find your brother and sister and tell them we're
ready to sit down."

I scrambled toward the back of the apartment and
searched for Connie and Frank. As I passed my parents'
bedroom, I heard voices drifting out. "Connie?" I called.

The bathroom was adjacent to my parents' room.

Connie opened the bathroom door and stuck her head out. Before I could utter a word, she grabbed my wrist and yanked me inside. As she closed the door, I saw Frank standing behind her.

"What happened?" I said.

"Nothing," Frank whispered. "Keep quiet."

My brother and sister stood near the door, listening intently. After a moment Frank turned the knob and cautiously opened the door a few inches. Excited to be snooping with them, I got down on my knees and wiggled my head between their legs, positioning my ear next to the opening. Uncle Joe and Uncle Sally Boy were talking in my parents' room.

"Awright, calm down, calm down," Uncle Joe said. "Just tell me what happened."

"I was over to Ma's place last Wednesday," Uncle Sally Boy said. "Checkin' up, seein' how she's doin', and I see the breadbasket is fulla unpaid bills. Plus, she got a late notice for last month's rent."

"How come?" Uncle Joe said.

"That's what I says to her. I says, 'Ma, what's with all the bills?' I says, 'Every month we all kick in and give you forty bucks to cover the rent, food, and whatnot.' She says to me, '*No quaranta dollari, no quaranta dollari. Only venticinque dollari. A venticinque.*'"

"What twenty-five dollars? We give to Mamma every month. She gets ten bucks from each of us."

"That's what I'm tellin' ya," said Sally Boy. "Almost half of it is goin' south. I collect the support money from you and Rocco, then I throw in my money and give it to Bill, like always. He's suppose ta put in his nut and bring it over to

Mamma's beginning of the month. Meanwhile, the son of a bitch is shortin' the envelope. The other day I brought over some groceries because the poor woman was eatin' some crap raviolis out of a freakin' can."

"You're shittin' me."

"I wish," said Uncle Sally Boy. "Last month I give him the envelope, there was thirty-five dollars in there. After I collected from you and Rocco, I put in my ten, plus an extra fin so Ma could go out and buy herself a new bra and some underwears."

"Jesus Christ," Uncle Joe groaned. "Didja say anything to him?"

"I did. I called him up and says, 'What happened?' He says, 'Whaddaya mean?' I says, 'Whaddaya mean, whaddo I mean?' You know how he plays stupid sometimes. I says, 'Mamma's short support money every month. Whaddaya you been doin' with the money?' I says, 'You're suppose ta kick in equal like the rest of us.' He says, 'Whaddaya talkin' about?' He says, 'I put in every month.' I says, 'You put in *ugats*. The poor woman is about to get evicted and live out on the street. 'Oh,' he says. 'She's gettin' old. She doesn't know what she's talkin' about.' You know him. Whenever you ask him about something, he's always got some bullshit excuse. I mean, you *believe* this son of a bitch? And then he's got the *balls*, the *fuckin' balls* … He's out there all lovey-dovey, kissin' and huggin' Mamma and singin' songs like nothin's wrong. You know—the good son … The phony bastard," Sally Boy muttered in disgust. "This is why Rocco didn't want to come today. When I told him, he hit the roof. And I don't blame him. I swear on Mamma, that she should get cancer in her eyes, if it wasn't for her birthday and all, I wouldn't be here either."

"Awright," Uncle Joe said, opening the bedroom door. "I'll talk to him. I'll straighten it out. From now on, I'll collect the money and bring it over to Ma's."

"Good. Because I've had it up to here with him. Plus, I got Rose on my back. She's ready to scratch his eyes out. Between the two of them, I'm startin' to get ulcers."

"Don't worry about it. I'll handle it. But let's drop it for today. It's Mamma's birthday, and we don't wanna get her upset, otherwise we'll never hear the end of it."

Frank carefully closed the door.

"Holy smokes," Connie whispered.

"Unbelievable." Frank shook his head. "The old man's so full of shit, it's coming out his ears."

"You think Mommy knows?"

"Probably," said Frank. "But I'm sure she's buried it like all the other crap she lets him get away with."

Connie stared down at me with a preoccupied look on her face. I couldn't tell if she was lost in thought or searching for an answer. I placed a hand over my chest. "And whaddaya want from *my life*?" I said, imitating my father's voice.

"Shush." Connie giggled, pressing a finger against her lips.

"This kid is not well," Frank said, pointing at me, his face deadpan. "I keep telling you, we have to have him looked at."

I laughed and Frank draped his hand over my mouth. "Keep it down, will ya? Or I'll make you go out there and kiss Grandma again."

"No way."

"Where's Mommy?" said Connie.

"She's in the kitchen. She told me to tell you we're ready to eat."

"Good—let's go. I'm starving."

"Is Grandma gonna be living on the street?"

"I ... I don't know," said Connie. "But whatever you do, don't say anything about this to anybody."

∾

At dinner everyone was seated around the table, hands clasped for prayer. My mother had just served up steaming plates of baked macaroni with meatballs and sausage, drenched in thick red gravy. The aroma was tantalizing. My father sat proudly at the head of the table and tapped his fork against his plate to get everyone's attention.

"Connie," he said, nodding at my sister.

Connie bowed her head and closed her eyes. As she said grace, I peeked over at Uncle Sally Boy. He looked pissed off. His hands were clasped, but his gaze darted around the table.

"Amen," Connie said, making the sign of the cross.

"Awright, let's dig in." Uncle Joe reached for his fork.

"Wait a minute," my father said. "*Sta' zitto.* Not so fast."

"Please," Uncle Joe said. "Go ahead. But if you're gonna make a speech, don't take too long, will ya? I'm ready to eat a chair over here."

Frank snorted, and my father shot him a hard look. Then he bowed his head, clasped his hands, and closed his eyes, taking a moment to collect his thoughts. "As I was about to say, thank God for all the good things he's given us.

It hasn't always been easy, but I'm grateful that he blessed my home and allowed me to put food on the table when a lot of people are struggling to make ends meet. If Papa were alive today, I know he'd be proud of his children. Even my brother Rocco, who couldn't be here to spend a few hours with his mother on her birthday because he had more important things to do."

Aunt Rose glanced at Uncle Sally Boy, then looked at the ceiling, mouthing the word please. When she lowered her head, she caught me watching her. I quickly looked away.

"I also wanna give thanks to God that he's allowed Grandma to be here with us so we can celebrate her seventy-fifth birthday. Amen." He made the sign of the cross and kissed the tips of his fingers. "Okay—*mangia*."

Napkins flapped open, bread and butter were passed around, glasses were filled with soda and wine, and gobs of Parmesan cheese were sprinkled over the macaroni. After everyone settled, all that could be heard were chomping mouths and grunts of satisfaction.

Sitting opposite my father, my mother pushed her food around with her fork. "Must be good," she said, sounding irritated. "Nobody's saying a word."

This was something my mother announced when praise for her cooking wasn't immediately forthcoming, an event that pretty much happened at every other meal.

"*Madonna me*," Uncle Joe raved, looking around the table with a huge grin. "I wonder who *made* this wonderful dinner?"

"And who made it?" My mother shrugged. "The man in the *moon* made it."

"It's delicious, Mary," Aunt Rose said.

"Great, Mom." Frank gave her a thumbs-up.

"I keep tellin' ya, Mare," Uncle Joe said, stuffing a big wad of bread in his mouth, "someday you gotta open up a restaurant. Place'd be packed every night. Am I right?" He turned to my father.

"When we got married, she couldn't boil eggs," my father said. "First meal she made for me was chicken. She cooked the whole bird and forgot to remove the gizzards— wax paper and all. Stunk up the whole apartment for two days. Remember?"

My mother grinned. "That's his favorite story," she said, turning to Aunt Rose. "I've been listening to that story for twenty years."

"That's 'cause he doesn't know how good he's got it," Uncle Joe said.

"Tell him." She jutted her chin toward my father, tucking a wisp of hair behind her ear.

"Next time he gives you *agita*, go on strike," Uncle Joe said. "We'll get Sally Boy and some of his longshoreman guys to set up a picket line."

"That's what I say." Uncle Sally Boy glanced at my father. "When things ain't right, shut 'em down."

"Hey, Sally Boy," Frank said. "You're a big union guy. What do you think of Joe McCarthy?"

"I think he's *a bum*." Sally Boy adjusted his napkin around his collar and flattened it out across his chest.

"Please," Aunt Rose said, "don't get him started."

"The bastard's got everybody on a witch hunt," Uncle Sally Boy said.

"My history teacher, Mr. Finkel, says McCarthy's pointing the finger at everybody in Hollywood and secretly trying to break up the unions."

"Aw, that's bullshit." My father scowled.

"Whaddaya mean, it's bullshit?" Sally Boy fired back. "The kid's right."

"We're lucky we got a guy like Joe McCarthy to weed out these communist bastards," my father announced. "This is the greatest country in the world, and if they don't like it, they should pack up and go back to wherever the hell they came from. Go back to where everybody's refrigerator is empty and they all wear the same clothes."

I tried to imagine a place like that. "How do they eat?" I asked.

"Mr. Finkel says McCarthy's financed by the bankers on Wall Street," Frank said. "He said McCarthy and his cronies are trying to use the same scare tactics the Nazis used on the Jews in Germany." Frank glanced at my father, trying to get a rise out of him.

"Oh, now, listen to these words of wisdom. *Mr. Finkel says, Mr. Finkel says* … Who the hell is Mr. Finkel—another Jew commie bastard? Ya see? This is where our tax dollars are going. They should lock his ass up for even teaching that crap."

"Whaddaya talkin' about, lock him up?" Uncle Sally Boy said. "This son of a bitch McCarthy and his stooges, they're usin' this communist bullshit as an excuse to go after everybody." He looked around the table as if pleading a case to a jury. "Got a guy in my place—we just voted him in, made him shop steward about a month ago. Jimmy Flannery, good man from Red Hook. The owner has it in for the shop because we're all union. Plus, he hated Jimmy. *Hated him.* And for what? The guy was tryin' to organize the workers to get the owner to improve safety conditions in the warehouse: better lighting, safety gear, and whatnot. The minute Flannery opened his mouth—*boom*. He's labeled a troublemaker. So what'd the owner do? He had a coupla goons break into the guy's locker and stuff it with communist pamphlets and some other bullshit, said he was a communist whatchamacallit."

"Sympathizer," Frank said.

"Right, sympathizer. Meanwhile, Flannery's a workin' stiff like the rest of us. Guy can't even *spell* communism."

"What happened to him?" Connie said.

"What happened?" Uncle Sally gestured with his hands pressed flat together. "Somebody dropped a dime, and the next thing you know, a car fulla G-men showed up at the plant and took him away. Now the poor guy's under twenty-four-hour surveillance, waitin' for his trial. No job, no paycheck—nothin'."

"Plus, he's got a wife and four kids," Aunt Rose said. "Can you imagine?"

"What's a G-man?" I said.

"Never mind," said my father, shaking his fork in my direction. "You eat your dinner."

"Why can't I know?"

"Because," he said, "little boys should be seen and not heard. You speak when the chickens piss."

"That's what you always say," I grumbled. "We don't even have chickens."

Connie laughed and then immediately covered her mouth as if to take it back.

"It means government," Uncle Sally Boy said, "men that work for the government."

"It's when some guys wearing dark sunglasses and trench coats knock on your door and take you for a ride," Uncle Joe added. "So be ready." He held up his fists in front of his face and made two mini jabs.

"Big deal," my father said. "That's one guy. What about all the commies they're weeding out all over the country? I just heard on the news the other day, they rounded up a whole bunch of 'em on the west side of Manhattan. There was, like, *twenty* of 'em. They found eavesdropping equipment, printing presses, recording machines—the works. It was in all the papers."

"Wouldja listen to him?" Sally Boy said, talking to my mother while pointing a thumb at my father. "There's no gettin' through to him. I'll tell ya what," he went on, turning to my father. "Someday, when some rat bastards set you up and the guys with the nice white shirts come to your job and cart you off, let's see if you'll be singin' the same tune. Maybe if you ask 'em nice, they'll let you bring your violin to the big house, and you can play 'em a nice tarantella."

"Never gonna happen," my father said.

"Oh, *really?*"

"That's right. Know why? 'Cause I got nothin' to hide. That's why. Every one of these creeps they pick up is tied to some communist organization trying to pollute us with all that liberal bullshit. I went on a job interview about six months ago for a government contract. The first question the guy asked me was 'Are you now or have you ever been a member of the Communist Party?' I said to him, 'Do you have a bank account?' He said, 'Yeah, why?' I said, 'Because Bill Caruso is one hundred percent red-blooded American and proud of it. And that, my friend, you can take to the bank.'"

Frank started humming "God Bless America," pursing his lips, making the droning sound like a kazoo. Without hesitating, my father reached over and slapped his face. Frank's head flew backward, and my heart galloped. He blinked a few times, disoriented, his cheek red with the outline of my father's fingers.

"Bill!" my mother shouted.

"C'mon, Bill," Uncle Sally Boy said. "Whaddaya doin' hittin' the kid like that?"

"What are you, a wise guy?" my father shouted at Frank.

"*Bellisario! Bellisario!*" my grandmother cried, clasping her hands and shaking them.

"Little snot-nosed bastard. This is *my house.*"

"Bill, for Chrissakes," said Uncle Joe. "Relax, will ya?"

I felt embarrassed, seeing my brother get whacked in front of relatives. It was like watching my father hold up shit-stained underwear for all to see. Frank grinned, and my gut tensed. It almost looked like he was begging for more.

"You see this little son of a bitch? You see how he's smiling?" My father wouldn't let up. "That's 'cause he's a little bitch. G'ahead, smile. You want somethin' to smile about? Here's somethin' to smile about." My father drew his hand back and slapped Frank's face again, harder this time. Frank's head struck the wall behind him with a thud. He tried to maintain his grin, but his expression wavered.

"Daddy, no!" I cried, scared for my brother. I moved to get up from my chair, and Connie latched on to my arm, yanking me down.

"Bill, for Godsakes." My mother threw down her

napkin.

"You shut up and mind your own business!" my father shouted. "This has got nothing to do with you."

Blood trickled from Frank's lip, but he seemed unaware. He started right up again, humming "God Bless America" with the same kazoo sound, only louder.

My father's face was purple with rage. He picked up his fork and held it in front of my brother's face. "G'ahead, ya little sissy," he growled. "I'll gouge your eyes out."

"Well, hey," Frank said. "You're a God-fearing, tax-paying, red-blooded American. Go ahead—gouge my eyes out."

My throat tightened. I felt like I was suffocating. I leaned into Connie, and she put her arm around my shoulders, squeezing me tight.

"Bill, you're scaring the children," my mother cried.

"You're such a model citizen," Frank said, his voice choking with spite. "Is that why you short support money for Grandma every month?"

"What?" My father blinked furiously. "Who told you that bullshit?"

"A little bird."

"Is that what you do?" my father said, sneering at Sally Boy. "I invite you to the house so you can poison my family?"

Confused, Sally Boy glanced at his wife and then at Big Joe.

"Don't look at me," Joe said, holding up his hands. "I didn't let the cat out of the bag."

"I didn't tell the kid anything," Sally Boy said. "Whatever family business we got with Mamma is between you, me, Joe, and Rocco."

My father turned to my mother. "You believe this shit? I can't even trust my own brothers. It's not enough that they spread rumors, they gotta turn my kids against me."

"Look, Bill," Sally Boy said, "I don't know where the kid got it from, but it's true. You haven't been pulling your weight. Rocco's mad as hell. He didn't wanna come and put on a show, listening to you serenade Mamma, actin' like everything's honky-dory."

My father's forehead glistened with sweat. "I told you before," he said, jabbing his finger at Sally Boy. "I put in equal every month. But you know what?" He held up a hand. "Don't worry about it—it's okay. Mamma knows. Mamma knows," he said in a kinder tone, nodding at his mother to solicit her support.

Grandma Angelina started babbling in Italian, looking and sounding as if she had no idea what anybody was talking about.

"C'mon, Bill," Uncle Sally Boy said, "skip the 'Mamma knows' bullshit. You're talkin' to another Caruso here. I mean, what the hell—you think we're all *stupid?*"

My father shouted at Uncle Sally Boy, and the two of them began arguing in Italian. My father's head was bobbing back and forth. At one point he stood up, his arm flailing, looking like he was going to start swinging again. I wanted to crawl under the table.

"Stop it! Stop it!" Aunt Rose cried.

Big Joe got up and wrapped his huge arms around my father from behind. "Bill—*sta' zitto*, will ya? Before you hurt somebody. It's over. It's *over*. We'll talk about this later."

My father let loose a slew of curses in Italian and

gradually calmed down, shrugging himself away from Joe's arms. "Little bastard." He tossed his fork on the table, glaring at Frank. "You're lucky. If Grandma wasn't here, I'd break your fucking legs."

Frank patted his lip with a napkin. "Yeah, I'm lucky," he said, holding out the bloodstained cloth toward my father.

"Please, a please," my grandmother pleaded. "A no fight ... a no fight." She wiped tears from her eyes with her handkerchief and made the sign of the cross.

"He's gotta ruin every meal," said my father, running a hand over the top of his head. "Every meal he's gotta ruin. Look ..." He nodded toward Grandma Angelina. "Your grandmother's crying. Poor woman can't even enjoy her own birthday. Ya happy now?"

"Yeah, it's my fault," Frank said.

"Son of a bitch," my father said. "What did I do to deserve such a rotten bitch-bastard? Somebody, please tell me."

"Hey," Frank said, "I didn't ask to be here."

The room grew silent, and all eyes turned to my father. He looked speechless, as if the notion were something he'd never considered. But after a moment his face hardened. "Aw," he blustered, "what the hell do you people know?"

The remainder of the meal felt like a dark cloud had drifted into the dining room and loomed over the table; chatter was quiet and sporadic. I couldn't take my eyes off Frank. He looked so wounded, I wanted to go over and hug him but was afraid my father would erupt again.

"Hey, champ, you hardly touched your pasta," Uncle Joe said.

"Not hungry." I moved my plate away.

"Eat your dinner," my father said.

"I'm not hungry."

"I said eat your dinner!"

I lifted my fork and took another bite of food. I could feel the weight of my father's eyes on me. In that moment I both feared and hated him. He lifted his glass and took a gulp of wine, eyeing me suspiciously as if he knew what I had been thinking.

FOUR

MY FATHER WAS having a hard time keeping up with the rent on our West Twelfth Street apartment. Mr. Kempt often knocked on our door, complaining about either late rent payments or too much noise. ("What's with you people? I feel like I'm back in Iwo Jima.") After several complaints, he told my father he'd be taking back the apartment when our lease was up.

In 1956 we moved to Bay Haven Apartments, a newly developed complex, Brooklyn's answer to affordable middle-class housing: thirty-one redbrick, six-story buildings surrounded by lush foliage and manicured lawns. Transected by a maze of cement walkways and asphalt driveways, the complex was within walking distance of the narrow, murky channel separating Brooklyn and Staten Island. My father rented a fourth-floor two-bedroom apartment with a view facing the main courtyard.

Bay Haven had the works: elevators, an underground garage, and a laundry room in the basement of every building. It also had a full-time maintenance staff. The only downside was that our new digs were about half the size of our old apartment. The place had only a tiny kitchen and dining area. My parents took the larger of the two bedrooms, and Connie and I shared the smaller room, just large enough for two small beds and a dresser. Frank slept in the living room on a fold-out sofa. "Nice layout," Frank said. "This place is so small I have to go out into the hall to change my mind."

Connie and I went to PS 200, just a few blocks from Bay Haven, where I attended kindergarten and first grade. I loved being around other kids. The teachers were friendly and read us stories. We sang and danced, made arts and crafts, and played kickball and other schoolyard games.

Jackie Di Gerardi and I were in the same first-grade class. Jackie was a lean kid with sandy-brown hair chopped back in a crew cut. His family lived on the fifth floor of our building. He also had siblings who were older, a sister in high school and a brother in the navy. Jackie's mother was a beautician, and his father, Anthony, was a professional musician who went by the stage name Tony Gerard—a short, hip-looking man with dark hair styled in a ducktail.

Almost immediately Jackie and I became inseparable. He would come down to my apartment, and we'd gobble up peanut butter and jelly sandwiches and watch hours of television, or I'd go up to his place and play games. He had an Erector Set and an entire army of miniature plastic soldiers. We held battles and knocked down each other's battalions. Jackie was the king of sound effects; he had a complete catalog of noises: tanks, jeeps, machine guns, sniper fire, dive bombers, explosions—you name it.

"Look out! The Japs are comin'!"

"Okay, men, we're goin' in!"

"Dot! Dot! Dot! Dot! Dot! Kish! Kish! Kish! Yawoo ... ka-*boom*!"

After first grade, Jackie and I were excited to find out we'd been assigned to the same second-grade class. A few weeks before school began, however, my father announced that I'd be going to Precious Mother, a parochial school just up the street from the house where Grandma Angelina lived in the basement apartment. Nobody had said a word to me beforehand.

"But I don't wanna go to Catholic school," I said. "Why do I have to go?"

"Because I want you to get a good education," my father said. "Not this public school crap, where the teachers getcha in and getcha out and you don't learn a damn thing. You listen to your father. He knows what he's talking about."

I was mad as hell. Both Frank and Connie went to public school, and they seemed to be doing fine. When they heard the news, they complained to my mother. "Ma, are you *serious*?" said Frank. "You're sending the kid to *Catholic school*?"

"What's wrong with Catholic school?"

"Why don't you just get the kid a lobotomy? It's cheaper, plus you can get the job done in one day."

"Don't be ridiculous. It just so happens that parochial schools offer a very good education. The teachers are supposed to be excellent."

Frank snickered. "Where'dja hear that, the old man?"

"No, no ..." My mother shook her head, as if the thought of taking cues from our father had never occurred to her. "It's common knowledge. Everyone knows Catholic schools have the best teachers."

"Everyone ..." Frank muttered. "You mean like that screwball you and Daddy watch on television every Sunday night?"

"Who?" My mother looked totally bewildered.

"You know who I'm talking about. The self-important fruitcake with the forty-pound crucifix around his neck. The guy who wears a yarmulke and looks like a Doberman pinscher."

Connie and I laughed until tears ran down our faces. "Bishop Sheen," she said, barely able to get the words out.

"Yeah, Bishop Sheen," Frank said.

"Don't be disrespectful," my mother told us. "If your father heard you talking like that, he'd hit the roof."

"Okay, then who?" Frank persisted.

"Huh? I don't know." My mother shrugged. "You know, just people …"

"Best teachers." Frank snorted. "That's a myth. Forget best. They don't even have *normal* teachers."

"Oh, *really?* Then what do they have?"

"They have nuns," Connie said.

"That's right," Frank said. "They got *nuns*—strict old bags who cram religion down your throat six hours a day. Is that what you want for the kid?"

"Aw, stop it, will ya?" My mother was wearing a sour expression by this time. "You make it sound horrible. Cousin Genevieve's little one goes to Catholic school, and he loves it," she added, glancing at me with a saccharine smile.

I didn't believe a word of it. Besides, who gave a rat's ass about Cousin Genevieve's little one. This was my life we were talking about.

"Johnny's got all his friends at 200," said Connie. "What about Jackie?"

"Yeah," I spouted. "Jackie and I are gonna be in the same class. You said it was all set. You *said.*"

"Ma, you gotta talk to Daddy," Connie pleaded.

"Make him change his mind."

My stomach rippled with dread. Not only was I not going to PS 200 with my best friend, but my parents were sending me to a place that sounded like a prison for kids.

My mother's eyes wavered with indecision, and for a second I felt a glimmer of hope. Then she said, "It's too late. Your father already paid the first month's tuition. And if that's what he wants, that's what he wants. I can't argue with him anymore. I already got high blood pressure."

"Ma, do you do everything that Daddy wants?" Connie said. "How about standing on your own two feet once in a while? Isn't that what you're always telling me?"

"I'll tell ya what," my mother said. "Someday, when you get your own kids, you can do what you want. In the meantime, mind your own business."

"Well, hey," Frank said. "*There's* an answer."

"That goes for you too."

"Believe me," said Frank, "if and when I get my own kids, my house won't look *anything* like this."

"And what's that supposed to mean?"

"Just what I said."

"What—you think it's easy raising three kids? Mr. Know-It-All over here."

"I hear you," Frank said. "But guess what? We didn't sign up to have kids—*you* did. If you thought it was going to be tough, then you and the old man should have opted for Plan B."

Frank's words seemed to go right over my mother's head. Her face became vacant, as if she'd suddenly checked out of the conversation. "Who does all the cooking and cleaning around here?" she asked, her eyes darting around the room. "Who does all the laundry and makes sure you kids have clean socks and underwear?"

"Ma, what are you talking about?" said Connie, throwing up her hands in frustration. "I'm down in the laundry room every weekend doing loads. Last Saturday I spent half the afternoon folding clothes and the other half in Bohack's, food shopping for the house."

My mother started to cry. "You kids don't appreciate anything. Nobody does ..."

"Okay," Frank said. "Here she goes, Mary on the cross."

Mary on the cross —this was my brother's favorite description of my mother whenever she went off on one of her self-pitying rants, something I often witnessed.

"Your poor father is out there breaking his back every day, trying to put food on the table." She continued to sob. "You kids don't know how hard he works. You don't remember the Depression. You don't remember how, after Daddy lost the business, he was out on Coney Island Avenue ten, eleven hours a day, selling onions and tomatoes just so we could have some money coming in."

"Ma, we don't remember the Depression because we weren't born yet," said Connie.

"Sometimes we didn't even know where our next meal was coming from."

"Ma—forget the Depression," said Frank. "How 'bout now? How about when the old man is in the bag every other night, and we have to move from West Twelfth Street into this matchbox because he's blowing rent money on booze?"

"That's not true!" my mother cried.

"How about when you can't afford to buy a nice dress,

or I'm walking around school with shoes that are ready to die on my feet, while the old man is buying himself new shirts and ties? Huh? How about that?"

"Me too," Connie said. "I've been asking for a new pair of saddle shoes for weeks."

"Those shirts were for his job," my mother fired back, choking with exasperation. "He needs them for work, for Chrissakes."

"C'mon, Ma, cut the bullshit," Frank said. "The old man's got drawers full of shirts. Why don't you just admit it? He's a selfish bastard pissing away money on himself, and damn the rest of us. He even stiffed his own brothers on support payments for Grandma Angelina."

"They settled all that," my mother argued. "Whaddaya want from the poor man? He helped carry his mother for years when Sal, Joe, and the rest of them didn't know how to put two nickels together. The pressure was always on your father. You kids don't know."

"Listen to you." Frank smiled. "You sound like his personal defense attorney. How much more bullshit you gonna take from him?"

"And what do you want me to do? You can't argue with him. He's got that hotheaded Neapolitan temper. Then after he gets a few drinks in him, he starts shouting me down."

"*So leave*," Frank said, raising his voice.

"Yeah," Connie said. "*Leave.*"

For a moment or two my mother pondered the idea, her eyes filled with uncertainty. I was thinking that if she left my father, I would be spared from going to Catholic school, but I knew that the odds of that happening would be the same as winning the state lottery. Not once, but *twice.*

"Leave and go where?" she said. "Your father and I have been together twenty years. Plus, I got three kids. Where the hell you want me to go?"

"*Anywhere,*" Frank said. "The old man doesn't give a shit about us."

"That's not true. Daddy's got some problems, but deep down he's a good man."

"Yeah, *right,*" Frank said, turning to Connie. "He's wonderful."

My mother went on and on about how hardworking my father was, and after a few minutes Frank got up from the sofa. "All right, that's it for me," he said, heading for the door. "I can't listen to you anymore."

"Where are you going?"

Frank didn't answer.

"I said, where are you going?"

"Out," Frank replied, without turning his head.

"You're not going anywhere."

"Watch me."

"Did you hear what I said?"

"Piss off."

"You lousy fuckin' bastard!" she shouted.

Hearing my mother curse sent a jolt through me. She would never curse at my father like that. One time she'd called the old man a son of a bitch, and he'd laid into her with a backhand.

Frank stopped at the front door and looked over his shoulder. "Nice mouth in front of the kid," he said. "Now I can see why you're sending him to Catholic school. That's where all good Catholics send their kids."

FIVE

FOR DAYS all I kept thinking about was Frank's description of nuns: "strict old bags who cram religion down your throat." The weekend before school started, my mother tried to get me into new school trousers so she could alter the cuffs. It was a lazy Saturday morning, and she followed me around the apartment in a white bra and a knee-length slip. Eventually she cornered me in the bedroom I shared with Connie.

"Put these on right now," she said.

I hopped onto my bed. "No."

"I said put them on."

"No—I'm not going."

"Lower your voice," she whispered, glancing over her shoulder. "You're gonna wake up your father."

"I don't care."

The night before, my father had returned late from his out-of-town job, and he'd been sleeping all morning.

"Johnny, did you hear what I said? Put these pants on."

"No!"

"If you don't put on these pants right now, I'm gonna call up the home for little boys and have them pick you up and take you away. Do you want me to call the home?"

Hearing that was like getting zapped with a ray gun.

The thought of being taken away was terrifying. I couldn't imagine being separated from Frank and Connie.

"Do you want me to call the home?" she said again, staring me down with penetrating eyes. "Because if you don't put these pants on, I'm gonna pick up the phone and call them right now."

I felt trapped. It was either Catholic school or a home for little boys.

"Okay, that's it," she said, turning. "I'm calling the home."

"No!" I cried, jumping up and down on the bed. "I'm not going! I'm not going to the home!"

"I said lower your voice," she rasped with clenched teeth. "You'll wake up your father."

"I don't care."

"You put these pants on right now. Do you hear me? I said *right now.*"

"Piss off."

"You little bastard," she snarled. "You kids think you're gonna put *me* in the grave—I'll put *you* in the grave." She moved closer to my bed and tried to grab my arm. I backed up against the wall, as far from her as possible. After a few swipes, she latched onto my wrist and yanked me toward her. I tumbled forward and landed on the wooden floor, bumping my head against the metal bed frame. The pain was excruciating, and I let out a scream.

"Get up," she demanded, tugging my arm.

A rumble came from my parents' bedroom. It was my father. He threw open the door and burst into the room wearing boxer shorts and a T-shirt, looking as if he'd woken from a dead sleep. "What the hell is going on in here?" he demanded. "My one full day off and I can't even get some goddamn rest in my own house!"

"This kid is driving me crazy."

"Why's he crying?"

"She's gonna put me in a home," I cried, rubbing the golf-ball-size lump rising on the back of my head.

"What the hell are you telling the kid?" my father said.

"He's not listening to me. I tell him something, and he tells me to piss off."

"So you're gonna put him in a home? Is that what you're telling him? What are you, a fuckin' animal?"

"No. I just—"

"Have you ever been sent away to a home? How about if I put *you* in a goddamn home?"

My mother opened her mouth, but before she could get a word out, my father slapped her face. He did it again and again. I'd never seen him go at her like that before. He knocked her against the bedroom door and continued slapping her into the small foyer. Frank was in the kitchen making breakfast. He heard the commotion and rushed back to see what was going on.

"Dad, stop! What are you *doing*?"

My father looked crazed. He had my mother pinned against the wall, slapping her repeatedly—left hand, right hand—until finally she slid to the floor, knees up, her slip straddling the tops of her thighs. My body tensed. She wasn't wearing panties, and she was sitting in a puddle of her own urine. Her vagina looked like a big wet open wound: brown-and-pink wrinkled flesh with traces of blood on it, surrounded by patches of dark hair threaded with gray. It was something I'd never seen before or even imagined being part of my mother's body. The sight of her opening and the smell of pee made me gag. I looked up at her face. Her eyes were askew, as if she didn't know where she was or what was happening.

My father went back into his bedroom and slammed the door.

"Mom, are you okay?" Frank hunched over my mother, struggling to lift her.

I started to dry-heave.

"Go back to your room," Frank said to me.

I couldn't move; the sight of my mother sitting helplessly in her own piss had me paralyzed with fear and disgust.

After a minute Frank realized I was still standing behind him. "I said go to your room." He pushed me away with one hand.

I went and sat on the edge of Connie's bed, licking tears from my lips, my head throbbing. Crumpled on the floor next to my feet were the blue school pants. It was all my fault. If I'd only put on the pants and kept my mouth shut, none of this would have happened.

SIX

PRECIOUS MOTHER WAS a three-story brick building built in 1930, located about a mile from Bay Haven. Just across the schoolyard stood the church, its austere brick walls punctuated by Gothic-arched stained-glass windows. Beyond that was the rectory.

On the first day, my mother walked me to school in near silence. The schoolyard buzzed with kids in uniforms: the boys in blue pants, white shirts, and blue ties; the girls in white blouses and blue jumpers.

"I want you to behave yourself today," she said, handing me a brown-paper lunch bag. She looked haggard and stressed. Her wiry hair was flattened on one side with a few bobby pins, and her lipstick, rouge, and face powder looked slapped on, making her look like a bag lady.

My stomach swelled with guilt. "Mom, please don't go."

"I put some extra cookies in the bag for you."

"Are you gonna be okay?"

"Don't worry about me. I'll pick you up at three. Wait for me near the entrance."

"Do you love me?" I asked.

My mother grimaced, then turned and started walking away.

"Mom." I grabbed her sweater.

"What?" she said.

"Do you love me?"

"Yes, I love you," she said, without emotion, and continued on her way.

The school bell blasted the yard with a sharp clangor as I stood on the sidewalk and watched her cross the street and disappear from sight.

Walking two abreast, we were led upstairs to a stuffy room crammed with wooden desks. My teacher was Sister O'Malley, a squat nun with no-nonsense eyes. She showed us the hand clicker she would use to signal the class. One click meant *stand by your desk*, two clicks meant *sit down*, and three clicks meant *line up against the wall*. She drilled us on the signals for several minutes and then made us stand silently next to our desks, ready for morning prayers. My eyes wandered around the room, trying to take in everything at once. The walls were plastered with scenes from the lives of Jesus, Mary, and the apostles.

At the front of the room, a tripod held a large illustration of Jesus nailed to the cross. Blood dripped from a gaping wound on his side and from his hands, feet, and forehead, where a crown of thorns spiked his skin. On the ground just below the cross, the Virgin Mary knelt with her hands clasped in prayer, looking up with a mournful expression. Underneath the picture, in big block letters, were ten sentences:

LOOK AT JESUS AS MARY DID.
SEE HIS BLEEDING WOUNDS.
SEE THE NAILS IN HIS HANDS AND FEET.
SEE THE THORNS IN HIS HEAD.

SEE HIS SIDE OPEN FOR US TO ENTER.
SEE HOW MUCH HE LOVES US.
HOW DO YOU THINK OUR LADY FELT?
HOW SHOULD WE FEEL?
IF JESUS LOVES US SO MUCH, WHAT ARE WE GOING TO DO FOR HIM TODAY?
MAY THE PASSION OF OUR LORD JESUS CHRIST AND THE SORROWS OF OUR MOTHER MARY BE ALWAYS IN OUR HEARTS.

During prayers, Sister O'Malley walked around the room with her hands clasped behind her back. The class went from one prayer to the next without missing a beat. The room was filled with a loud drone, like thirty beehives buzzing in unison. Over the summer I'd forgotten many of the prayers I'd learned in catechism class at Saint Fingar. I remembered a few words of each prayer, and then my voice would trail off and I'd fake the rest, reciting gibberish to the cadence of the class.

Sister O'Malley worked her way toward the back of the room, and my scalp prickled. She was spot-checking students, leaning close to their faces to hear what they were saying. After a few stops she turned, heading back to her desk. Then she paused, catching my eye. I looked away, but it was too late. She sauntered over to my desk and circled behind me, leaning over my shoulder and placing her ear inches from my head. I could smell the starch from her stiff white collar and feel her hot breath hitting my neck. My voice faded to a murmur as I stood there moving my lips.

"Okay, stop! *Stop!*" She waved her arms over her head. The room quickly fell silent. "You," she said. "What is your name?"

"Me?" I repeated, pointing to myself, pretending to be surprised.

"Yes, you. Do you see me talking to anyone else?"

"No, but—"

"Well, then, I must be talking to you. What is your name?"

"John."

"John what? And you will address me as Sister."

"John Caruso, Sister."

"John Caruso," she repeated, nodding and looking at the rest of the class. "Well, Mr. Caruso, I have a simple question for you. Are you familiar with the prayer created by the apostles to give praise and honor to our Holy Father and his only son, our Divine Savior and Lord Jesus Christ?"

Her words rattled over my head like machine-gun fire, and I stood there like a post, trying to decipher what the hell she said.

"Well, *speak up*. Are you hard of hearing?"

"I didn't understand what you said."

"You what?"

"Sorry, Sister. I meant, I didn't understand what you said, Sister."

The room erupted with a chorus of loud groans. I shifted my gaze and met a sea of shocked faces.

"You mean to tell me that you don't know the Apostles' Creed?"

Apostles' Creed. Apostles' Creed. Some words jumped into my brain, and I felt a rush of confidence. "Oh, sure." I nodded, nearly snapping my neck. "You mean, like, 'I believe in God, the Father Almighty, the Creator of Heaven and Earth …' You mean like that?"

Out of the corner of my eye I noticed a kid with a crooked tie and huge eyes. He looked terrified. His face was frozen, staring at me as if waiting for a bomb to go off.

"That is *precisely* what I mean," Sister O'Malley said, exasperated. She looked up and made the sign of the cross. "Holy Mother of God, please give me strength."

"Oh, yeah, Sister, I know it."

"You do, do you?"

I swallowed, praying she wouldn't ask me any more questions.

"Well, then"—she clutched the large crucifix that hung from her neck just below her breasts— "perhaps you'd like to recite it for the class."

The room filled with an eerie silence. My legs were trembling.

"Well?" she said. "C'mon, c'mon … We haven't got all day."

I cleared my throat, and as I spoke, I punctuated every two or three words with a stiff nod. "I believe in God, the Father Almighty, Creator of Heaven and Earth, and … and …" My mind raced to recall the rest of the prayer, but I couldn't remember shit. Fragments of different prayers and recitations jammed my head like needles in a pincushion.

"And *what*, Mr. Caruso?"

"And to the Republic for which it stands, one Nation under God, and … and blessed is the tooth of thy wound, Jesus."

The class exploded with laughter. I moved my cheeks up in a twisted smile, pretending to laugh along with everyone else, really fighting back tears.

"*Silence,* all of you!" Sister O'Malley commanded. "Of all the blasphemous ... Where did you take catechism lessons?"

"Saint Fingar," I mumbled.

"Saint Fingar. Is that how they taught you to recite the Apostles' Creed at Saint Fingar?"

"No, Sister."

"Then say it properly."

I looked around the room, scrambling to remember the words. "Uh ... Our Father, who art in heaven, uh ... uh ..."

"This is *outrageous.* Are you a *pagan?*"

"No, Sister. I'm Italian."

Sister O'Malley's eyes narrowed. She grabbed the knot of my tie, pulling me closer to her face. "Don't play with me, mister. I'll smack you right down to the principal's office and you'll be out on your ear. Do you hear me?"

"Yes, Sister," I gasped.

"Good. Because you're first on my list of troublemakers." She shoved me away. One side of her long black veil shifted and hung over her shoulder like a lopsided cape. "Go stand in the corner and ask our Divine Father for forgiveness," she said, flinging the veil back over her shoulder. "As for the rest of you, this is my first and last warning. I expect you to be able to recite the Apostles' Creed and all the other prayers in your sleep. Is that understood?"

"Yes, Sister," the class answered in unison.

I stood at the back of the room in silence, catching an occasional peek from various kids. One boy smirked, then looked away; a girl grinned, as if delighted to see me punished.

The first day of school, and already I was the number one troublemaker. I would have given anything to start the morning over or trade places with another kid. The class began reciting times tables out loud. I saw my empty desk in the middle of the room and thought about Jackie, the kids at PS 200, and Connie and Frank. Where were they, and what were they all doing? I looked at the Virgin Mary, kneeling and praying at the foot of the cross. LOOK AT JESUS AS MARY DID. SEE HIS BLEEDING WOUNDS. HOW DO YOU THINK OUR LADY FELT? HOW SHOULD WE FEEL?

Images of my mother filled my head. She looked just like the Virgin Mary: tired and mournful. The noise in the classroom faded, and I was back at home, watching her getting slapped around. Sharp pangs gripped my stomach. I saw the dazed expression on her face. She looked so helpless. I wanted to tell her I was sorry. I closed my eyes, hoping that if I wished and prayed hard enough, she would hear me.

SEVEN

SISTER O'MALLEY WAS free with her hands. Every day some kid got pushed, pinched, or slapped for talking in class or not addressing her properly. She also took delight in coming up with innovative punishments, like locking you in the dark coatroom for an hour or whacking your palms and knuckles with a wooden ruler. Another of her favorites was making you pray with your hands clasped while kneeling on Number 2 pencils for a prescribed period; you were sentenced to five-, ten-, or fifteen-minute stints depending on the infraction. While you were on your knees praying for Jesus to come down and put you out of your misery, she would continue teaching as if everything were normal. The whole class would have one eye on O'Malley and one on whoever was squirming in pain. It was like being in a windowless room slowly losing oxygen, with everyone too terrified to utter a peep.

I never told my parents what was going on at Precious Mother. I was convinced they would side with my teacher and give it to me even worse, especially my father, who blew a gasket after I got a C- in conduct on my report card. "What are you, a wise guy?" he said, smacking the back of my head. "You better cut the clowning around, buddy, and pay attention to the teacher, because I'm gonna come up to the school and check up on you. If I see you horsing around in class, I'm gonna take off my belt and give you a good whipping in front of everyone." My classroom door had a small square window in it that I monitored for days afterward, thinking he would actually show up and put his strap to me.

One morning my mother looked totally unraveled—barefoot, her hair a mess, wearing a frayed, coffee-stained housecoat. "Let's go," she said, gathering my things. "You're gonna be late."

Earlier that morning she had been arguing with my father about not having enough money for food. "This is *ridiculous*," I'd heard her say. "I can't keep asking my brothers for money. They got their own families to worry about." Things got heated, and my father left the apartment.

"I made you an egg," she said to me now.

"I'm not hungry."

"Your body needs fuel. You can't go to school without some food in your system."

"I'm not hungry."

On the mornings when I did manage to eat a hard-boiled egg or a buttered English muffin and drink a glass of milk, my stomach would quake on the way to school, and usually I'd vomit everything up on the sidewalk.

"Ma, I don't feel well," I said, draping a hand over my forehead. "I think I got a fever."

My mother always knew when I was faking. Occasionally, she would let me stay home when I sweetened the pitch and promised to help her with the housework. Often this worked like a charm, especially on days when the house was a disaster and my father was on her back about dust piling up under the bed or crud growing in the refrigerator. When it came to cleaning and organizing housework, my mother didn't know where to begin. For me, it was a piece of cake. I figured out that all she needed was a plan and someone to tell her what to do. (*"Okay, Mom, I'll start on the bathroom, and you work on the kitchen. Then we can have lunch, and then you can start on the living room and I'll do the bedroom."*)

"I don't care what you got," she said. "You're going to school today."

"I can help you clean," I said with a bright ring to my voice.

"Forget that. No cleaning today."

"I can't find my homework. Did you see my homework?"

"It's already ten to nine! You're gonna be late!"

"I think I left it in my room."

I headed toward the back of the apartment, but my mother grabbed my collar and threw me out the front door, slamming it shut. Seconds later the door opened again, and she tossed out my bookbag. I rang the buzzer and pounded on the door. "Ma, let me in, please! I'll be good, I swear. Just let me stay home this one time."

"I can't take it anymore!" she screamed from behind the door. "*I can't take it!*" She opened the door a few inches, and I saw her mouth and one eye peering out over the safety chain. "You're gonna put me in the grave!" she screamed, and slammed the door shut again.

I'd never seen her so crazed. I continued pounding on the door and ringing the buzzer until she opened the door again. I rushed forward, but she blocked the entrance and clobbered me with a wooden spoon. "Get out! Get out! Get out! Get out!" She tried to push me back into the hall, but I wedged myself in the doorframe, covering my head with my arms. She whacked me with the spoon a few times more, then threw it against the wall. "I can't take it anymore!" she screeched, pulling at her hair and twisting the skin on her cheeks. Seeing my mother's face contorted like that horrified me. She looked like Medusa or some other grotesque character from a Hollywood horror movie. "You're killing me! You're killing me!" she shrieked, and scurried back to her bedroom, her hands shaking above her head.

In the kitchen, my eyes welled with tears as I watched the faucet drip onto a stack of soiled dishes. My head and arms throbbed with pain, but somehow all I could think about was my mother, and that she might hurt herself—and that I would be responsible if I left her alone in the apartment.

I tiptoed to my parents' bedroom and placed my ear against the door. Not a sound. I knocked softly. No response. I waited a moment and knocked again, but there was still no response, so I opened the door and slipped into the room. My mother lay on her side beneath the covers, facing away from me.

"Mom?"

She didn't answer. My heart pounded against my ribs.

"Mom?"

"What?" she said.

"Do you want me to get your special pills?"

"Mommy already took," she said, adjusting the covers around her shoulders.

She seemed so helpless. I reached out and touched the

top of her head, then gently ran my fingers through her tangled hair, the same way she would sometimes stroke mine when I sat on the couch with my head in her lap.

"Does that feel good?"

She moved her body closer to the edge of the bed where I was standing. I began massaging her head with both hands, digging my fingers deep into her scalp. The more pressure I applied, the louder her moans of pleasure. The intimacy felt overwhelming.

"Yes, Mommy," she said in a childlike voice. "Just like that ... just like that."

Hearing her call me "Mommy" was confusing. Did she really think I was her mother? Her mood was tranquil, and she seemed content with my being in control. Whatever I had done to upset her, whatever pain I had caused her, it was now all gone. Giving her pleasure made me feel redeemed, and I finally relaxed. I moved my hands to massage her neck and shoulders. After a minute or two she turned and drew back the covers, pulling me onto the bed. Still wearing my school clothes, I snuggled in beside her, both of us lying on our sides, her arms around me.

"My little Janoots," she murmured, kissing the top of my head.

Across the room I glanced at my parents' wedding photo atop the chest of drawers. My father was decked out in a black tuxedo, his dark hair neatly parted. Beside him my mother looked statuesque, dressed in an elegant white gown. Pleased to be nestled in my father's arms, she was holding a plush bouquet of flowers, her young, beautiful face smiling right at me.

EIGHT

FOR A WHILE, my father was out of work, though the reason for his unemployment was unclear. A few times he landed a job out of town only to return home a couple days later.

"What happened?" I asked once.

"Oh," he said with a *c'est la vie* chuckle, "they made a mistake. They were lookin' for an electrical engineer—I'm a mechanical engineer."

Another time he said, "It's the craziest thing. I got up there and found out the company had gone out of business and closed the plant. Who knew?"

Frank had heard from Gaetano, my mother's cousin, who had helped my father get started in the business, that my father had been laid off from a few of his consulting jobs. Apparently, he had inflated his credentials, and when his employers realized he didn't have the skills needed for the job, they fired him.

At home I'd listen to him trying to scrape up work. He'd be on the phone, wearing a T-shirt and boxer shorts, drinking endless cups of coffee and farting his brains out. I'd know it was a business call because he'd speak loudly and distinctly, in a confident, officious tone. "Yes, that's correct, sir. When I was working up there at Sperry, I was in their gyroscope division. We designed a range of close-tolerance gauges, jigs, and instruments—all fine-precision equipment, you understand."

There was one call that didn't go well. As the conversation slid downhill, my father talked faster and faster, trying to convince the interviewer to give him a job. "Well, how 'bout procurement? If you need a good man, I know how to purchase ... I can negotiate ... I do estimates ... I also know how to expedite. Do you need a good expediter?" When the person finally ended the call, my father slammed down the receiver. "Drop dead, ya bastard!" he yelled at the phone. "I hope ya *rot in hell!*"

My mother took a job as a salesclerk in a dry-cleaning store to bring some money into the house. "We have to cut back," I heard her tell Connie and Frank. The new austerity didn't sit well with them, mainly because the cutting back didn't apply to my father, who continued to give my mother a weekly shopping list of his favorite meats and delicacies. Being the loyal wife, she made sure he continued to enjoy prime rib, sirloin, Italian sausages, and specialty cheeses, while she served us beans and franks, fish sticks, and pasta.

While the old man was job hunting, he was always around the house. I'd come home from school, and it would be just the two of us. He'd make me a snack and then ask me the same question: "Okay, what do we have for homework?"

At the dining room table, we'd go through each of my assignments. Rather than helping me figure out the stuff I had trouble with, he zeroed in on appearance and penmanship. He couldn't spell to save his freaking life, but his cursive handwriting was impeccable; it flowed with a clean, dignified, John Hancock flair. All my assignments had to be neat and orderly. With his index finger he'd point to the spot on the page where he wanted me to start writing. If I was a little bit off the mark or the numbers and letters weren't formed to his liking, he would make me erase them and start over. Every minute felt like torture and made me want to jab a fucking pen in his neck.

"*Neat. Neat*," he stressed, tapping my head with a pencil. "When the teacher sees that your homework is sloppy, you look like a horse's ass."

After a while I caught on. What he was really looking for was praise—not from me, but from my *teacher.* He constantly asked what she thought of my completed homework. "What did she say? Did she like it? Wha'd she think?" As if the assignments were meant for him and I was just the messenger.

Every day I prayed that he'd land a job in Mongolia or some other place halfway around the world.

Shortly after I entered the third grade, Grandma Angelina suffered a heart attack. The doctors at Coney Island Hospital warned my father and his brothers that, because of her age and diet, things didn't look good.

My father and Big Joe had been visiting her the afternoon she passed away. She died about fifteen minutes after they left the hospital. Her doctor phoned Uncle Sally Boy, who immediately called our house. When my father came home, my brother hit him with the bad news.

"Whaddaya talkin' about?" my father railed. "I just left the goddamn hospital. Mamma's fine."

"Bill, he's serious," my mother said. "Sally Boy called here a few minutes ago. Mamma probably passed while you were on your way home. Sally Boy is on his way to the hospital, where he's gonna meet Rocco and Joe."

My father looked stunned. "But I was just there." He rubbed a hand across his forehead. "I was ... I was by her bedside all afternoon. I even helped the nurse give her a sponge bath." As he spoke, his eyes watered. He went to his bedroom and shut the door. After a moment we heard him bawling uncontrollably.

"I better go see how he's doing," my mother said, hoisting herself up from the couch.

Connie looked down at the floor, her eyes darting nervously. She then looked up at Frank.

"Hey." Frank shrugged. "Somebody hadda tell him."

We sat listening to my father wail along with the muffled sounds of my mother's voice attempting to console him.

"God." Connie winced. "He's really taking it hard."

"He sounds like he's dying in there," I said.

"That's the guilt kicking in," Frank said.

"C'mon, Frank. It's his mother, for Godsakes."

"What, it's not true? Please ... gimme a break."

Frank prided himself on being detached from the Caruso drama. Part of me felt the same way, at least when it came to my father's mother. It wasn't just that Grandma Angelina was old-world Italian; my relationship with her had always been distant. Even the language barrier couldn't account for our lack of connection. Most of the time, looking into her eyes had felt like peering into the window of an abandoned house. I thought of her mostly as someone I had to appease to make my old man happy.

"Whaddaya think's gonna happen now?" Connie asked.

"Whaddaya *think*'s gonna happen?" Frank said. "It's gonna be the old Caruso shuffle. They're gonna have a big funeral, where everybody's gonna cry on everybody else's shoulder. Then they're gonna put Grandma in the ground next to her husband, and a week later the old man and his brothers are gonna start blaming each other for not taking better care of her." Frank let out a hard snort. "What a crew … what a freakin' crew."

§

Friends and relatives crowded into Testa's Funeral Home. Big Joe, Sally Boy, and Rocco showed up, along with some of my father's other brothers and sisters who had come from out of state—people I'd never seen before. Everyone was somber and dressed in black.

The room where my grandmother had been laid out was dimly lit, the walls covered with gray drapes. About ten feet from her casket, mourners sat in rows of folding chairs, some with their heads bowed in prayer, others staring into space like zombies. The air was heavy with the cloying scent of flowers, a nauseating smell of orchids and carnations. On one side of the casket, a bunch of floral arrangements sat perched on tripods, each with a small, handwritten card.

Connie and I walked up to the casket and knelt. The sight of us kneeling in front of our dead grandmother incited a wave of cries and moans. It sounded like a chorus of professional mourners. "Aw, look how sweet—the kids," one tearful woman said. "God bless the kids."

My grandmother's hands lay folded across her abdomen, a rosary twined around her thumbs. Her eyes were closed, and her hands and face were caked with powder, but I could still see wrinkles in her cheeks and forehead. It reminded me of *The Mummy*. I was surprised to see that her dead face held a familiar expression, a look of confusion that I'd often glimpsed when I went to her house for lunch. With gaunt cheeks and furrowed brows, she'd sit across from me at the kitchen table and study me intently while I ate one of her creepy sandwiches. She always looked as if she had no idea how the world or anything worked and was searching my face for an answer.

"C'mon, let's go," Connie whispered, making the sign of the cross. "Other people are waiting to pay their respects."

Near the back of the room, my father was standing with Big Joe, Sally Boy, and Rocco, who appeared to be doing most of the talking. Rocco was all business and no bullshit. He was built like a little bull: a short, stocky man with a barrel chest and a flat-top crew cut. I don't think I ever saw him without a pissed-off look on his face. He worked six days a week operating a fruit-and-vegetable concession stand in the Bronx. A few times he came to visit us with his wife and two sons, Rocco Jr. and Cosimo. Cosimo was around my age. Both of them were like their old man: cocky Brooklyn scrappers with Neapolitan bugs up their asses.

I walked over to them, mainly to say hello to Big Joe and Sally Boy. My father put his hands on my shoulders from behind and drew me close.

"How ya doin', Johnny Boy?" Uncle Rocco said, his voice deep and gravelly. "You awright? Everything awright?"

It was the first time I'd seen him wearing a suit. It looked as if he'd put it on right off the rack: the pant legs and sleeves were too long and made his arms and legs look like stovepipes.

"I'm okay," I said, tired of being asked.

"Ya gettin' big there," he said, poking my shoulder. "Ya gettin' big. Ya mus' be eatin' ya Wheaties."

"He misses his grandma," my father said.

It pissed me off whenever my old man tried to put words in my mouth. I didn't miss my grandmother, and hated the way he said "his grandma." It made me sound like a baby.

"Yeah, I bet he does," Rocco said.

I could feel the tension between Rocco and my father. Ever since my father had shorted support payments for his mother, they hadn't been on speaking terms.

"He was Mamma's favorite," my father boasted. "Janoots used go over to her house every day for lunch. She would always make him something nice, right?" My father leaned over, trying to catch my eye. "Right?" he asked again, gripping my shoulder.

I shrugged, looking away. The thought of my lunchtime sessions with Grandma Angelina brought up images of her musty apartment and disgusting sandwiches. It was either tuna fish sopped with mayonnaise, or gabagool (oily Italian lunch meat) on white bread with a dab of mustard, along with bitter-tasting Sicilian black olives and a glass of warm milk. I never told the old man, but most days I'd skipped lunch at her place and headed over to Mario's Pizzeria for a slice and a Coke.

"You gotta forgive him," my father said. "He's a little

upset today."

"It's okay." Sally Boy nodded. "We're all a little upset."

"He misses his grandma," my father said again. "Did you pay your respects and say goodbye?" He leaned forward, tightening his grip on my shoulders. He had already seen me and Connie kneel in front of the casket, and I didn't want to give him the satisfaction of making me perform like a trained seal in front of his brothers.

"I asked you a question," my father said.

I could feel Uncle Rocco's eyes on me. His face was filled with a self-satisfied, contemptuous grin, as if to say, *You see? Even you know your old man's an asshole.*

"Yes. I paid my respects. Didn't you see me?"

"Hey, watch it there, mister," my father shot back. "I don't like that tone of voice."

"Well, you saw me up there with Connie." I shrugged free of his grip. "Why are you asking me?"

My father grabbed my ear and twisted.

"Leave me alone, will ya?" I batted his hand away, and he slapped my face.

"Don't *ever* talk to me like that again."

"Jesus Christ, Bill," Uncle Sally Boy said. "Hell is wrong with you?"

"He knows better than to disrespect me like that."

Big Joe put his arm around me and drew me close to his side. I noticed a few onlookers watching us, and I edged away from him, embarrassed.

"Look at him," Uncle Rocco said, fixing my father with a stare. "Big man ..."

"Mind your own business," my father said. "Nobody

was talking to you."

"Remember when we were kids?" Rocco said, turning to Uncle Sally Boy. "Remember how he used to twist our ear like that and whack us around? Do this. Do that. He thought he was Mussolini—treated us all like we were his personal servants. We used to call him El Duce. 'Member? Now he's got his wife and kids to knock around."

"Listen, sonny boy," my father said. "When I was ten, I was wiping your ass. You used to piss the bed, and I was the one who had to change the sheets. I changed everybody's sheets. And when Pa had a hard time making ends meet, I was out on the street selling newspapers to help feed the family. So please, save the bullshit for someone else."

"Here he is," Rocco said, "the good son. Where's your violin?"

My father cursed in Italian. "Why don't you do us all a favor and go back to the Bronx where you belong, with the rest of the *cafones*—let Mamma rest in peace."

Uncle Rocco hated when my father referred to him as lower class. He unbuttoned his jacket and stepped forward, ready to pounce. "Fuck you, ya cheap bastard. If Mamma knew you were dippin' into her monthly nut, she'd be turning over in her fuckin' casket."

The air was heavy, and the floral smell intensified. My stomach was queasy, and the room wobbled. I headed for the exit, but after two steps I barfed up a fountain of yellow vomit on the carpet, a chunk of it clipping Rocco's trousers.

"Ya sister's ass!" Rocco blurted.

"You okay, Johnny Boy?" Big Joe said.

"Somebody get a chair!" Sally Boy called out.

"He's okay," my father said. "He just needs a little

air."

One of the funeral attendants brought over a chair, and people gathered around us. I sat down, feeling mortified. Uncle Sally Boy loosened my tie, and Aunt Rose rubbed a moist hand-wipe across my forehead.

"What happened?" my mother asked, rushing to my side.

"I don't know," Rocco said, wiping vomit from his shoe with a handkerchief. "We were talkin', and the next thing I know, the kid throws up all over the place. And I just got this suit out of the cleaners."

"Whaddaya complainin' about?" said my father with an aggravated singsong. "It's good luck, for Chrissakes."

"Don't worry." Rocco sneered, flicking vomit from his fingers. "I gotcha good luck right here."

NINE

"WHAT IS YOUR name?" Frank squinted while holding the tips of his fingers close to his lips, pretending to inhale a cigarette. He was sitting on my belly and had my arms spread wide and pinned to the floor with his knees.

"Johnny," I said, giggling.

"Johnny what?"

"Johnny Caruso."

"Tish! Tish!" He mock-slapped my face with a sweeping forehand and backhand. "Don't you *dare* lie to the commandant! Where do you live?"

"Brooklyn," I answered, trying to control my laughter.

"Where?"

"Brooklyn! Brooklyn!"

"Where in Brooklyn?"

"Bensonhurst! Bensonhurst!"

"No such place! Tish! Tish! Don't you *dare* lie to the commandant!"

This went on for ten minutes, with me laughing so hard I nearly pissed myself.

A few nights a week, Frank worked the counter at a nearby luncheonette. He usually came home around seven thirty. I'd hang out in my parents' bedroom and wait by the window to catch him walking up the courtyard. I always knew when he was coming because he whistled his favorite tune, "Swingin' Shepherd Blues," a popular jazz instrumental. His whistle was loud and clear and echoed off the surrounding buildings, sounding just like the cool jazz flute on the record. It was as if he wanted the whole neighborhood to know it was him.

Frank owned a secondhand record player that he'd bought with his earnings, along with a small collection of jazz records—totally different from the Italian opera records my father played on his old Victrola. Frank played Louis Armstrong, Charlie Parker, Miles Davis, John Coltrane, Chet Baker, Count Basie. Occasionally he brought home a new album and snapped along in rapt enthusiasm. He knew all the musicians and their nicknames. "Know who that is?" he'd shout, jabbing his finger at the turntable. "That's Satchmo." "Know who this is? That's the Yardbird." I had no idea how the musicians had gotten their nicknames, but they sounded cool and made me want to listen to their music.

৯৹

When Connie turned fourteen, my mother decided my sister needed her own room. I was moved out to the living room, where I slept on the convertible sofa bed with Frank. He and I shared the hall closet and one of the two chests of drawers in my parents' bedroom. Space was tight, but I didn't mind; it felt comforting to be close to my brother at night.

Frankie was popular in high school and played saxophone in the school's dance band. One Friday evening he came home around six thirty, showered, and rushed to change into his band clothes: black pants, black shoes, and a powder-blue jacket with snazzy dark-blue lapels. I sat on the edge of my parents' bed and watched him scurry from the dresser to the closet and back again, covered with talcum powder. "Panic *project*. Panic *project*," he said, tripping over himself as he struggled to get dressed.

"What time is the dance?"

"Eight o'clock," Frank answered, checking himself out in the mirror, "but we have to rehearse some new tunes, and I haven't even seen the sheet music."

"You gonna eat before you go?" I asked, hoping he would stay a bit longer.

"No time—I'm already late. Besides," he said, slipping on his band jacket and raking back his wet hair, "eating is for wimps."

As Frank was leaving, my father stopped him near the front door. "I want you back here at ten o'clock," he said, tapping the face of his wristwatch.

"Whaddaya mean?" Frank said in disbelief.

"Just what I said."

"Dad, the dance is *over* at ten. And then everybody hangs out until ten thirty, eleven. I can't just leave. I'd look like a complete Neanderthal."

"I don't care. I want you back in this house at ten."

"But why?"

"Because this is *my* house," my father said, "and as long as you're living under *my* roof, you do as I say."

Frank slung his horn case over his shoulder and walked out of the apartment.

That evening I watched some television and opened the sofa bed around ten thirty. I dozed off and woke up some time later to the sound of paper rattling. My father sat at the head of the table, in boxer shorts and a T-shirt, browsing a newspaper. A wedge of light coming from the kitchen cast an eerie, oversized shadow of his body onto the wall next to him.

"What time is it?"

"Never mind," he said without looking up. "Go back to sleep."

I could tell he was furious; he'd skim a page for about thirty seconds, then flip it over and go to the next one, intermittently checking his watch. I lay silently in bed, thinking about Frank: where was he?

Minutes later I heard him whistling in the courtyard. I was relieved he was finally home but dreaded the ticking bomb waiting for him. I peered over my shoulder to see if my father had picked up on Frank's soulful whistle, but he just sat there riffling through his newspaper, tuned out in a heap of rage. In that moment I realized my old man would never know my brother like I did.

Frank's keys jingled in the lock. The instant he appeared in the doorway, my father shot up off his chair. "Where the hell were you?"

"The dance ran late."

"I told you I wanted you back here at ten o'clock sharp!"

"Dad, I just toldja, the dance ran late. We didn't start to pack up until ten twenty."

"Don't give me that bullshit. It's close to eleven thirty! When I tell you ten o'clock, I mean ten o'clock. Not a minute later."

"Dad, I'm in the band. I just can't pack up and leave."

"Oh, I'm in the *band* ... I'm in the *band.*"

"Well, what do you want me to say?"

"Mister Big Shot over here. The big sax man, playing that nigger music for all the girls. Right? Are you the big man with the horn?"

Frank picked up his horn case and walked away.

"I'm not finished with you. Don't walk away from me when I'm talking to you!"

"What?" Frank said. "I've heard this like twenty times already."

"And don't *what* me."

"Well, whaddaya you want? I'm tired. I've been going since seven thirty."

"What do you have to say for yourself?" My father turned his head sharply as if to give Frank his good ear.

Frank headed toward the bathroom. "What can I say. You missed a good gig."

As he passed, my father whacked him from behind, clipping his head with an open hand. "G'ahead, ya fuckin' snot-nosed bastard—I'll cripple you!"

"Drop dead," Frank said, talking over his shoulder.

"What did you say?"

My father followed Frank and smacked his head full force. Frank turned to respond, and my father jammed his foot into Frank's side and laid into him with furious punches to his stomach and upper body. Frank doubled over, groaning and gasping for air. The sound of my brother's helpless and pain-filled voice was overwhelming. My legs stiffened, and my gut was paralyzed with fear.

"Get the hell out of my sight," my father said with utter disdain.

After washing up, Frank came back to the living room, slipped out of his clothes, and got into bed next me.

He was breathing heavily, and I could feel tension radiating from his body.

"Frankie, are you okay?" I whispered.

He pulled the covers over his shoulders and turned on his side, facing away from me.

"Frankie, are you okay?" I whispered again, placing my hand on his shoulder.

"Go to sleep," he said, moving away.

I lay on my back feeling helpless. I wanted to cuddle next to him and let him know I loved him. Frank's breathing grew heavier. He sniffled a few times, then began to weep. It was the first time I'd ever heard him cry. I turned to face him and put my hand on his shoulder again. I edged closer and could smell his spicy cologne. His weeping grew louder. I was sure he was going to pull away again, but he didn't. I wrapped my arm around his waist and kissed his back. Frank didn't budge or say a word, but I didn't care; I was happy to be snuggled up next to him.

TEN

"MA, I'M NOT takin' him to the beach with me," Connie said.

"Why not?"

"Because I'm goin' with my girlfriends."

"So what?"

"Whaddaya mean, *so what?* We're all teenagers, *that's* so what. I'm the only one in the crowd who's always got their kid brother with them. I feel like I'm walking around with a clubfoot."

"What's a clubfoot?" I said.

"You'll take him with you this one time."

"But that's what you always say. Then there's the next time, and the next time, and the *next time.*"

"What's the big deal? He's not gonna bother anybody."

"Yeah, right," Connie said. "Except when he's a pain in the ass."

"He's your kid brother."

"Why don't you take him? You never take him anywhere."

It was true, I rarely went places with my mother, except for occasional visits to see her sister in Williamsburg, or on boring shopping trips to downtown Brooklyn. When she pressured my sister to include me in her plans, it made me feel like an unwanted tagalong.

"Never mind that," my mother said. "He's your brother. You take him with you to the beach, or you're not going anywhere."

"Ma!"

"That's it and that's all," said my mother, turning away. "I don't wanna hear another word."

Connie was irate. "Get your towel," she said, tugging on my T-shirt. "You give me any trouble today, and I'll box your ears back."

"What's a clubfoot?"

"Aw, shut up."

℮

My father finally landed a job working for an aircraft company somewhere upstate. Everyone was relieved. With the old man gone during the week, Connie would sometimes invite a few girlfriends to our apartment after school. They'd sprawl on the couch and living room floor and do their homework while watching *American Bandstand*. They practiced all the new dances, like the Stroll and the Madison, and they knew the names of all the regular kids on the show and talked about them as if they were personal friends. They would also talk about boys in their school and compare notes on who was dating and who had a crush on whom. Guys were "dreams," "walking dreams," "living dolls," or (my favorite) "the living end." I didn't have a clue what that meant, but it sounded like something I should aspire to.

I liked it when Connie's girlfriends came to visit; it

made me feel like I was one of the big kids. Plus, they showered me with attention, which made me look good in front of my sister. Their acceptance allowed me to hang out with Connie and be a part of her life without feeling resented.

Once I did an imitation of Elvis, shaking and twisting my hips while strumming an air guitar and singing "Hound Dog." Her friends went berserk.

"God, your kid brother is *so* cute!"

"How adorable!"

"Hey, Connie, can I take him home with me?"

"Take him home?" Connie said. "How 'bout you take him for keeps?"

Connie dated different guys but never talked about them with my parents. I found out about her boyfriends by listening to her yap with her girlfriends and eavesdropping on her phone conversations. For some reason she dated mostly Italian lugs, who were good-looking but didn't sound too bright. There was Vincent Palumbo, for example, whose family owned Palumbo's Meats & Poultry on Bath Avenue. "Vincenzo," as Connie liked to refer to him, was a sharp dresser and popular in school. "Are you kidding? *Everybody* admires Vincenzo," I heard her tell one of her girlfriends. "Palumbo's is one of the biggest family-owned business in Bensonhurst," she added, sounding like she was dating one of the Medicis.

Unfortunately for my sister, "Vincenzo" was a little too popular. Two months after they started dating, it was brought to her attention that he'd been secretly exploring other options. One of my sister's friends spotted Vinny in the balcony of the DeLuxe movie theater with his tongue down the throat of Susan DeLuca, one of Connie's classmates.

To say that my sister was pissed was an understatement. I listened to her rip Vincent a new asshole over the phone, then watched her take a sharp pair of scissors to his photo and turn it into confetti. "Lousy bastard!"

"What happened to Vincenzo?" I said with an overblown Italian accent.

"None of your goddamn business!"

Then there was Nunzio DePasquale, who worked weekends as a stock boy in an auto-supply store on Eighteenth Avenue.

"Nice name," said Frank sarcastically.

"What's wrong with Nunzio?" Connie said. "I think it's a beautiful name."

"Please," Frank said. "If you tried, you couldn't get more greaseball than *Nunzio*."

Nunzio was a beefy high school senior with buff arms, a huge neck, and enough pomade in his hair to lubricate a school bus. I couldn't understand what Connie saw in him. Granted, the guy was handsome, with a chiseled jawline and dark, sultry eyes, but when he opened his mouth he sounded like a baboon. The first time she introduced me to him, he said stuff like "Jeetjet?" for "Did you eat yet?" and "'Sco" for "Let's go." I got the feeling that my sister was trying to rescue him from something, but if she wanted to rescue someone, why couldn't she rescue me?

One afternoon I came home from school early and caught Connie and her new dream boy making out on the couch. Her skirt was hiked up to her thighs, and he had his hand under her sweater. The moment she saw me, she freaked out. "What are you doing home so early?" she said, quickly pulling away from Nunzio and adjusting her clothes. The sight of this palooka with his paws on my sister set me off. "What are *you* doin'?" I demanded.

"Nothing," Connie said. "We were just talking."

"Why was he touching you like that?"

"We were just talking, that's all."

"He was touching you; I saw him."

"Johnny, it was nothing," Connie insisted, trying to sound rational. "We were just touching a little bit. We're friends. It's no big thing."

Nunzio seemed amused. He sat back and clasped his hands behind his head like he was taking in a ballgame. "Relax, will ya?" he said with a smile. "We wasn't doin' nuttin."

"Who asked you?" I said.

"Man," Nunzio said to Connie. "The kid always like this?"

"Keep your fuckin' hands off my sister."

"Whoa, whoa, whoa ..." He held up a hand, fingers spread wide. "Whodaya think ya talkin' to over here?"

Connie sprang up from the couch and slapped my shoulder. "*Hey, you.* You don't talk to my friends like that."

"I don't care. You tell this greaseball to keep his hands off you."

"Wow," Nunzio said, "kid brother's got some mouth on him."

"I'm sorry," Connie said. "I don't know what's wrong with him today."

Nunzio stood up.

"Where are you going?"

"It's gettin' late," he said, glancing at his watch. "I

gotta get backta work."

"Can you stay for just for a few more minutes?"

"Naw, really. I gotta split."

Connie continued to apologize and tried to talk him into staying, but Nunzio wasn't hearing it. He tucked his shirttail into his pants and was out the door in a flash.

"What the hell is wrong with you?" Connie said. "And where the hell do you get off calling him a greaseball? Are you out of your *mind*?"

"I didn't want to see him touching you like that. I was tryna protect you."

"Protect me from *what*, you idiot?"

"From him feeling you up."

"Well, thanks a ton. I'll be lucky if he ever talks to me again. Besides," she added, hands on her hips, "that's what teenagers do. They touch each other."

"Yeah, but this is different."

"How the hell is this different?"

"You're my sister, no?" I choked out, fighting back tears. "I don't want anybody touching you."

Connie paused, staring at me. "Oh God," she said, clutching her forehead.

I thought I'd been protecting her, and now I felt I'd done something wrong. "I'm sorry," I said.

"Oh, now you're sorry. Thanks mucho."

"Well, what do you want me to say?"

"Listen, someday I'll explain it to you," she said. "But in the meantime, please do me a favor and mind your own business. I'm a big girl. I don't need anyone to protect me. Okay?"

☙

Connie had transformed what had once been our shared bedroom into her own private boudoir. My bed had been replaced with a modern desk that my mother had bought for her on sale, and my father had put up bookshelves. She'd made her own floor-length, lavender chiffon curtains that she hung over the drab window shade and painted one wall Degas pink, decorating it with a print of a pirouetting ballerina in a fancy white tutu. Pictures of Bobby Darin, Paul Anka, and James Dean covered the remaining walls, along with a school banner and some other high school crap. At the official unveiling, I walked in and thought I was in somebody else's apartment.

"Nice curtains," I said, gliding my hand up and down the smooth fabric.

"Don't touch them!" she said. "Your hands are all sweaty."

My sister made it clear that she didn't want me or anyone else intruding on her space. She put a sign on her door that read "PLEASE KNOCK!" When she wasn't home, I'd sometimes hang out in her room and listen to her 45s or work at her desk. If one thing was out of place, she knew I'd been in there. "I'm not going to tell you again," she'd warn me. "Stay the hell out of my room when I'm not here, or I'll break your little fingers."

One day I was rummaging in the hall closet, looking for my baseball glove, when Connie walked into the apartment carrying a load of schoolbooks cradled in her arms.

"Where are you coming from?" my mother said, following her to her room.

"I was hanging out with Ann Gottlieb," Connie told her. Ann was my sister's best friend, a tall, soft-spoken girl who lived with her family in a small rowhouse on a tree-lined street a few blocks away, in the "nice neighborhood" populated mostly by Jewish people who owned their own homes and had private driveways and backyards.

"How is Ann?" my mother asked.

"She's fine. We were studying for the science final, and then we helped her mother move some books and things into her new home office."

"Her mother is a teacher?"

"Joyce is a child psychologist," said Connie with a hint of smugness.

"Oh, a psychologist," my mother said, impressed.

"She's a real brain. She has a master's degree in special education and a doctorate in psychology. She's also well-traveled. After college she lived in Paris for a year and went all over Europe."

"She must come from money."

"That's what I want to do someday."

"What, travel?"

"I want to be a doctor and work with children," Connie said, plopping her books down on her desk. "And then I wanna go to Paris and Italy and see all the museums. Especially the Louvre." She pronounced "Louvre" with a grotesque French accent.

My parents never took us to museums or even discussed them. Such places seemed foreign and unavailable to me. But Connie had been to the Guggenheim and the Metropolitan Museum of Art on class trips and talked about art and artists as if she were an authority, which bugged the shit out of my father. When she was in lecture mode, she'd miraculously lose her Brooklyn accent, like the time she treated us to a discourse one evening at dinner: "I mean, *God*, Van Gogh didn't emerge as an artist until he was in his early thirties—his *early thirties!*"

"Oh, *rah*-lee, *rah*-lee?" my father responded with mock curiosity, sounding like a snooty English aristocrat with a mouth full of marbles and a rod up his ass. "Please, my dear, do tell."

"A *doctor?*" my mother said. "Forget about it. To become a doctor, you're talkin' *what?*—at least eight to ten years of schooling."

"You're right, Ma," Connie said, frustrated. "But then guess what? After the eight or ten years—*bingo*. You're a doctor for the rest of your life."

"I guess. Just seems like a lot of schooling. What does Ann's father do?"

"He's a lawyer."

"Oh, a lawyer. He works in Brooklyn?"

"I don't know."

"Between the two of them, I'm sure they do well for themselves."

"They're doing a lot better than we are."

"Are they religious?"

"*Ma.*"

"What?"

"What is this, Twenty Questions?"

"I'm just asking."

"I know, but you do this all the time. It drives me nuts."

"I'm just curious. Can't I even ask a simple question?"

I found my glove wedged between some old blankets, pulled it out, and moved over to stand in the doorway of my sister's room.

"Well, let me ask *you* a question," Connie said. "How come *you* never went to college?"

"Who could afford it?" my mother said. "Only rich people went to college. My father worked as a busboy and waiter most of his life. You kids don't know how easy you got it. Forget college. Thirty, thirty-five years ago, we were lucky to have a roof over our heads."

"Yeah, but didn't you ever want to get an education?"

"Of course I did. I wanted to do a lot of things. It just wasn't in the cards for me. At eighteen, my sister Lena and I worked in a bra factory nine, ten hours a day to help out the family. Working conditions were horrible. All day long, forty sewing machines going nonstop. The noise was deafening. Plus, we had little or no ventilation, and one bathroom for an entire floor. *Forget it.* Sometimes there'd be a dozen girls lined up to use the toilet. My sister and I and some of the other gals brought our own pots to work so we could take them into the storage room and pee when we needed to. You don't know ..." My mother paused and nodded, her eyes welling with tears. "Even if we could afford college, my father wouldn't hear of it. Whaddaya think, it was like today, with all the freedoms you kids have? Back then, neighborhood women didn't go to college. We stayed home and cooked and cleaned and took care of the family."

Connie glanced at me, then back at our mother. The thought of my mom working ten hours a day and pissing in a pot was unimaginable.

"I didn't know that, Ma," Connie said. She stepped

forward and wrapped her arms around our mom. I dropped my glove and did the same. My mother wept, and we hugged her tight. "We love you, Ma," said Connie.

ELEVEN

MY FATHER WAS on a rampage. "Are you out of your mind?" I heard him shouting at my mother in their bedroom. "You let a stranger into our apartment without my knowledge! Are you crazy?"

The bathroom sink had been leaking, and my mother had called a repairman to come and fix the sink during the day, when no one was home.

"For Chrissakes," my mother said, "what's the big deal? Everybody does it. The damn sink's been leaking for a week already."

"I'm not *everybody*. This is Bill Caruso you're talkin' to! I don't want strangers sneaking around the house when nobody's here."

"What strangers? They work for Bay Haven; it's their *job*."

"I don't give a damn if it's the President of the United States. I don't want anybody in the house when nobody's home—*period*."

"Dad, what's anybody gonna take?" Frank said, stepping into the bedroom. Connie and I trailed behind him.

"Whatever," my father said. "We got things up here."

"What things?" Frank said.

"Things."

My father walked over to the chests of drawers and opened the top two drawers, one after another. "I knew it," he said, shaking his head. "Look at this." He gestured with a hand. "Somebody's been in here. My undershorts are all messed up and pushed to the side. That's not how I left it." He fumbled around for a bit, examining his belongings, then slammed the drawers closed and hurried to his closet, where he reached for the top shelf and pulled out a bottle of Napoleon brandy, his private stash that he kept hidden behind his violin case. "Son of a bitch," he said, carefully inspecting the label. "Just as I thought."

"What?" asked my mother.

"Somebody's been in here drinking my goddamn brandy."

"How do you know?" Frank said, fighting back a grin.

"I mark the label with a pencil every time I take a shot —that's how I keep track."

"Who the hell here drinks brandy?" My mother turned to me, Connie, and Frank. "I don't. The kids certainly don't."

"Oh, yeah?" My father held the bottle near his face. "Well, somebody must have. This thing is off by almost a quarter of an inch; pencil marks don't lie."

"That's ridiculous," my mother said.

"G'ahead." He held the bottle close to her face, pointing to a mark he'd made on the label. "Take a look, then tell me I'm crazy."

My mother reluctantly glanced at the bottle and turned away.

"And why is this book out?" my father asked, pointing to one of his drafting books on top of the small bookcase next to the bed.

"I thought you took it out to read," my mother said.

"I did. But I put it back in the bookcase."

"Well, maybe you forgot. The book's been sitting there for a couple of days. I thought you were reading it. For Godsakes, what's the difference?"

"I *know* I put that book back on the shelf. Somebody's been in this room," he insisted, looking around, searching for more evidence.

"Why don't we tell him the truth?" I said calmly, stepping closer to my mother.

It was as if I had whipped out a pistol and fired two rounds in the air; everybody froze in their tracks.

"Oh God ..." I heard Connie murmur from behind.

"No—" I said. "Let's tell him, so he knows."

"Tell me what?" my father said.

"The handyman," I continued. "After he fixed the leak in the bathroom, he came in here, opened your drawers, and futzed around with your underwear. Then he went into the closet, helped himself to a couple of shots of brandy, and sat on the bed and read your book. Only thing is ... the guy messed up and forgot to put it back in the bookcase."

Complete silence. My father looked totally perplexed. He stood there staring at me as if I'd spoken Swahili. My heart was pounding like a fucking jackhammer. After a moment, his tense expression gave way to a smile. He giggled like a kid, and within seconds everyone was laughing. I exhaled, feeling like I'd defused a bomb.

"C'mere, you," he said, pulling me closer. He wrapped his arm around my neck. "What are you, a wise guy?" He squeezed me tight, kissing the top of my head.

For the rest of the day, I was the apple of my father's eye. He gave me a buck and told me go out and blow it on whatever I wanted.

"That had to be the all-time best," Connie commented later. "Did you see the look on the old man's face? He didn't know *what* the hell was goin' on."

"Neither did I," Frank said. "For a minute I thought the kid had lost his marbles. 'Why don't we tell him the truth?'" he mimicked. "What the hell were you thinking?"

"I don't know." I smiled and shrugged. "It just popped out of my mouth."

"You were too funny," Connie said.

"Kid was *lucky*," Frank said. "With the old man, ya never know. Thank God he wasn't half-tanked with a wild hair up his ass. Things coulda gone south in a hurry."

A few weeks later, on my eleventh birthday, my father took me to Coney Island. There was something magical about Coney Island during the summer. The sunbaked beach was a patchwork of blankets and towels, and the boardwalk and fairway swarmed with people going from one ride and concession stand to another, their faces glowing with excitement.

My father talked about Coney Island as if it were a sacred oasis—the go-to destination where he and his brothers went to escape and have fun when they were kids. The minute the D train pulled into Stillwell Avenue station and we stepped onto the platform, we were smacked with that unmistakable aroma of roasted peanuts, popcorn, and cotton candy. Within the span of two minutes my father turned into another person. It was almost like watching the Wolfman shed his whiskers, claws, and fangs and morph back into a human. He held my hand as I dragged him around to all the big rides: The Parachute Jump, the Wonder Wheel, the Bobsled, the Cyclone roller coaster. "Okay, where are we goin' next?" he'd say after each ride. I felt like the adult taking *him* out for *his* birthday.

We drifted up and down the Bowery—a long, crowded walkway lined with rides and attractions—and stopped at every other shooting gallery, penny arcade, and sideshow. Afterward we polished off a few hot dogs at Nathan's and headed over to Steeplechase Park, a huge amusement complex. Inside the Pavilion of Fun, we went on just about every ride, including the Human Pool Table, the Whip, and the Bowery Slide.

At one end of the pavilion was the Blowhole Theater, a small stage with an open seating area that held about two hundred people. My father and I sat in the front row and watched a team of dwarf clowns manically run around, poking fun at patrons who unknowingly entered the stage after leaving the mechanical horses, a ride that circled the exterior of the building. The stage was booby-trapped with moving floors and a jittering staircase that hapless fun seekers had to traverse in front of a sea of laughing onlookers. The floor also included a few strategically placed high-pressure air nozzles that shot air upward, causing women's dresses to fly over their heads. People laughed boisterously, including my father, who couldn't get enough of the pandemonium.

Later that afternoon, we went to catch a bus back to Bensonhurst. While we waited at the bus stop, my father smiled, resting his hands on my shoulders. His forehead, cheeks, and hairy arms were red from the sun. "Did you have a good time today, buddy?"

"I *did*. The slide and the Cyclone were my favorites."

"How about the clowns?"

"Oh yeah, the clowns! Forget about it, they were great!"

My father kissed the top of my head. "We'll do it again."

The bus was scheduled to arrive in fifteen minutes. The two of us were exhausted and happy just to stand and relax in silence. We watched other passengers line up behind us, their hands filled with food, soft drinks, stuffed animals, and other crap they'd won at shooting galleries. Suddenly there was some commotion.

"That's terrible," said a distraught woman, pushing a child in a stroller. "Someone should call an ambulance, for Godsakes."

Peering over my father's shoulder, I saw a man flat on his back, his body convulsing. A few people looked on, but most passed him by. "Dad, look."

My father rushed over, and I followed. The man had a small gash on his forehead and appeared to be having a seizure. He made gurgling sounds, and his eyes darted uncontrollably. A yellow taxi idled just a few feet ahead of us where a cloud of gray exhaust oozed out of the tailpipe and wafted over the man's body. "Tell the driver to cut the engine," my father said.

I dashed over and told the driver what was happening. He cut his engine, hopped out of the taxi, and followed me back to the man. "Holy cow," he said. "I didn't even know anyone was back here. Did someone call an ambulance?"

"We don't know," I said.

"I got a two-way radio in the cab. I'll have the dispatcher call it in."

The man in the street started to convulse more rapidly, his jaw shifting from side to side. My father's face was awash with concern. "Can you hear me? Can you hear me?" The man didn't respond. My father held on to his forearms and pressed them against the asphalt. "Just relax," he said. He seemed to know what he was doing. He held the man in that position for a good two or three minutes. After a while, the convulsions waned and the man's eyes started to focus. He seemed more aware of his surroundings. Seeing him regain consciousness was like watching a child wake from a bad dream.

"You're gonna be okay," my father said.

The man didn't speak. He just stared at my dad, looking helpless and confused. My father helped him sit up. "You're gonna be okay," he repeated. He unbuttoned the top buttons of the man's shirt and loosened his collar. The guy blinked a few times with a quizzical expression, as if to ask, *Do you mean me?*

A small crowd had gathered and looked on in near silence, their faces mostly blank with apathy, though I noticed a few people in the crowd observe my father with admiration. Seeing that made me feel proud of him. Until he had jumped in to help, no one seemed to care what happened to the man. He could have cracked his head on the curb and dropped dead or been run over by the cab backing up. Either way, he had been completely vulnerable.

A short time later, a police car pulled up to the curb.

"What's goin' on here?" asked one of the officers.

"This man had a seizure," my father said. "He needs medical attention."

The cop looked like a seasoned veteran—tough Irish eyes, sergeant's stripes. "Okay. We'll take care of it." He squatted, resting his forearms on the tops of his thighs. "What's goin' on there, buddy?" he said to the man. "How we feelin' today?"

"You don't understand," my father said. "This man just had a seizure."

"I said we'll take care of it," said the cop.

A second cop emerged from the patrol car. "What seems to be the problem?" he said.

"This man just had a seizure," my father told the second cop. "He needs to see a doctor."

"Mike, talk to this guy, will ya?" said the first cop.

"Awright, listen, pal. If you just step back and let us do our job, we'll take care of it."

"Yeah, but you don't understand," my father insisted. "This man fell down. He needs—"

"I said back off." The second cop raised his voice, holding up his hands. "We'll take it from here. We appreciate your help. Now please, let us do our job, okay? We do this all day long."

My father was becoming agitated.

"C'mon, Dad," I said, tugging on his arm. "They'll take care of him. He'll be okay."

Minutes later an ambulance showed up and two EMS workers in white uniforms attended to the man. They checked his pulse and examined his eyes and ears. One of them placed a gauze pad over the gash on his forehead and helped him to his feet. As they escorted him to the ambulance, he and my father made eye contact.

"Poor guy," my father said. "Let's hope they don't treat him like another piece of meat."

TWELVE

JACKIE D. AND I played touch football with a gang of kids on the "Big Grass," a wide stretch of patchy lawn not far from Bay Haven's main entrance. One afternoon our team was in the hole, something like twenty-four to fourteen, and Nicky DeMayo, one of the older kids, tossed a twenty-yard Hail Mary in my direction. I raced past a swarm of defenders and managed to snatch the ball out of the air after bobbling it on the tips of my fingers—a once-in-a-lifetime miracle catch. Just before I cleared the end zone, I felt a hand graze my leg.

"Gotcha," said a short, dorky kid with a tangle of brown hair. He stared up at me through thick, horn-rimmed glasses that made his peepers look like floating olives.

"*Bullshit.* You only got me with one hand."

I couldn't believe it. I had just made the touchdown of the century, and now some extraterrestrial claimed it was a no-go.

"No way, I tagged you with two hands!"

In seconds we were surrounded by a dozen kids, all ranting and taking sides.

"What happened?" Nicky said.

"Nick, I don't know where you found this guy," I said, pointing a finger at the kid, "but he's sayin' he tagged me with two hands, which is total bullshit."

"I did too," said the kid. "After he caught the ball, I came down low and touched his leg with both hands." He held out his hands as if presenting them as evidence. "Ask anybody."

"*Your ass!*" I yelled in frustration. "I was like three steps ahead of you! You clipped me with one hand ... *one fuckin' hand.* You barely touched me—I had you by a mile, you bug-eyed freak!"

The kid shoved me, and I shoved him back twice as hard. He lost his balance, and as he stumbled backward, I noticed a Star of David pop out from under his sweatshirt, dangling on a chain.

"Fuck you, ya kike!" The words shot out of my mouth like an angry bolt of lightning.

"Who you callin' a kike?" he said.

"*You,* ya fuckin' kike."

I had no idea what a kike was, but I knew it was a derogatory word because my father sometimes used it when talking about Jewish shopkeepers. "Never trust a Jew," he told me. "They're always ready to Jew you outa something."

"Johnny, lighten up," Jackie said.

"Fuck, that. This kid's yankin' my fuckin' bird over here."

The two of us exchanged heated insults for about five minutes, barking each other down like wild dogs. Jackie and Nicky tried to intervene, but I wasn't letting up. I was convinced I was right, and nobody was going to tell me different. Finally, our squabble had cut the mood like a sudden downpour and ended the game.

I got home around four thirty and was surprised to see my father sitting at the dining room table in his work clothes.

He was nursing a highball and looked livid.

"Get over here, you," he said.

"Wha'd I do?" I asked, cautiously stepping toward him. My brain riffled through a list of recent fuck-ups: hiding a pair of torn school pants under my dresser; accidentally breaking one of his favorite beer glasses and not telling him; getting busted by the Bay Haven maintenance staff for hurling water balloons off the roof of our building ...

"Did you call some kid out there a *kike*?"

I froze. His gaze sliced through me like a scorching poker.

"Answer me."

I swallowed, and hot blood rush to my cheeks.

"*Answer me!*" He slapped my face so hard my legs buckled.

"*Get up*," he said, tugging my collar. "Now I'm gonna ask you one more time. Did you call some kid out there a kike?"

"Yes," I whimpered.

"I got a call from a Mrs. Weintraub. She said you called her son a kike in front of all the other kids. *That true?*"

"Yes," I said, wiping tears from my eyes. "But we were playin' two-hand touch, and then ... then we got into an argument, and the kid pushed me."

"I don't care what the hell he did. You don't call somebody a kike in front of a bunch of kids! What if the whole neighborhood gets wind of this? I've never been so embarrassed in my life."

"What about the Jewish guy from the deli?"

"What about him?"

"You said he was a kike the time he tried to

overcharge you for beer."

"Never mind what I said!" He screamed. "You do as I say, not as I do!"

I still didn't know what kike meant, but it was too late for that. Now the whole neighborhood was going to find out, and my old man would turn me into dead meat.

"Let's go," my father said, grabbing my arm and shoving me toward the door. "We're going to see Mrs. Weintraub, and you're gonna apologize to her son."

The kid and his mother lived two buildings over from ours. All the way there my father prodded me along the walkway. When we arrived at their apartment, Mrs. Weintraub, a buxom woman with intelligent eyes, answered the door. "You know, Mr. Caruso, I appreciate your concern, but you really didn't have to come over."

"That's okay," my father said, adjusting his tie. "I like to straighten things out as they happen. This way he and I won't have any misunderstandings. Is your boy around? Johnny here has something he wants to say to him."

Mrs. Weintraub opened the door a little farther, and the sounds of meat sizzling on the stove drifted into the hall from her nearby kitchen, along with a waft of fragrant aromas. The whole floor smelled like liver and onions.

"Kenneth!" she called over her shoulder.

Her son appeared and stood next to his mother. He had changed his clothes and looked much younger than he had outside. He also wasn't wearing glasses, which made his face appear more innocent. He wasn't a Jew to me now, or even Christian—he was just another dumb kid, like me.

"Johnny has something he wants to tell you," my father said, yanking me front and center. "G'ahead." He poked my shoulder.

"I apologize for calling you names."

"And what else?"

I cleared my throat. I felt so embarrassed I could barely look the kid in the eye.

"Say it!"

"And ... and I won't do it again."

Mrs. Weintraub started to say something, but my father grabbed my arm with one hand and began slapping my face with the other, striking me once for every word he pronounced through clenched teeth. "The next time ... I hear you ... using ... language ... like that ... there will be ... hell ... to ... pay! *You hear me?*"

My face burned with an icy agony. I tried to defend myself with my free arm, but it was useless. I just kept telling myself that at some point it would end. My face and eyelids swelled, and I could barely make out a blurred image of Kenny and his mother.

"Please, Mr. Caruso, that's enough! Please stop," Mrs. Weintraub begged. Both she and Kenny looked horrified.

"That's okay," my father said. "This young man has got to learn to respect other people. I swear"—he glared at me —"I don't know where the heck he gets it."

Back at home I found Frank in the kitchen, talking with my mother. He took one look at me and his jaw dropped. "What the hell happened to you?"

"Daddy beat me for calling a Jewish kid a kike," I cried.

"Jesus Christ," my mother said. "Let me put some cold water on that face."

"You gotta be kidding me," Frank said, tilting my

head toward the overhead light. "Ma, you see this? Kid's face is all bruised."

"I see it, I see it." My mother rushed to the sink and soaked a dish towel in cold water.

"Where's Daddy?" Frank asked me.

"I don't know. He said he had to go someplace and told me to go home."

My mother wrung out the towel and laid it on my face. It felt cool and soothing. "Hold it there for him while I get some ice," she told Frank.

My brother held the towel to my face, occasionally lifting it to inspect my cheeks. "How's your nose? Can you breathe okay?"

I nodded.

My mother emptied an ice tray into another towel and wrapped it tightly around the cubes. "Here," she said, handing it to Frank, "put this on him. He'll be all right."

Frank held the ice over my eyes, then gently moved the cloth around, pressing it against different parts of my face. After a moment he tilted my head toward the light again. "Jesus Christ, Ma," he said. "When are we gonna pack our goddamn bags and get the hell out of here?"

"It's not that easy," my mother said.

"Oh, yeah?" said Frank, cupping my chin in his palm, holding it up toward my mother. "How about this? Is *this* easy? This kid looks like he went twelve rounds with Joe Louis."

❦

My father returned home about an hour later. I was sitting on the couch watching television. He dropped some packages in the kitchen and strolled through the living room to his bedroom without saying a word. I kept my eyes fixed on the screen, thinking of how much I hated him and wished he would drop dead. A minute later he came back into the living room.

"What are you watchin'?" he asked, trying to sound friendly.

"TV," I said without looking up.

"I know you're watching TV. Anything good?"

"A show."

He paused, and I could feel him smothering in guilt. He went into the kitchen, then returned to the living room a few minutes later. "Did you eat?" he said.

"Not hungry."

"Are you sure?"

I didn't answer.

"I bought some ice cream," he said. "You want some? It's your favorite, cherry vanilla."

"Said I'm not hungry."

My father retreated to the kitchen again. I heard him run the faucet and shuffle some plates. I had visions of going in there, picking up a knife, and repeatedly stabbing him in the back.

He soon returned. "Are you interested in a movie? I think they got *Ben-Hur* playing over at the Oriental. If we leave now, we can make the early show."

I couldn't believe my ears. My eyes were still swollen and my cheeks puffed. I turned my head, and he was looking at me, his face a pitiful mask of guilt and remorse.

"Listen, I didn't mean to be so ..."

Before he uttered another syllable, I turned back to the TV. My father vanished into the kitchen, and a few minutes later he left the house without saying a word.

It was about three a.m. when the intercom buzzed and woke Frank and me. My mother opened her bedroom door, and a wedge of light sliced into the living room.

"Frank, who is that?" she called out.

"Shit," he mumbled. "Now what?"

The buzzing persisted.

"Frank!" my mother called again. "Who is that?"

"How the hell do I know?"

"Well, answer it and find out who it is."

"Why don't *you* answer it?"

My mother didn't respond. The pace of the buzzing became more rapid.

"Frank!" she shouted.

Frank whipped back the covers and hopped out of bed, heading for the dining area. "Hello," he said into the intercom.

"Is this the home of Bill Caruso?" a man said.

"Who is this?" Frank said.

"It's Lou from Champ's Corner. We got your father here. We wanna bring him up."

"Who is it?" my mother said.

"Some guy named Lou from Champ's Corner. He says he's got the old man with him."

"All right, buzz him up," my mother said.

Connie came out of her room in a bathrobe. "What

the hell is going on?"

"It's the old man," Frank said, slipping on a pair of jeans.

Shirtless and barefoot, Frank switched on the dining room light and opened the front door. My mother shuffled into the living room adjusting her housecoat, Connie trailed behind her. I heard the elevator door open, then voices and scuffling in the hall.

"Jesus Christ," my mother said. "What the hell happened?"

I sprang out of bed to have a look for myself. My father was drooping between two men holding him up by his arms. His shirt hung out of his pants, and his tie was twisted off to the side. Below his waist his fly was open. His crotch and pant legs were soaked where he had obviously pissed himself.

"I think he had a little too much to drink," one of the men said, trying to sound respectful.

"Thanks, fellas," Frank said. "We'll take him from here."

My mother and Frank braced my father between them, slinging his arms over their shoulders. As they carried him in, my father turned and glanced at the men. "Thank ... thank you, gentlemen," he said, slurring his words, "but I ... I really didn't need your assistance."

I lay in the sofa bed, my whole body numb except for my face, which felt raw against the pillow. Eventually I closed my eyes, wishing I were from another family, in another neighborhood, on another planet—wishing I would somehow disappear.

THIRTEEN

"IMPOSSIBLE," MY MOTHER said.

"Nothing is impossible," Frank replied.

"And what are we gonna live on? Your good looks?"

I sat on the couch listening to Frank and Connie work on our mother. Earlier in the week, I'd overheard them hammering out a plan for the four of us to move someplace where my father couldn't find us. To me, the thought of the four of us living together, away from my father, sounded like a place the nuns and priests often described as heaven. Only without the blissful clouds and winged angles.

"Ma, listen to me," Frank said. "I got a real job now. No more jerkin' my banana at the luncheonette for a dollar fifteen an hour. I'm just starting out, but there's a guy in print production who's leaving, and they're talking about making me the new production assistant."

Frank had just turned nineteen and had landed a job as an office assistant for an advertising agency in Manhattan. He had also been attending Hunter College a few nights per week.

"Right," Connie said. "Plus, Ann Gottlieb's mother is recommending me to one of her doctor friends who's looking for someone to help organize her files. And I just applied for a part-time job at the public library on Eighteenth Avenue."

"And if *you* get a job, say in another dry-cleaning store somewhere, we'll have plenty of money," Frank said. "Probably more bread than the old man's bringing home now. No more scraping from week to week while we watch him piss away house money on booze."

My mother looked stricken with indecision. "I don't know ..." she said, blinking and touching her lips. "I mean, it's not that easy. There are too many ifs."

"Ma, we gotta get the hell outta here," Frank insisted. "We can't live like this anymore. This shit is killing us."

Hearing Frank and Connie gave me hope. For the first time, I believed it might be possible for us to live away from our father.

As my mother mulled it over, she noticed me sitting next to Connie. "Go outside and play," she said.

"Why?" I asked. I hated when she tried to cut me out of the conversation. It made me feel like an afterthought.

"No," Frank said. "Let the kid stay. He's a big boy now, and this concerns him too. What do you think?" he asked.

"I wanna leave, just like you guys. But how come *we* have to leave? Why can't *he* leave?"

"Good point," Frank said.

"Wow," Connie said. "I never thought of that. Why don't we all just get together and ask *him* to leave?"

My suggestion and Frank's and Connie's responses were a triple shot of reality, too much for my mother to absorb in one dose. She considered the idea for maybe four seconds, then started bawling like a toddler. "You kids don't know what it's like," she sobbed. "I try ... I try ... But I can't anymore. I just can't."

Connie and Frank weren't fazed by her tears. Neither was I. Seeing their unflinching, stolid faces made me think that my mother was just running through one of her "Mary on the cross" routines.

"What is it, Ma?" Frank said, sounding annoyed. "What do you mean you can't?"

"Yeah, Ma," Connie added. "Can't what?"

"I can't." My mother continued to shake her head, wiping her eyes with the corner of her faded apron. "It's not that easy. I can't just pick up and go like that. With what? We have no savings, *nothing*."

"We'll work it out," Connie said. "We'll make it happen."

"And then there's all the relatives, and the church ... What's everybody gonna say?"

"The *church*?" Frank exploded. "Who gives a rat's ass what the church thinks? The Pope isn't living under this roof. He doesn't know what the hell is goin' on up here. The church ..."

"If you're so worried about what the family thinks, why don't you ask them all to move in with us so they can see what a son of a bitch your husband really is?" Connie said.

"You shut up!" My mother sprang up from her seat. "I swear, I can't take it anymore!" She tugged at her hair. "You kids are making me crazy! One of these days I'm gonna jump out a window—I swear to God, I'm gonna jump right out of a window!"

"Really, Ma?" Frank said. "You're gonna jump out a window? Really?" He popped up from the couch, rushed over to the windows, and pushed them open one after the other. "G'ahead, they're open. You gonna jump? Jump."

I couldn't believe my brother was inviting my mother to kill herself. Connie looked equally shocked. We both knew that Frank had a low tolerance for bullshit, but this was beyond anything we'd ever seen. My mother froze, her tears ceasing. A cool wind filled the living room, pulling one of the drapes over the sill.

"G'ahead," Frank repeated. "*Jump*. We're waiting."

My mother's face was drenched with shame. She sank into her chair and buried her face in her apron.

"You're full of shit," Frank said. "You don't deserve children."

"What do you want from me?" she sobbed.

"Nothing, Ma," Connie said, her voice filled with frustration. "We don't want anything. Not a goddamn thing."

My mother's head rose from her apron. "But what can *I* do? What can *I* do?" She shook her hands in front of her, her fingers curled and tense.

"You can pack up and move the fuck out!" Frank shouted. "*That's* what you can do!"

Frank had become friendly with Gordon and Emily Peterson, a young couple who lived on the third floor of our building. Gordon, a bearded, pipe-smoking Brooklyn College professor, wore tan desert boots and tweed jackets with elbow patches. His wife, Emily, was a social worker, a strikingly beautiful blonde who would sometimes go to work dressed in a colorful African gown or Indian sari.

I stopped by their apartment once to summon Frank to dinner. Their home was like a museum. One entire wall of their living room was covered with books and record albums. The other walls featured original abstract paintings and a tiger skin next to an authentic African shield crisscrossed with two spears. Framed black-and-white photographs hung among the paintings, several of them showing Gordon in an African village. Smiling in his safari outfit, he stood in front of a straw hut along with a group of half-naked tribesman wearing face paint and feather headdresses. Some photos showed Emily in India. In one she was posing with a group of Indian women near the entrance of the Taj Mahal. In another, she sat atop an elephant.

The few times I encountered the Petersons in Frank's presence, I got the feeling he was embarrassed by me. "This is my kid brother," he announced the first time. "They just let him out on pass." I wasn't quite sure what "out on pass" meant, but I laughed along, pretending not to be offended. I wanted to look good in the eyes of these people, whom my brother held in high regard because they were way more educated and cultured than our parents or any of our relatives. Connie once commented how "erudite" she thought the Petersons were compared to the neighborhood's working-class families. "Are you *kidding*?" Frank replied. "These people *invented* hip."

When Frank wasn't working or in school, he was usually in the Petersons' apartment. My father was envious of the time Frank spent with them. "What are you doin' hanging out with those oddballs?" he once asked.

"You don't even know them," Frank said.

"I don't have to know them. I can tell just by looking at them. The guy needs a shave and a haircut, and half the time his wife is dressed like a circus clown."

"Right." Frank chuckled. "They're *oddballs.* Meanwhile, Gordon is a college professor with a doctorate in anthropology, and his wife has a master's degree in sociology. They've been all over the world."

"*So*— he has a doctorate," my father said with a shrug. "What the hell does that *mean?*"

"It means he's pretty damn smart. Where's *your* doctorate?"

"It's up your ass!"

Gordon often turned Frank on to new authors and lent him books. I had no idea what they were about, but I thought the titles were cool. What were *Gulliver's Travels* and *The Adventures of Huckleberry Finn* compared to *Naked Lunch* and *Tropic of Cancer?* Sometimes I would skim through their pages and read a paragraph here and there. I wanted to understand them, but most of the time the stuff went over my head.

My father was constantly on my back about reading. He'd frequently cram the importance of education down my throat, but I rarely saw him with a book in his hands. The extent of his "library" was the small bookcase next to his bed, which contained a few technical and religious books among yellowed and dog-eared back issues of *Reader's Digest.*

I liked the idea of reading books because Frank and Connie were into them, but I didn't enjoy reading itself. Every so often my father would treat me to one of his "reading lessons." He would have me stand in front of his old reel-to-reel tape machine and record my voice as I read out loud from a schoolbook or one of Connie's old Classic Comics, *Black Beauty,* or some other bullshit. It didn't matter what I was reading; it felt like torture. I was self-conscious and labored over every sentence.

The more I struggled, the more heated he became. "Stand up straight and speak up!" he'd tell me. "When you read, you want to be comfortable. You're reading a *story*. That's all it is." Every once in a while, he'd pull the book from my hands and read what I had just read, only he'd read it in an overblown, theatrical voice, as if auditioning for *King Lear*. Then he'd rewind the tape and play back both our renditions. "You hear the difference? Now *that's* reading."

Once my father sat me down on the couch and gave me a copy of George Orwell's *Animal Farm*, Frank's latest borrowed book. "I want you to read this and tell me what you think it means," he said, making it sound like some kind of IQ test.

I felt like I had a gun to my head. I distinctly remember the front cover of the book; it showed a group of pissed-off horses, cows, sheep, and chickens. They were all huddled together in the entrance of a barn—definitely not Old MacDonald's spread. I read maybe four or five pages, and my eyelids grew heavy. About an hour later, my father woke me up and asked what the book was about. "I don't know," I mumbled. "Something about some angry animals?"

"What can I do?" He walked away, shaking his head. "I guess somebody's gotta be the shoemaker."

FOURTEEN

IT WAS THE Fourth of July, and my father had found a paperback copy of Aldous Huxley's *Brave New World* sitting on top of Frank's dresser. Gordon had given it to Frank, and it had become one of his favorite books. He told Connie that Huxley was "a visionary way ahead of his time" and that he had a "crystal ball." Gordon had written some words for my brother on the inside cover: *For my buddy Francesco. Good luck on your journey! —Gordy.*

Frank knew what he wanted and seemed to have direction and purpose, which I admired. What was my purpose and my journey? I didn't know. Other than my drunk father handing me a literal map to success, no one had ever discussed my future with me, let alone suggested any goals or plans for getting anywhere. When teachers and other kids asked me what I wanted to be when I grew up, I'd make stuff up depending on who was doing the asking. Most of the time I'd tell people I wanted to be a scientist, the same bullshit my father fed strangers when they asked him what he did for a living. I'd answer with the same confident manner, which always impressed. ("Wow, a *scientist*. Any particular area of science?" "I'm not sure at the moment, but I'm thinkin' about goin' in for jet propulsion.") In reality I didn't know dick about science. My grades were miserable, I could barely do long division, and the closest I came to comprehending jet propulsion was farting in the bathtub.

That morning, my father asked me to help him hang an American flag outside our living room window, something he did every Independence Day. He was in a pissy mood, and when I yanked on the cord and pulled up the window blinds a little too fast, he wigged out.

"Easy with that! You'll fray the goddamn cord."

"I'm sorry. I didn't mean to—"

"What the hell's the matter with you?" he said. "Can't you see it's a delicate instrument? You don't just pull down hard on something like that. You take your time." He lowered the blinds, then carefully raised them again, gripping the cord with his pinky extended, the same way he held his violin bow. "Easy ... easy," he said, his eyes following the blinds all the way to the top of the window casing. "I swear, I gotta tell you people everything."

Our flag was fit for an aircraft carrier, the biggest in the neighborhood. After we hung it, he sent me to the deli for two six-packs of beer and a mountain of cold cuts. I knew he was getting ready to dig in for the day and tie on a load. When Frank came home later that afternoon, the old man was half-looped.

"Where the hella you been?" he asked.

"I was hanging out with Gordon," Frank said. "He and his wife bought a new stereo."

"Gordon, huh? Let me ask you a question. Is this your book?" He held up *Brave New World* as if it were a stash of drugs.

"Yeah, why?"

"Where did you get it?"

"Gordon gave it to me."

"I know where you got it. Why are you reading this filth?"

Frank looked both bewildered and amused. "Filth?" He grinned. "What are you talking about? Huxley's considered one of the greatest—"

"It's *filth!*" My father hurled the book against the wall, its pages fluttering. "And I don't want it in my house!"

"Have you read it?" Frank asked.

"I don't have to read it! I already know what it's about."

Frank sneered with a familiar sadistic glint in his eye. "Oh, really?" he said, stroking his chin with his fingers and nodding in mock earnestness. "Then please, tell me. What's it about?"

"It's about drugs, test-tube babies, and whatnot. That's why the church banned that crap years ago!"

Frank laughed.

"What's so funny?"

"Here you are commenting on a book you haven't even read." Frank continued to laugh. "You're taking your cues from the church, and you don't even know what you don't know. *Listen* to yourself."

"Listen, buddy boy," my father said, jabbing a finger in Frank's face. "I know you're a big-shot advertising man up there in Manhattan with the rest of the phony bastards, but when you're in my house, you can take all that Madison Avenue bullshit and shove it! I don't want you bringing this crap into my house. Do you hear me?"

"Well, hey," Frank said, extending a hand toward my father, "now *there's* an intelligent response. It's good to know you're an open-minded, critical thinker with your own thoughts and opinions."

"And tell your friend *Gordy* that if he wants to poison somebody's mind, he and his fruitcake wife should get their own goddamn kids."

"Why don't you tell him? I'm sure he'd relish the exchange of ideas."

"I will. And don't think I won't."

Frank picked up his book and noticed that the front cover was torn. He opened his mouth to say something, but then headed for the bathroom. My father blocked his path. "Gimme that," my father said, holding out his hand.

"Whaddaya mean? It's my book."

"I'm gonna burn that shit."

"You're not burning anything."

"I said give me that."

Frank hid the book behind his back, and my father lunged forward, trying to snatch it from him. They tussled with each other, and Frank pushed my father away, causing him to stumble backward and fall on his ass. My father's eyes turned wild with rage, and I thought for sure my brother wouldn't make it out of the house alive.

"You son of a bitch!" My father struggled to lift himself from the floor, but before he could regain is balance, Frank ran out of the apartment, slamming the door behind him.

The old man's face was beet red; I'd never seen him that angry. He charged for the front door, both hands struggling to open the spring lock and turn the doorknob at the same time, a simple maneuver any of us could have done blindfolded. After a few seconds, he ran back into the living room and made a beeline for the window. I jumped out of his way, barely avoiding getting mowed down.

He yanked down on the cord for the blinds with all his might—it wasn't a "delicate instrument" this time. The blinds shot up with a clatter, and he threw the window open with a thud, rattling the casing. "You fuckin' bastard," he hollered down at Frank, "I'll kill ya!"

I dashed into my parents' bedroom, and from the window I watched Frank in the courtyard. He was looking up at my father, smiling and waving the book. My father's image was reflected in the windows of the building across the courtyard. There he was, with his strap T-shirt and hairy chest, his head and torso leaning out the window, hands braced far apart on the outer sill above the huge flag. He looked like a crazed war veteran angry at the world.

A short distance away, a cluster of women sat on beach chairs and community benches, knitting sweaters and enjoying the afternoon sun. They were all gawking at my father, their mouths open in disbelief. When Frank noticed the onlookers, he got their attention and pointed up at the old man as if to say, *Can you believe this lunatic?*

"Scumbag! Scumbag!" my father shouted, his voice ratcheting up to an even higher level of rage. "Wait till I get my fuckin' hands on you!"

Frank tucked the book under his arm, wagged his head, and smirked while rubbing his index fingers, one over the other, in a *shame on you* gesture. My father went ballistic. He leaned so far out the window I thought he'd fall. "G'ahead, ya little sissy!" he screamed at the top of his lungs. "You come back here, and I swear I'll put you in a fuckin' hospital!"

Frank turned and walked out of the courtyard, shaking his head. As I watched him disappear from view, my stomach sank. I thought I'd never see him again.

My father slammed the window shut and paced back and forth, cursing his head off. After a minute or so he pushed open the door and came into the bedroom. I thought for sure he'd start swinging.

"What the hella you doin' in here?"

"Noth … nothin'," I said. "I … I was just—"

"Well, if you're doin' nothing, then go do it outside where you belong."

As I walked out of the room, he pushed me against the doorframe. "Let me see you turn out like him," he warned, holding a stern finger up to my face, "and I swear, I'll put *both* of you in a hospital."

Frank moved out of the apartment after that day. He didn't tell anyone, just packed some clothes in a suitcase and split. When I heard the news, I was devastated.

"How can he just leave like that without saying a word?" my mother asked Connie.

"Ma, you sound surprised."

"Of course I'm surprised. Why would you think I wouldn't be surprised?"

My father stalked around the house. "Good! Now he'll get a chance to see how tough it is out there." He acted as if he couldn't care less, but I knew that Frank's sudden exit had affected him.

My parents bickered about who was to blame. My

mother called all of our relatives to see if anyone knew of Frank's whereabouts. Nobody had a clue.

In the midst of all the family drama, no one asked me how I felt. I was happy that Frank had finally gotten away from my father, but I missed him sorely. I was also fearful of not having him around to speak up for me when the old man exploded and decided to turn my face into a human speed bag.

Connie told me Frank was living in a rooming house on Twenty-First Avenue, about a mile from Bay Haven. She said she'd known where he was all along and that he'd told her to keep it secret until he got settled. A few days later, Frank sent for me. His place was in a musty old three-story Victorian house with big wooden banisters and a wide, creaky staircase covered with a tattered carpet. Frank's room was on the top floor.

I knocked on the door, and Frank quickly opened it.

"Frankie, are you okay?"

"Yeah … yeah," he said, pulling me into the room. "Did you tell anybody you were coming?"

"No, nobody."

"The old man doesn't know where you are, right?"

"*Nobody*," I said. "He asked me where I was going, and I made up some bullshit, told him I was going to the park."

My brother looked unsettled. His hair was messed and his eyes red.

"Frankie, I was worried about you. I didn't know where you were. I missed you."

"I'm sorry, but I had to get out of there. I can't take the old man anymore."

"Yeah, I know—me too."

"Make yourself at home," Frank said, pointing to an unmade bed with a faded green bedspread. I sat down and sank into the droopy mattress. The room looked like it hadn't been decorated since the turn of the century: a plain oval rug, a wooden rocking chair, a desk with a lamp, and a framed mirror above a small dresser. Frank's suitcase lay open on the floor, clothes dangling from the sides. His saxophone case stood upright against the wall between the two small windows facing the backyard. On top of the dresser was a carton of orange juice. Next to that was a big loaf of Wonder Bread and open jars of peanut butter and jelly, a butter knife sticking out of each.

"I haven't had breakfast yet," Frank said, making himself a sandwich. "Are you hungry?"

Seeing my brother in a strange room in a strange house gave me an uneasy feeling. The place was worlds away from our cramped apartment and the din of constant fighting. But it wasn't only the space; something had changed in Frank. Just a few weeks before, he and Connie had been trying to talk my mother into moving, and now he had done it on his own. He'd liberated himself. The closeness I'd always shared with him suddenly seemed tenuous.

"Do you want a sandwich?" he said.

I hesitated, searching his face for reassurance that things were still the same with us.

"*What?*" he demanded. "C'mon, you want a sandwich or not?"

"I'm not hungry."

He took a quick bite and sat down next to me on the bed. "I'm glad you came over. I wanted to talk to you alone.

There's a lot of stuff goin' on. I'm not comin' back home."

"Never?"

"Never."

"What about what you and Connie were talkin' about?"

"About what?" he said, speaking with his mouth full.

"You know, all of us moving out and living together someplace, away from Daddy."

He took two more bites of his sandwich, wolfing it down like a hungry animal. "That's not gonna happen. Things are different now. I don't want to live with Ma either."

"Well, what about me?"

"What about you?"

"Can I stay here and live with you?"

Frank stared at his saxophone case on the opposite wall. I could almost hear his wheels turning. He closed his eyes, took a long, deep breath, and shook his head.

"Why?" I said. "There's room here. I can sleep on the floor."

"Sleep on the floor ..." Frank turned to look directly at me. "Johnny, you don't understand. I can't take care of you. I can just about take care of myself. Besides, even if I could, the old man wouldn't have it."

"First he's gotta find us, no?"

Frank snorted. "Are you kidding? If he knew you were with me, he'd send bloodhounds looking for us."

"C'mon, Frankie. I won't be any trouble. I promise."

"Oh God." Frank rubbed his eyes with the heels of his palms. "I knew this wasn't gonna be easy." He took a deep breath, collecting his thoughts. "Johnny, listen to me. I asked you to come here so I could talk to you man to man." His

124 JOHN CALIFANO

face was gripped with concern, and for a moment I thought he was going to tell me something shattering like he had cancer.

"What is it?"

"I enlisted in the army."

"Whaddaya mean? You mean like the real army? The *army* army?"

"No, dummy. The fake army."

"When?"

"Last week. I just got my papers. I'll be shipping out from Fort Dix in two weeks."

"How long you gonna be away?"

"A couple months. I signed up with the reserves. I have to do eight weeks of basic training, and then serve one weekend a month for five years and a few weeks in the summer."

"Five years. *Holy shit*." I stared at the floor, trying to imagine what it would be like not having my brother around.

"What can I say?" Frank said. "It's a drag, but for now that's the way it's gotta be."

He got up and leaned against the dresser, chugging juice from the carton. My chest grew heavy, and tears welled up in my eyes, but I didn't want him to see me cry. I looked away and noticed his torn copy of *Brave New World* on the nightstand next to the bed. The front cover was partially open, and through blurred eyes I spotted Gordon's inscription: *Good luck on your journey!* But what was *my* journey?

I looked at Frank. His face was expressionless. He took another swig of juice and shrugged, his eyes staring right through me.

FIFTEEN

SOON AFTER FRANK split, my mother started spending more time in bed. Her doctor increased her dosage of Miltown, and some days she got up only to make trips to the bathroom and the kitchen. Whenever she decided to check out like this, my sister picked up the slack. Connie was a senior in high school and worked two part-time jobs. She also did the shopping and made dinner every night. One time I heard her blast my mother while she lay in bed, the covers pulled up over her head. "What is it, Ma? Now that your darling son is gone, we all have to pay for it?"

"Leave me alone!" my mother screamed. "I'm sick! I'm sick!"

"Me too," Connie said. "I'm sick of doing all the work around here. Why don't you try getting out of bed and putting on some makeup instead of walking around the house looking *mezzo morto*."

The fact that my mother was zonked out on tranquilizers and living between the sheets didn't seem to trouble my father. As long as she kept her mouth shut, he didn't have to deal with her erratic mood swings. They slept in the same bed but were miles apart, my mother on one side with her back to him, her head barely sticking out from under the covers, my father on the other side lying on his back, snoring so loudly I could hear him from the living room. Sometimes I'd peek in on them and wonder how they could live like that. They looked like two strangers sharing a flophouse mattress.

Even though my mother was on mental hiatus, my father wasn't about to give up any of his perks as king of the castle. There was an unspoken expectation that my sister would step in as the woman of the house. Every week my father would give her a list of Italian specialties—cheeses, olives, cold cuts—and she'd run around like a lunatic between school and work to make sure he got what he wanted. She'd fix him a highball when he came home and cook him steaks with just the right amount of seasoning and tenderizer. If his steak wasn't cooked to his liking, he'd explode like an irate customer in a high-end restaurant.

Once Connie made the mistake of serving him beer in one of our regular milk glasses instead of his special beer glass, which always had to be chilled. "What the hell is wrong with you?" he shouted. "You *never* pour beer in a goddamn milk glass! Plus, this glass is warm. How many times do I have to tell you?"

"I'm sorry," Connie said.

"What?"

"I *said* I'm sorry."

As she turned to walk away, my father grabbed her hair.

"Ow! What are you doing? That *hurts.*"

"What did you say?" my father challenged her, bringing her face close to his own. His eyes were narrow and piercing, his grip so tight his knuckles had turned bone white.

"What are you talking about?" Connie asked. "I didn't

say anything."

"I wanna know what you said."

"I said I'm *sorry.*"

My father turned his head, positioning his ear close to her mouth. "What are you *sorry* about?"

Connie looked terrified and confused. "I'm ... I'm sorry." Tears streamed down her cheeks.

"I can't hear you." He moved his head even closer to her mouth, his gaze fixed on the floor. "What are you *sorry* about?"

"I'm ... I'm sorry about the glass."

"What *about* the glass?"

"I'm ... I'm ... sorry for pouring the beer in the wrong glass."

"*And?*" He tightened his grip, twisting her head to one side.

"You're hurting me!" Connie cried. The fear and pain in her voice filled my stomach with pangs.

"And?"

"And *what? What?* I don't know what you what me to say!"

"Are you going to do it again?"

"No."

"No, what?"

"No, I won't don't it again."

"Won't do what again?"

"I won't pour beer in the milk glass anymore."

"Good." My father shoved her head away. "Next time you try that phony *I'm sorry* bullshit with me, I'll slap the shit out of you. That crap may work with the parents of some of your highfalutin friends, but don't try that bullshit around here."

Connie rushed to her bedroom. Before she opened the door, she stopped and turned, facing my father. "*I hate you!*" she shouted at the top of her lungs.

My father unfastened his belt buckle and pulled the belt from his trousers, looping it in half and whacking it against his thigh; it sounded like a cracking bullwhip. Connie dashed into her room and slammed the door.

"G'ahead, ya little bitch. Run and hide! You're just like your *mother!*"

After this, Connie developed a twitch; every time she was stressed, her midsection would twist to one side as if she were trying to readjust her clothing. She had never really been thin, but in three months she gained twenty-five pounds. She would go through a couple of sleeves of Fig Newtons or Oreos as if it were nothing. I remember overhearing Aunt Rose talking to my mother about it: "When is your daughter gonna stop eating? She's gonna get as big as a house."

Connie was sensitive about her weight. She bought a bunch of diet magazines and low-calorie beverages to help her reduce, but nothing worked for her. It was around this time that she and I started going at each other hammer and tongs. I was the perfect scapegoat: her pain-in-the-ass kid brother whom she had to look after in addition to catering to our drop-out mother and half-crazed father. I helped with the housecleaning, but whatever I did wasn't enough; she was always on my back about something. Whenever she went on one of her rants, she addressed me as *mister* or *buster*. I'd hear shit like "When are you gonna do the laundry, *mister?* The towels in the hamper are ready to walk away," or "Okay, *buster*, let's get crackin' in the kitchen. It's your turn to do the dishes." The one sure way I knew to get back at her was to make fun of her weight. In name-calling I always got the best of her, and I took pleasure in seeing her boil. One time we got into a heated argument, and she slapped me. "You little *brat!*" she sneered.

"Fuck you, ya big pig!" I shot back.

"Little jerk!"

"Klutz!"

"Moron!"

"Fuckin' *pig!*"

"Listen to that mouth," she said. "You're lucky I don't wash it out with soap."

"You should talk."

"Wait until I tell your father."

"G'ahead and tell him. He's your father too."

Sometimes Connie would eat in the middle of the night. I'd hear her tiptoe through the living room to the kitchen. Once I got up to see what she was doing. The kitchen was dark except for the dim light from the open refrigerator, illuminating Connie's pale blue slip and bulging thighs. She sat hunched over a pan of leftover lasagna, forking it into her face like a bank robber stuffing cash into a satchel. Seeing my sister go at food like that creeped me out. "Whaddaya doin'?" I said.

She didn't even look up. "Nothing," she answered, talking with her mouth full. "I'm just having a little snack. Go back to bed."

I watched her for a few more seconds, feeling a combination of pity and disgust. What was she doing to herself? This was my older sister with sparkling eyes and big ambitions, who loved art and was popular in school. The one with a great sense of humor and big Jackie Gleason laugh, who wasn't afraid to speak up to my parents. She kept gorging herself like a ravenous beast until she noticed I was still watching. "I said go back to bed," she choked out.

I wanted to tell her to stop, but we'd been fighting so much that I thought whatever I said wouldn't make a difference. "You know," I said, "if you don't stop eating like that, you're gonna get as big as a house."

"Get the fuck outa here, you little creep!" Connie started to get up and lost her balance. Her knees fired off two loud pops as she tipped backward, grunting and bracing herself against the floor with her arms.

"I'm sorry," I said.

She picked up the fork and hurled it at me, clipping my shin. "I said get the fuck outta here!"

"Fuck you, ya big pig!" I shot back. "Now I hope ya *float away!*"

SIXTEEN

GEORGE ADAMCZYK (pronounced "a dumb chick") was the son of one of the rental agents at Bay Haven Apartments. He and Connie had graduated from Lafayette High School in the same year, but they never really connected until one afternoon when Connie stopped by the Bay Haven office to pay the rent. There she found George—tall, athletic, and good-looking—helping out his father. Through the wonders of animal magnetism, he and my sister soon became an item.

Unlike Connie, whom my mother often chided for being "boisterous," George was quiet and projected an inner confidence. He was an only child and lived with his parents and grandfather on the bottom floor of a two-family house a few blocks from Bay Haven.

I liked George. He was different from the gorillas Connie had dated in the past. He played chess and took the time to teach me all the basic moves. He was also good at baseball and basketball but mainly spent time on track-and-field stuff like shot put, discus, and javelin. I'd sometimes see him in Bensonhurst Park, alone in one of the empty ball fields, warming up with jumping jacks and push-ups. He'd toss a discus or hurl a javelin, usually with a handful of onlookers checking him out through the perimeter fence. In 1960, nobody else did that stuff in Bensonhurst Park.

Connie was obsessed with her newfound love. Every other sentence out of her mouth began *George* this or *George* that. It was my sister's first serious relationship, and she was protecting and nurturing it as if George were a wounded bird that had fallen out of a nest. I would sometimes hear her yakking with George on the phone in baby talk: "How's my little Torgie? Did he go bye-bye with his parents this weekend?" One time I heard her ask, "Did you make wee-wee this morning?" Fucking *wee-wee*. How out to lunch was *that*?

Sometimes I wondered what attracted George to my sister. He was trim and athletic, and my sister was overweight and engaged in a constant battle with her bulging thighs. I think the only exercise she got was shopping, cooking, and tending to my father. She was self-conscious about her appearance and would compensate by babying George. At first, I thought, leave the poor guy alone, will ya? He's a grown man out in the park tossing javelins; he doesn't need a fucking nursemaid. After a while, though, I concluded that, for all his manliness, George didn't mind my sister's mothering.

෨

The stretch of Bay Lane closest to Bensonhurst Park was ideal for stickball. It had three manhole covers evenly spaced, about forty feet apart. Me, Jackie D., Big Frenchie, Chicken Head Murphy, and a few other kids were playing single, double, triple. I was in the middle of the street, waiting for Jackie to throw out a pitch, when a car approached from behind, honking its horn. I'd been at bat maybe five minutes, and this was the fifth car wanting to pass.

"Okay! Okay! Hold your horses!" I shouted at the driver.

The car was a dark green, two-seater, open-top convertible with a fancy chrome grill, bug-eye headlights, and a brown leather strap buckled across the hood. I stepped away to clear the street, but the driver didn't budge. And he kept honking the horn.

"What the hell is he waiting for?" I hollered. "He's got enough room to drive a freaking truck through here."

"Johnny—it's *your brother*," Jackie said.

"What? Where?"

Jackie jutted his chin toward the car. The driver wore a paisley shirt and dark, JFK-style sunglasses, his hair trimmed in an army buzz cut. I did a double take. "Frankie!" I called out and hustled over.

"Brother mine—what are you up to?"

"Whaddaya doin' here?"

Frank smiled. "Where else should I be?"

"I mean, you know ... When'dja get back?"

"A few days ago. I stopped by the house to grab some stuff, and Connie told me you were out here."

"How come you didn't *call* me? I missed you."

"I was gonna, but things have been crazy." Frank played with the radio dial, flipping it back and forth between channels. "I been hung up trying to find an apartment and all," he said, settling on a jazz station. "What can I say? Life happens."

Frank pulled over to the side of the street, and I trailed behind him. He looked like he'd just rolled in from Beverly Hills: cool and confident, a pipe jutting from the side of his mouth.

"Where'dja get the wheels?" I asked.

"It's Gordon's." He dipped his head toward the driver-side door, admiring himself in the tiny rearview mirror mounted on the front fender. "He let me borrow it for the afternoon."

"Cool."

Frank flicked open a shiny lighter and held the flame over the bowl of the pipe, taking several puffs.

"What's with the pipe?"

"You like it?"

"I don't know. Looks weird. Like, who smokes a pipe?"

Frank continued to puff away. After he got the thing going, he removed his sunglasses, sat back, and draped his arm over the passenger's seat, twirling the glasses in his hand as if he were on a movie shoot. He'd been away only a couple months and had lost that fresh-out-of-high-school demeanor, along with most of his acne.

"What can I tell you?" he said. "It's classier than smoking cigarettes like every other Brooklyn greaseball."

I laughed.

"How's the old man these days? I didn't see him up at the house. He's probably over at Champ's Corner knocking back whiskey shooters."

"You shoulda seen him right after you shipped out. He was walking around the house cursing Gordon up and down, blaming him for everything. 'That liberal bastard and his fruitcake wife, poisoning my son with all those books and all that communist bullshit!'"

"Communist bullshit ..." Frank sniggered. "He's so

ignorant, he doesn't even know what he doesn't know."

Bad-mouthing the old man always got my brother's approval, and I never hesitated to cash in on it. It was the one surefire topic of conversation I knew would keep us connected.

I opened the car door and hopped into the passenger's seat.

"Where you going?" he said.

"Can you take me for a spin?"

"I have to drop some stuff at my apartment and get the car back to Gordon."

"C'mon, just a quick spin. I've never been in one of these things."

Frank glanced at his watch. "Okay. Quick spin around the block, then I gotta split."

The car smelled showroom new. I ogled the leather-wrapped steering wheel and handsome wood-paneled dashboard studded with an array of smart-looking buttons and dials. Jackie and the other kids came over and circled the car, gawking at it like it was a centerfold pinup.

"Hey, Frankie, nice ride," Jackie said.

"Yeah, she's a real beaut," Chicken Head Murphy said.

"Thanks, fellas. If you want to buy it, I'll give ya a discount. It's four grand, but I'll let you have it for thirty-eight hundred."

Everybody laughed.

"Johnny, you coming back?" Jackie said. "You're up three-zip."

"Yeah, I'll be back in minute. We're just goin' around the block."

Frank jostled the pearl-handled stick shift. "You ready to motor?"

"Let's do it!"

He turned up the radio, revved the engine, and popped the clutch. The whole gang watched as we shot down Bay Lane, wheels screeching. My head swelled, proud to be riding shotgun next to Frank. We cut over to Cropsey Avenue and zipped in and out of traffic. Every time he gunned the engine, my legs tingled with adrenaline. As we passed the front entrance of Bay Haven, I looked around, hoping other kids from the neighbored would spot me cruising down Cropsey in a two-seater Morgan. At one point, Frank slowed for a red light, and the car glimmered in the reflection of a storefront window. The whole time I kept thinking, *He's back, thank God, he's back.*

୬

My father's fifty-sixth birthday was approaching, and Connie and my mother decided to celebrate it with a dinner to which they would invite Frank as a surprise. It would be just the five of us. I didn't think Frank would go for it, but after a couple of ear-bending phone conversations with my mother, he agreed.

When my brother walked through the door, Connie and my mother made a big to-do, acting surprised to see him.

"Ma—Frankie's here!" Connie cried, loud enough for my father to hear.

"Welcome home," my mother said, smothering Frank with hugs and kisses as if she hadn't seen him in years. I could tell the charade was a little more than Frank had bargained for. He smiled and stood there enduring my mother's embraces, his arms hanging at his sides, looking to the ceiling as if to ask, *What the hell have I gotten myself into?*

"Hey, Bill!" my mother called out. "Look who came to visit—it's your son Frank. Come say hello."

My father was in the living room, camped out on the couch with his feet up on the ottoman, watching *King Kong*, the Sunday-afternoon feature.

"Happy birthday," Frank said, coming to attention and saluting my father.

"Well, if it isn't Audie Murphy," my father said, referring to the famous war hero turned big-time screen actor. "What are you doing here? I thought you went AWOL."

"I was downstairs visiting Gordon and his wife, and I thought I'd stop by to wish my old man a happy birthday."

I wasn't sure if my brother meant it that way, but it came across as if his wishing my father a happy birthday was secondary to visiting Gordon. I thought for sure my father would launch into a tirade.

"Well," my father said, his voice ringing with sarcasm, "it's nice that you remembered your *old man*." The TV roared, and the screen filled with the black-and-white image of King Kong standing on top of the Empire State Building, beating his chest and swiping biplanes out of the sky like dragonflies.

"Are you kidding?" Frank laughed, holding his hand up and twisting his wrist and fingers as if they had been mangled in battle. "How could I possibly forget?"

"Very funny," my father said. "All right, let's skip the

bullshit. Are you staying for dinner?" Underneath his guarded manner, I sensed that my dad was pleased that Frank showed up and actually wanted him to stay.

"All depends," Frank said.

"On what?"

"I don't know." Frank smiled. "Is it safe? I mean, you know … Do I need to sweep the house for land mines?"

My father snorted a laugh and wagged his head, muttering a few choice words in Italian that translated into something like *what a fucking pain in my ass.*

Connie and my mother had cooked a humongous meal: eggplant parmigiana and breaded veal cutlets, Frank's favorite. My sister had done most of the shopping and cooking. Since Frank's return, my mother's mood had improved. Just knowing that her oldest son was safely back from the army had given her a real boost. She'd even managed to put on a new housedress and some makeup.

During dinner Frank talked about basic training: the constant inspections, the long hours doing KP (kitchen patrol), the endless marching with heavy backpacks.

"So—did you learn anything?" my father said, challenging Frank.

"Yeah. I learned how to drive a five-ton half-track through a wooded area, shoot an M-1 rifle and dismantle it blindfolded, and rip out a guy's lungs with a bayonet. Unfortunately, I couldn't put that on my résumé when I reapplied for my old job at the ad agency. But when I interviewed with the new head of the department, he ate it up. Guy's an ex-marine, with a metal plate in his head from Guadalcanal. He told me I had all the right skills to become an account exec."

Everyone laughed except my father, who seemed mildly amused, though there was disappointment in his eyes.

"Did you see Elvis?" my mother said.

"Yeah," Frank answered with a straight face. "We bunked together. The guy snores like crazy."

"Really?"

"Square business. Plus, he's a real fruitcake. Every night he went to bed curled up with a teddy bear and his favorite blankie, singing 'Love Me Tender.'"

"*C'mon ... get out*," my mother said.

Connie and I laughed.

"Ya see?" Frank said, pointing to my mom. "Can't fool *her*."

"Ma, he's pulling your leg," Connie said. "Elvis was stationed in Germany and discharged two years ago. Don't you read the papers?"

"What the hell do *I* know?" My mother placed a hand against her chest. "All I heard was that he was in the service."

After dinner Connie brought out a homemade three-layer chocolate cake and set it on the table in front of my father. My sister had a real knack for making things look special; she'd decorated the cake with fancy whipped-cream curlicues, along with a handful of flickering candles neatly arranged around the top.

"Boy oh boy, is that for *me*?" my father said.

We sang "Happy Birthday" and watched him blow out the candles with one enormous breath.

"Make a wish, make a wish!" Connie said.

"I don't need to make a wish," my father said, his voice low and melancholy. "I already got my wish. Everybody's here. That's enough for me."

Connie handed my father a cake knife, and he carefully sliced the cake and dished out a piece to each of us, a ritual he'd performed for all of our birthdays.

"I put up a pot of coffee," my mother said. "Should be ready in a few minutes." She signaled to Frank with a discreet nod.

"You know what?" Frank said, looking around the table. "How about a little music?"

"Good idea," my mother said.

As a surprise, Frank had bought a new violin case for my father, a fancy, black, crushed-leather job with a red velvet interior. Earlier in the week, he'd given the case to Connie and asked her to switch it with my father's old, ratty-looking case that he kept on the top shelf of his closet.

"How 'bout it, Pop," Frank said. "Can you play us a little tarantella?"

"Who, *me*?" said my father, sounding completely surprised.

"Yeah, why not?"

"Aw, c'mon. You don't wanna hear me play the violin." The old man loved the spotlight—roughly translated, this comment meant: *I'd love to play the violin, so please don't stop begging me.*

"What are you talking about?" Frank said. "Of course we do. Let's take a vote." He raised a hand high above his head. "All those in favor of hearing Daddy play some of his old Italian favorites, raise your hand and say aye."

"Aye!" we all said, raising our hands.

"There ya go," Frank said. "The ayes have it."

My father's face lit up with an ear-to-ear grin. "Okay, you guys win. G'ahead, go grab the violin."

Frank started to get up from the table, then paused and sat down again. "I got a better idea. Why don't you get it?"

"What? You can't get the violin for your old man?"

Frank scrambled for an answer. "No, it's not that. It's just, you know, I think it would be better if *you* got it. I mean, it's your baby, right?"

"What? I'm asking you to get my violin. Is that too much to ask? It's my birthday... Maybe you could do something nice for your old man once in a while."

"All right. You want me to get the violin? I'll get it. Where is it?"

"In my closet on the top shelf, where I always keep it."

Frank got up and headed for my parents' bedroom, and I could see my father's agitation growing. The jubilant smile he'd had on his face minutes earlier had taken a powder, and I could hear the Caruso war drums beating in the distance. "See what I mean?" he said, talking to my mother. "And then you wanna know why I get *agita.*"

"Okay, don't get excited," she said. "He means well."

"I'm not excited. Who's excited? I just asked him to get my violin. I mean, is that too much to ask?"

"I can't find it!" Frank called from the bedroom.

"He can't find it," my father said. "You *believe* this? It's in my closet, sitting right up there on the top shelf, and he can't find it. "*Puttana diavolo* ..." *The devil's whore.* He slapped his leg in frustration. "Even on my birthday ..." He stood up and headed for the bedroom with a deliberate stride.

"I knew this wasn't a good idea," Connie said.

"What's the big deal?" I said. "Why doesn't Frankie just get the violin and give it to him? He'll still be surprised."

The three of us sat listening to the muffled sounds of bickering in the bedroom.

"We'd better go see what's goin' on in there," my mother said.

In my parents' bedroom my father and brother were arguing in front of the closet.

"What are you, *blind?*" my father said, pointing to the violin. "It's right there!"

"All right. So go ahead and get it," Frank said. I could tell by my brother's devilish smile that his mindset had changed. This was no longer about surprising my father with a new violin case; he was enjoying seeing the old man get heated in a test of wills.

"No," my father said. "I want *you* to get it."

"But I don't wanna get it. It's your violin. Why don't *you* get it?"

My father had that wide-eyed, tight-jawed, crazed look I'd seen on his face a hundred times before. Connie's midsection twitched, and she grabbed my hand, squeezing it tight.

"All right, Frank, that's enough," my mother said. "Take down the case for your father."

My brother's face settled into a smug grin. He reached into the closet and retrieved the case with both hands. "Here," he said, handing it to my father. "Happy birthday."

"Thank you," my father said, tersely. He started to turn away and suddenly noticed the bright sheen of the case's new leather along with the fancy red ribbon that my sister had tied to the handle. "Wait a minute ..." He peered up at the closet. "But where's my ...?"

"It's a birthday present," my mother said. "Frank got you a new case and wanted you to get it yourself so you'd be surprised."

My father's anger dissipated. He examined the case, holding it like someone holding a newborn for the first time. "You got this for *me*?" he said, turning to Frank.

Frank didn't answer, he just stared back at him, maintaining his smug grin.

"But I didn't know," my father said. "Really." He looked around at all of us. "I mean, I had no idea ..." He moved backward until his legs hit the bed frame, where he plopped down on the mattress, his eyes fixed on the case in a baffled gaze.

"Well," said Frank, "I guess now you know."

My father's chest rose up and down a few times, and then he burst into tears, his shoulders shaking. "I'm sorry!" he cried, lowering his head and rocking back and forth, one hand clutching the case, the other latching onto my brother's arm. "I'm sorry ... I'm sorry."

In all his confrontations with my brother, I had never seen my father become this unraveled. I glanced at Connie, and she looked just as shocked.

"Hey, c'mon, Dad," Frank said, patting him on the back. "It's okay ... It's okay. We'll let bygones be bygones." Frank peered over my father's head and smiled triumphantly. I watched him closely, hoping to see a glimmer of compassion, but it was like searching for a rose in the Arctic. He actually enjoyed seeing my father in agony. I felt sick and looked away in disgust.

My mother stepped closer to the bed, and Frank moved back. "C'mon, Bill," she said, putting her arm around my father. "Let's go have some coffee and another piece of cake. You'll feel better." She helped my father to his feet, and the two of them lumbered toward to the living room, my father holding the case close to his chest with both arms.

"You didn't have to do that," Connie said in a heated whisper.

"Do what?" Frank asked.

"C'mon, Frankie, you saw he wasn't going for the case. Why didn't you just give it to him, for Godsakes? Don't we have enough trouble in this house?"

"Yeah," I said. "It still woulda been a surprise."

"Hey, what can I say," Frank said. "He's a big boy. He knows how to buy his own booze—he can get his own violin case."

SEVENTEEN

SISTER VERONICA was my seventh-grade teacher. She was tall and young, with a pretty face and wonderful, plump breasts neatly tucked away under her black habit. Her brown eyes were filled with life and set under brows so thick they almost touched each other. Every few weeks she'd tweeze them, leaving a light-gray pattern around each. To me her brows were endearing, and I thought she was cute as hell for thinking she needed to pluck them.

Once, at the end of a history lesson, she asked if anyone had any questions. My hand was the first in the air. "Did you tweeze your eyebrows last night?"

My question caught her off guard. I hadn't meant to put her on the spot; it was just my dumb way of letting her know I liked her and thought she was special.

"Well, as a matter of fact, I did," she replied. "And thank you for pointing that out to the class, Mr. Caruso."

"I thought so." I beamed. "My sister, Connie, plucks her eyebrows, and they look just like yours."

The thing I loved about Sister V. was that she wasn't jaded like some of the older nuns at Precious Mother, most of whom were Irish-American and vocal about having given their life to Christ. I didn't know why she had decided to become a nun, but I got the feeling she wasn't entirely on board with the Catholic program.

I could also tell that some of the older nuns were jealous of her because all the kids liked her. She always tried to make lessons fun and would sometimes have us sing Broadway show tunes. Her favorite was "Do-Re-Mi" from *The Sound of Music*. She would have the boys and girls sing different verses while she stood up front, waving her arms, ruler in hand, looking like a real conductor.

Precious Mother had a firm stance on physical exercise and schoolyard games: it allowed no recreation period, no dodgeball, no relay races—none of the fun stuff that my buddies who went to public school regularly talked about. Listening to them made me feel as if I were doing hard time at Dannemora.

One afternoon Sister V. took our class down to the schoolyard and had us do toe touches and jumping jacks for thirty minutes. It wasn't the same as schoolyard games, but just getting some sunshine and fresh air in our lungs was a huge relief.

Not surprisingly, when Sister Gilhouly, the principal, got wind of this incident, she had a shit fit. Gilhouly was serious business, a stern nun whose watery eyes peered at you over wire-rimmed glasses pushed far down on her nose. Everyone joked that Gilhouly was one of the children of the damned, a fictional group of English schoolchildren who could set a house on fire just by staring at it. If Gilhouly singled you out for something, she would lower her head and shoot you one of her death-ray stares over the top of her spectacles—a look that made you want to hide under a desk. My buddy, Freddy Bufano, a wiry kid with ginormous buckteeth, did a killer imitation of Gilhouly. His death stare was so perfect, you didn't know if you should shudder or piss yourself laughing.

That day, shortly after our schoolyard workout, we went back to our classroom and sat quietly, listening to Gilhouly out in the hallway where she was reprimanding Sister V. in a furious whisper. The way Gilhouly was carrying on, you would have thought Sister V. had taken the class outside for a smoke break.

"What if one of the children had sprained an ankle?" the old windbag said. "What would I have told their parents?"

"I thought a little exercise might help the children—"

"We are a *learning institution!* If parents wanted their children to do jumping jacks all day, they would have sent them to public school."

Sister V. walked back into the classroom and closed the door behind her. Arms outstretched and palms turned up, she said, "Well, I tried."

Connie was a freshman and had been attending Long Island University in downtown Brooklyn. One morning, while we were getting ready for school, she and I got into a blowout. She was insisting I put on a pair of old galoshes that belonged to my brother.

"It's pouring outside," she said. "If you don't put these on, you're gonna ruin your shoes, and then I'll never hear the end of it from your father." (Connie had a habit of conveniently removing herself from the family lineage. Whenever she got heated with me, she made a point of referring to our dad as "*your* father.")

I didn't have any rain boots, but there was no way in hell I was going to wear Frank's galoshes. They were too big and made my feet look like Goofy's from *The Mickey Mouse Club.* "Forget it," I said. "I'm not puttin' those on."

Our argument woke my father, who was sleeping off a hangover. He came charging out of his bedroom, wearing only boxer shorts. "What the hell's goin' on here?"

"It's raining out, and he won't wear galoshes," Connie said, one hand on her hip. "He says they make his feet look big. I swear, I don't know what I'm gonna do with him."

My father grabbed the galoshes and pushed them into my chest. "Put on the goddamn galoshes!"

"I'm *not* wearing them," I said, folding my arms.

My father slapped me repeatedly—right hand, left hand—his eyes wide and threatening. I held my arms over my head and tried to back away, but he didn't let up. He slapped me from the dining area all the way into the kitchen, where he rammed me against the wall and kneed me in the stomach and thighs. "I don't wanna hear another word out of you!" He grabbed my hair and dragged me back out of the kitchen. "You put on those galoshes and get your ass to school. And I want you back here by three thirty—no dillydallying after class. Now *get movin*!"

My cheeks were bruised and puffed, my thighs spasming from being kneed. I limped to school, flipping him the bird every twenty feet, cursing under my breath. ("Fuckin' drunk bastard … I hope you fall down a flight of stairs and drop dead!") I also hated Connie for ratting me out. She had broken our unspoken agreement: when it came to the old man, always cover each other's asses, no matter what.

When Sister Veronica noticed me in class, she

stopped her lesson and asked me to step out into the hall. "Good *Lord,*" she said. "What happened to you?"

"Nothing." I started to turn away, but she crouched in front of me and examined my face.

"Listen, John, I know you don't believe me, but you can talk to me; you can tell me if something is wrong."

I swallowed, fighting back tears. I wanted to spill my guts and tell her everything, but I was afraid that if word got back to my father, he'd come up to school and beat the crap out of me in front of everyone, as he often threatened to do.

"Did you have a fight with one of the older kids?"

"My father woke up on the wrong side of the bed," I said, hoping that would satisfy her.

"Your *father* did this to you?"

The alarm in her voice scared me. "Please don't say anything."

"When did this happen?" She held my chin in her hand, gently turning my head from side to side.

"This morning. If my father finds out I told anybody, he'll kill me."

"I understand." She brushed back a few strands of hair dangling over my forehead. "How about we talk after class? Would you like that? It'll just be between you and me," she added.

My mouth was dry, and I couldn't speak. Blank faced, I nodded and stared at her, all the time thinking I had just made the biggest mistake of my life.

For the rest of the day, my head was buzzing. I was convinced that my talking with Sister V. would somehow get back to my father. The old man had a thing about divulging family business to anyone outside the house. I remembered one day, back in first grade, when my teacher had sensed that something was troubling me. She pulled me aside and asked what was wrong. It had seemed like a simple question, and I gave her a simple answer: I told her my parents had been fighting and that my father had slapped my mother. When I mentioned this to my father, he blew up. At the time I was sitting on the toilet seat watching him shave. In a blur, he put down his razor and slapped my face so hard that my head flew back like a screen door caught in a windstorm. I was stunned; it was the first time he had ever whacked me in the face, and I didn't understand what he was so angry about. "Don't you ever, *ever* tell anybody our business!" he said, jabbing his finger into my face. I left the bathroom crying, feeling as if I had violated some sacred family code.

After the three o'clock bell, I waited until the class cleared out. Just as Sister V. and I sat down to talk, Mr. Jefferies, the school maintenance man, showed up with a metal toolbox and announced he needed to repair the radiator. Sister Veronica suggested we go up to the convent on the top floor of the building. As we climbed the stairs, the rosary beads around her waist bounced against her leg, the sound echoing through the stairwell.

Outside the nuns' quarters was a small reception area —a plain room with a gray vinyl couch and a few folding chairs around a coffee table. One of the cinderblock walls was adorned with a two-foot crucifix, along with an oddly placed electric clock mounted above it. An image of my father tapping the face of his watch filled my brain.

"Please have a seat," Sister V. said.

I parked myself on the couch, and she sat on one of the metal chairs opposite me. I told her about my fight with

Connie and my father wigging out, kicking and slapping me.

"Oh my goodness," she kept saying. "You poor thing."

It was comforting to hear an adult outside of my family express genuine concern, but at the same time I couldn't escape the feeling that I was betraying my father.

"That's horrible," she said when I'd finished. "What about your mother—wasn't she home?"

"She was sleeping. But he hits her too."

"Good heavens."

"He beats *all* of us."

"Listen," Sister V. said, her voice filled with worry. "How about if I talk to—"

"No, please don't talk to anybody."

"Just listen for a minute. If you let me, I can talk to Father Michaels. He's good with this kind of thing. He can call your father—"

"No! You don't know my father. If he finds out I spoke to you, he'll *kill* me. You gotta promise you won't say anything to anybody."

"Okay." Sister V. leaned back in her seat. "It was just an idea. I won't say anything."

"You promise?"

"You have my word." She held one hand above her head and placed the other over her heart. "Scout's honor."

We sat in silence for a few moments. My leg bobbed up down, which I wasn't aware of until I noticed her glance at my knee.

"Oh!" She snapped her fingers. "I almost forgot! I'll be right back."

Sister V. popped out of her chair and stepped into the convent, leaving the thick wooden door halfway open. The scent of incense wafted into the reception area. I leaned to the side to get a better view of the nuns' living quarters. A long hall just inside the entrance led to a kitchen and, beyond that, a dining room. Everything seemed quiet and private—a club exclusively for women. None of the kids I knew in school had ever been inside the convent; it was the forbidden zone. Catching a look-see through the open door gave me a naughty-boy rush, like copping a peek up a woman's dress on the subway.

Moments later Sister V. returned to the reception area with a glass of milk and a plate of chocolate chip cookies. "I baked them last night."

I hesitated, but she nodded as if to say, *Go ahead; it's okay.* I grabbed a few cookies, and she sat quietly, watching me stuff myself. The starched white habit that encased her cheeks made her face look like it was gripped in a vise. Her head was completely covered, and I tried to imagine what her hair looked like. Her eyebrows had grown pretty full; I wondered when she would tweeze them again.

"Did you always want to become a nun?" I said, taking a gulp of milk.

"Why do you ask?" She tried to conceal a smile.

"I dunno." I shrugged. "You seem different from the other nuns."

"Different how?"

"I dunno. You just seem, you know … *nicer.*"

Sister V. smiled. She leaned forward and helped herself to a cookie. "You know, when I was your age, being a nun had never occurred to me. As a matter of fact, I dreamed of someday singing on Broadway."

"Really?"

"That's right. I knew all the Broadway show tunes and would put on shows for the kids in my neighborhood with my younger brothers and sisters."

"Did you ever sing on a stage? I mean in front of an audience?"

"I did. In high school I sang in musicals, and I was in a number of plays."

"What happened?" I asked. "How come you didn't become a singer?"

"Well, I wanted to, but my parents wouldn't hear of it."

"Wha'd they say?"

She laughed. "My mother thought I was stark-raving mad!"

"What's wrong with being a singer?"

"Nothing." She shrugged and gazed down at her lap, carefully dusting crumbs from her legs. "It's just that, you know … things don't always work out the way you plan. When I was growing up, my family didn't have a lot of money. My father became ill, and I had to take a job to help out … That's just the way it was." A trace of sadness had crept into her voice. "Then, when I got older, I had a girlfriend who entered a nunnery, and, well … I decided to join her." She looked up at me finally. "But enough about me. What about you? Have you given any thought to what you might like to do when you get older?"

My brain fluttered through a Rolodex of impressive careers, none of which I had any interest in. "I wanna be a scientist," I said, hoping she wouldn't question me further.

Sister V. looked puzzled and amused. "A scientist?"

I nodded. My science grades were barely passing, and

I was failing math. I probably would have had a better shot at convincing her I wanted to play center for the Harlem Globetrotters.

"How did you come up with that answer?" she asked. "Wanting to be a scientist is very admirable, but do you even *like* science?"

"Not really."

Sister Veronica studied me for a moment, and I wanted to slither under the couch.

"To be honest, Sister, I don't know what I wanna be. Most of the time I feel like I'm not good at anything." As I spoke, my voice quivered; it was the first time I'd said that to anyone.

She clasped her hands and hunched forward. "Well, that's okay. Not knowing what you want to do in life is a good starting point. You're still very young. You don't need to have your future planned out yet."

"But you said that when you were my age, you knew you wanted to be a singer on Broadway."

"That's true. But God had a different path for me. It's different for everyone. Believe me—someday you'll find your special calling, the thing that you really want to do in life. And when you do, you'll know it. You just have to follow your heart and have faith in God."

It all sounded great; I wanted to believe that someday I would find my "special calling." But following my heart and having faith in God seemed like empty phrases to me, like the weekly penance the priest gave me after hearing my bullshit confession from behind a metal screen in the stuffy wooden booth. It felt as superficial as sticking a Band-Aid on a tumor. What the hell did some faceless priest know about my true feelings and fears? Where was God, Jesus, or the Blessed Virgin when my drunk father slapped my mother senseless and beat the fuck out of my brother and me?

I had lost track of time. When I glanced at the clock, my stomach twinged. My father had been expecting me home by three thirty, and it was already close to four. "He's gonna kill me," I said, clamping a hand to my forehead.

Sister V. told me not to worry, and then she did something I'll never forget. She went into the convent and returned a few minutes later with a note addressed to my father:

Dear Mr. Caruso,

Please excuse John's getting home late this afternoon. He needed some help with his math assignment, and I asked him to stay after class so I could work with him.

Thanks for your understanding.

Sincerely,

Sister Veronica

"There," she said, handing me the signed note. "Now we both have a secret that we don't want anyone else to know."

EIGHTEEN

MY PARENTS NEVER discussed sex with us. Their attitude was similar to that of most of the other parents I knew: *They'll find out on their own, just like we did.* I knew that women had babies, but I wasn't quite sure how they came to fruition. I thought that maybe the women woke up one day and decided to have a kid. Then they got big bellies, wore maternity clothes, and had mysterious food cravings. When I told this to Connie, she laughed. "I swear," she said, "men don't know *anything.*"

Connie knew all about reproduction. She described the mechanics of sex to me in great detail: erections, sperm, eggs, the whole deal. She referred to it as "sexual intercourse"—it sounded so mature. My twelve-year-old brain reeled in awe and disbelief, as if she were describing interplanetary travel. Like every other preteen Catholic-school numbnuts, I'd been indoctrinated with the prevailing notion that sex was *fucking*—a dirty and sinful act that people weren't supposed to talk about. It was considered lewd and lascivious and was only enjoyed by horny men with big hairy dicks and sluts who "put out." I didn't even know what *fuck* actually meant. All I knew was that the word had something to do with sex, and in the neighborhood parlance it was often used to underscore anger, discontent, and doubt:

"*Fuck* you." "I'm *fucked.*" "Hey—what the *fuck?*" "*Fuck* if *I* know."

Connie had a romantic and idealized interpretation of sex, something I admired. She told me sex was a beautiful thing that happened between a man and a woman, and that it was better when two people loved each other and waited until they were married before they "consecrated their love for each other." The way she described it made it sound like some ethereal, out-of-body experience. This reinforced my own secret, idealized notion of romance. I'd listen to The Flamingos' heart stopping rendition of "I Only Have Eyes for You" and fantasized about falling in love with a dream girl who had presence, charm, and talent, someone I could kiss and cherish twenty-four hours a day for the rest of my life. The only problem was that half the time I was so angry and obnoxious I couldn't have attracted a lobotomized vixen. I had developed a quick wit and a sharp tongue. In a crowd of kids, my first impulse was to show off and make myself the center of attention. If anyone responded with the slightest hint of rejection, I was quick to open the bomb-bay doors and drop a payload of nasty insults on them.

In 1962, puberty roared in on me like a bullet train. My voice started to change, and I graduated from hurling eggs and water balloons off the roof to flirting. Jackie D. and I were part of a clique of about fifteen kids that hung out on the back stoop facing Bay Lane. The whole scene was a dating frenzy; kids would go steady and break up with each other as if they were trading baseball cards.

When my father noticed that I was becoming more social, he started to move in on me. "Goin' outside for a little grab-ass?" he'd say with a chuckle, trying to sound like one of the boys. "Got some little *twat* out there?" At first, I didn't think much of it; I figured it was just his stupid way of trying to relate to me. But then he started doing something that I didn't remember him ever doing to Frank. Every so often he'd corner me on my way to the bathroom or stop me as I was leaving the apartment. "How's my little *peeshock*?" he'd say, grabbing my crotch. "Is he gettin' big or what?" Or "Where's my big guy? Better watch that thing. Someday it's gonna getcha in trouble." Whenever this happened, I'd clam up and push him away, and he'd laugh it off. More than having him grab my crotch, I hated that he made my penis sound as if it were something he owned. Sometimes he would pass me in the apartment and fake a jab toward my groin, making me flinch. It was like living with a bully from school. I wondered if my friends' fathers did the same to them.

That summer Harriet Voriotis was also twelve. She and her family lived three buildings over from mine. Her parents seemed different from most of the working-class parents in the neighborhood. Her mother, Samantha, reminded me of Joan Baez: intelligent, with radiant dark eyes and straight brown hair that hung down one side of her face, covering her cheek. Harriet's father was a poet who read his work in Greenwich Village. Who else in Bay Haven wrote poetry? It was like living next door to an astronaut.

I was attracted to the Voriotises. They were youngish and seemed like forward-thinking people. I especially liked Harriet, a slightly chubby girl with a quirky smile. She was popular in the neighborhood and had her own sense of style; she wasn't afraid to be different. While other girls wore pastel pedal pushers with bright polka-dot tops, Harriet sported cut-off jeans, black high-top sneakers without socks, and wore either a gray sweatshirt or one of her father's oversize button-down shirts that hung halfway down to her knees.

I didn't know what it was about Harriet, but whenever she was around, I managed to transform myself into a complete jackass. One afternoon Jackie and I were hanging out on the stoop along with half a dozen other kids from our side of Bay Haven.

"Hey, guys, has anyone heard the Bristol Stomp?" Harriet asked.

"What the hell is the Bristol Stomp?" Jackie said.

"It's a new dance. All the kids are doing it on *American Bandstand.*"

Jackie put a hand over his mouth, muffling a laugh.

"Well, how's it go?" I asked. "Can you show us?"

"I forget the words, but from what I remember, I think it goes something like this." Harriet hummed the melody and danced on the pavement, stomping her feet in short bursts while snapping her fingers.

I sprang off the stoop and stood next to her, studying her feet. "You mean like *this?*" I kicked my legs out and stomped my feet in spastic movements, acting like Frankenstein crushing an army of invading roaches.

Jackie laughed, setting off a wave of guffaws from the other kids.

"You know, Johnny, you think you're funny, but you're a real jerk," Harriet said. She walked away, and I followed her, still doing my crazy dance.

"How about like *this?*" I hollered.

A few days later, I was hanging out among a gang of kids in The Square, a cozy public gathering area in the center of Bay Haven. It was a warm night, and the air buzzed with chatter, along with Dion's "Runaround Sue" blasting from three or four transistor radios all tuned to the same station.

In the middle of the crowd, I noticed Harriet talking with some girlfriends. She looked great—tight-tight jeans and an ice-blue sleeveless blouse with a dagger collar that highlighted her tan cheeks and arms. The instant our eyes met, she looked away.

I wiggled my way through the crowd toward her. "Nice blouse," I said.

Harriet ignored me, turning her head away. Her girlfriends followed suit.

"Testing!... One!... Two!... Three!... *Testing!*" I announced, cupping my hands around my mouth.

"I'm not talking to you," she said.

"What? Wha'd I do?"

Harriet grimaced and turned away again.

Just then I felt Jackie's arm around my neck. "What's goin' on?" he said, bobbing his head and snapping his fingers to the music.

"Nothin'," I said. "She's not talkin' to me."

"Not talkin'? How come?"

"Hell if I know." I shrugged.

"Hey, Harriet!" Jackie called out. "Can you show us that dance again?"

"Listen, jerk," said Denise Bagliardi, a tall, skinny girl who wore gobs of makeup and kept her hair stacked like a beehive. "Why don't you make like an egg and beat it? And take Mr. Cool here with you." She chucked her thumb in my direction.

Harriet turned her back to us, and one of her white bra straps slipped out from under her blouse and looped down her upper arm. Jackie reached over and curled his finger under the strap, lifting it up as if it were a rare specimen. "What ... the ... hell ... is ... *this?*" he said.

Harriet smacked Jackie's hand away, sending a loud *whack* echoing across The Square, drawing the attention of more onlookers.

Harriett's face flushed. "Well, if you must know—it's a training bra." She quickly pulled the strap back over her shoulder and out of sight.

"What are you training for? You got nothin' there," I said, jutting my chin toward the two small mounds barely protruding from her chest.

"Ooh!" the onlookers chorused. More kids crowded around to see what was going on. Other kids started shouting out comments and goading me on.

"Hey, listen," Jackie said. "Until you grow a pair, you can always use it as a slingshot."

"Ooh!"

"Very funny, moron," said Nancy Gallagher. "Twelve —is that your age or your IQ?"

"Ooh!"

"Wait a minute, wait a minute," I said, flapping my hands to quiet everyone. "I got an even *better* idea. Why don't you cut out the tips, put glasses in the holes, and use it as *goggles?*"

"Ooh!"

Harriet looked embarrassed and angry. Suddenly she burst into tears, cupping a hand over her mouth. Like a trapped animal, she turned in different directions, trying to find the best escape route. Finally, she charged through the crowd in front of her, shoving me aside with both hands.

A couple of days later, Jackie and I had just walked out of Tony's candy store when Jackie gave me a sharp elbow to the side. "Twelve o'clock," he said. I looked up, and the blood drained from my face: Harriet and her mother were heading straight for us. I wanted to bolt, but before I had a chance, they were a few feet in front of us.

"Johnny, would you mind if I had a word with you?" Harriet's mother asked.

"I gotta go," Jackie said. He turned and headed in the opposite direction.

"I'm sorry," I said, pointing at Jackie, "but I was just about to go too."

"It's okay, Johnny. I just want to talk to you. Do I have permission to talk to you?"

I didn't know what to say. I thought it was some kind of trick. No adult had ever asked me for permission to do anything. I nodded.

"Good." She smiled. "Because, when you think about it … we're really all friends here. And we all want to get along with one another. Am I right?"

I glanced at Harriet. Her face was expressionless, but I sensed that she was still pissed and fighting to conceal her lingering hurt and anger.

I nodded again.

"You know," Harriet's mother said, "sometimes we say things to each other that we don't really mean—"

"I didn't mean it," I said. "I was just … I was just joking. We were all hanging out in The Square, you know, just foolin' around—honesttagod." I held up my hand.

"I believe you. But whether you meant it or not, what you said was mean and hurtful to Harriet. That was the first time Harriet ever wore a bra."

"Mom, *please*," Harriet pleaded, her face contorted with embarrassment. She turned to leave, and her mother draped an arm around her shoulders and drew her closer.

"No, that's okay, sweetheart, that's okay." Her voice was confident and soothing. "There's nothing to be ashamed of."

Harriet buried her face in her mother's shoulder and sobbed. The sound sent a wave of guilt through me. I offered my hand, wanting to console her, then drew it back, fearing it would make things worse. Her mother continued to speak, hugging Harriet tighter and resting her chin on top of her daughter's head. "You know, women wear bras all the time," she said to me. "That's part of being a woman. Your mom wears a bra, doesn't she?"

I nodded.

"How about your sister, Connie? I imagine she wears a bra too."

"Yeah, I think so. I mean … yeah."

Women, breasts, bras—just thinking about all that stuff made me want to curl up in a ball and die right on there on the sidewalk.

"Well, at one point, I'm sure your sister wore a training bra. Can you imagine someone saying such hurtful things to your sister?"

I remembered the time I'd found one of Connie's bras on a stack of clothes in the laundry basket. I had wrapped it around my head like a bonnet and paraded around the apartment. Connie was furious. "Gimme that, *you jerk!*" she'd shouted, chasing me down. I imagined her glaring at me now, eyes wide, lips tightly pressed together: *Ya see, mister?*

This is what I'm talking about.

I looked at Harriet's mother and shook my head.

"Can you see how what you said to Harriet might have hurt her feelings and embarrassed her in front of all the other kids?"

My mouth went dry. I nodded, aware of the lump forming in my throat.

"Wasn't very nice, was it?" she said.

There was a long silence. Overhead, the distant whine of an airplane filled my ears.

"No," I mumbled.

"Is there something you'd like to say to Harriet?"

I shifted my gaze toward Harriet, and her mother gently turned her in my direction. "Harriet, Johnny has something he'd like to say to you."

Harriet's eyes were red. Tears and streaks of dark eyeliner ran down her cheeks.

"I'm sorry for what I said to you about the bra."

Harriet sniffled a few times and ran the back of a hand under her nose. "Why do you always pick on me?" she said. "Every time I'm outside, you're always picking on me. I didn't do *anything* to you."

"I know you didn't. I'm sorry. I apologies. I mean I … I apologize."

"You promise not to pick on me anymore?" There was a slight *pretty please* in Harriet's voice, and just hearing it made me feel like an even bigger shithead.

"I promise."

Harriet sniffled and wiped her cheeks.

"Do you accept Johnny's apology?"

Harriet nodded.

Her mom tucked a clump of shiny brown hair behind her ear and peered into her daughter's eyes. "Is that a yes?"

"Yes, I accept your apology," Harriet said, barely making eye contact with me.

"Can you two shake hands, and let's all be friends and treat each other with respect?"

I offered my hand again and waited for Harriet to respond. After a few seconds, she wiped her palm against her leg and we shook.

"Good," her mother said, rubbing the tops of both our heads. "You're both good kids. And thank you for listening to what I had to say." She rested her hand on my shoulder. "It really means a lot to us."

I felt as if a big weight had been lifted off my chest. For days all I could think about was Harriet's mother and the kind and considerate way she'd spoken to me. It had been like experiencing an encounter with a beautiful creature from another galaxy. She'd even told me I could call her Samantha. I couldn't help feeling envious of Harriet. I wished my mother were as understanding as her mom.

It took a while, but Harriet and I became better friends over the course of that summer. I went from an annoying jerk to a self-appointed bodyguard—"Anybody messes with Harriet, they gotta answer to *me*."

NINETEEN

THE SCHOOL HIRED Mrs. McNulty, a soft-spoken laywoman, to teach Class 8B. Class 8A was taught by Sister Margaret Catherine Nimitz, the oldest and most feared nun in school. Nimitz had been teaching eighth grade at Precious Mother since forever. She was a hard-looking woman with a perpetual scowl and a lantern jaw that cracked like a boxer's knuckles when she shifted it from side to side. She had a reputation for smacking kids around at will—boys, girls, she didn't differentiate. If you were caught disturbing the class, or if she even suspected you of causing trouble, she wouldn't hesitate to bat you around like a piñata.

Freddy Bufano and I had gone through the sixth and seventh grades together. When I found out we were both assigned to 8A, Freddy was the first person I called.

"You believe this shit?" I said.

"What fucking luck."

"We got a *whole year* with that hag."

"Foggetaboutit," Freddy said. "We're doomed. After what happened last year with Capelli, old Nimitz is gonna be on the warpath."

The year before, Class 8A had seen a lot of action under Nimitz, especially her blowout with Tommy Capelli, the toughest kid in the school. Capelli appeared older than his age and walked with an irreverent, bad-boy swagger. He looked as if he'd just stepped out of the Sicilian version of *Blackboard Jungle:* three-quarter-length black leather jacket, toothpick in mouth, cigarette cradled behind one ear, and hair coiffed into a meticulous pompadour.

Capelli was always in some sort of trouble. I think he spent half the year in the detention hall and the other half in the principal's office. He had this mysterious air about him; you never knew what he was thinking or what he was going to do next. He wasn't a bully—he would never hit you up for lunch money or push you around just for the hell of it—but his mere presence intimidated the shit out of everyone. He'd walk into a crowd of kids hanging out in the schoolyard, and everyone would get quiet. His favorite expression was *walio*, meaning *boy.* If Capelli liked you, he'd approach you from behind and flick the back of your head with his finger. "Hey, *walio*."

One day Capelli got into a scrap with Nimitz during the lunch hour. It was Ash Wednesday, and everyone was buzzing around the cafeteria with black ashes smeared on their foreheads—the place looked like a convention of chimney sweeps. Freddy and I were sitting and eating when we heard a blaring squelch from the speakers at the front of the cafeteria. It was Capelli. He was up at the microphone stand next to the announcement table, his forehead smeared with a cross of ashes the size of a baseball card. "Testing!" He flicked the mic with his finger. "One ... two ... tree! Testing!"

"Hey, Tommy," somebody called out, "sing us a song!"

"Hey, *walio*," Capelli said into the microphone with a

big shit-eating grin. He stuck his hand inside his shirt and under his armpit, moved his body close to the microphone and proceeded to flap his arm up and down, producing an astounding array of high-quality fart sounds. The cafeteria went berserk with laughter. I was downing a container of chocolate milk and laughed so hard, milk shot out of my nose. Freddy almost choked on his sandwich.

One of the lay teachers cautiously approached Capelli and tried to coax him away from the mic, but Capelli seemed completely oblivious. He had hit the sweet spot in his armpit and was on a roll. Moments later Sister Nimitz entered the cafeteria from one of the side entrances. She went right for Capelli and whacked him across the face with a sweeping backhand. *Whap!* Capelli's head whipped back like a rag doll, causing him to lose his balance. Nimitz lunged forward to strike him again, and he deflected her hand and punched her in the stomach, sending her flying backward onto the announcement table. "Ya keep ya fuckin' hands offa me!" he shouted, jabbing his finger at her.

The entire cafeteria gasped in shock—striking a nun was unheard of; it was the Catholic Church's equivalent of killing a cop. Nimitz cradled her stomach with both arms, and a few teachers rushed to her aid. Sister Gilhouly shouted down Capelli, directing him to her office. Gilhouly was no stranger when it came to slapping kids around, but after seeing Capelli bury one in Nimitz's stomach, she was wary about using her hands and kept a safe distance. Someone called the police, and a half hour later two cops showed up and took Capelli away in a squad car.

For days afterward, everyone talked about Capelli and how they couldn't believe he'd belted Nimitz. Some girls said hitting a nun was a sacrilege and that Capelli was going straight to hell. But Freddy and I and a few other kids thought he had more brass than Yankee Stadium and that old Nimitz had gotten what she deserved.

When we got to class on the first day of school, Nimitz laid down the law, using the same speech she'd treated years of eighth graders to on their first day in 8A. "There are some troublemakers in this room," she announced, her eyes scouring the class as she waved her infamous black notebook above her head. "And I know *exactly* who you are. I don't know what they let you get away with in the lower grades, but if you think you can get away with any tomfoolery in my class, well, my little darlings"—she stared us down, her wrinkled face giving way to a menacing grin—"just you try me."

Nimitz had a bunch of oddball habits, especially concerning her teeth. She had false upper dentures and kept an extra set in a glass of water on her desk. The water magnified the teeth and made them glisten and undulate as if they had a life of their own, a constant reminder of her caustic presence. Sometimes, when she worked herself into a shouting frenzy, her upper teeth would loosen in her mouth, garbling her words. Without the slightest embarrassment, she would remove the teeth, swap them with the fresh teeth sitting in the glass, and continue ranting. "Look out!" Freddy once warned the class. "She's *reloading!*"

I tried my best to stay out of Nimitz's way, but after I failed a few math exams the old crow was onto me. One afternoon she wrote a math problem on the blackboard. "One and five-sixths times four and one-half," she announced as she wrote. "Who wants to come up and give it a try?"

The hands of a few eager brainiacs shot up in the air, trying to get her attention, and I slithered down in my seat, hoping to go unnoticed.

"Let's see …" She looked around the room. "How about Mr. Caruso? Let's see what *he* can do with this."

I knew I was fucked—*big-time.* My face flushed as I crept out of my seat and walked up to the blackboard. Nimitz handed me the chalk, and I stood there squinting at the problem, pretending to study the two fractions. They could have been hieroglyphs; I didn't have a freaking clue where to begin.

"First of all," she said, "which is the numerator and which is the denominator?"

"The numerator?" I asked.

"Yes, the numerator. Do you know the difference between the numerator and the denominator?"

"The numerator is the bottom number, and the denominator is the top?"

"Are you asking me or telling me?"

I didn't respond, I just stared at the blackboard, praying she would call on someone else.

"Who can tell me which number is the denominator?" she asked the class, without taking her eyes off me.

"The bottom number," someone called out.

"Thank you," she replied, still not looking away from me.

"I meant the bottom number," I said, lying through my teeth.

"So now you have to convert this into an improper fraction," Nimitz went on, picking up another piece of chalk and tapping it hard against the board. "How do you do that?"

She circled each of the fractions.

I stayed focused on the blackboard to avoid eye contact. "Multiply?"

"Yes, *multiply*. That's what we're doing here. But multiply *what*?"

"The numerator?"

"For the love of Saint Peter! You've been in my class three months, and you don't know the difference between the numerator and the denominator. You're too busy fooling around back there with those other two geniuses, Mr. Bufano and Mr. Angelica. *Dumbbell!*" In an instant, she shoved my head into the blackboard with a loud thud. A sharp, pulsating pain shot over the top of my head from one ear to the other.

"Shame on you," Nimitz said. "You have the lowest grades in the class. I'd be surprised if you even knew what two plus two is. Can you tell me what two plus two is?"

I felt totally humiliated, as if she'd pulled my pants down in front of the entire school. Nimitz stood there glaring at me, her insistent gaze pressing me for an answer.

"Four," I muttered.

"Well, praised be the Lord. He can add two and two. There may be hope for him yet. For your assignment tonight, I want you to revisit the chapter on fractions and complete all the problems at the end of the lesson," she said, glaring at me. "And I want that on my desk first thing in the morning. Now go back to your seat and ask the Lord for forgiveness."

As I turned to walk away, Nimitz walloped the back of my head with an open hand. "*Ya blame fool!*"

‰

After school that afternoon, Freddy walked me home. A deep rage was welling up inside of me like bubbling magma.

"You okay, man?" Freddy said.

"I'm fucking *pissed*."

"I don't blame you. Man, she gave you some shot. I thought your head was gonna go right through the blackboard."

"I didn't even see it coming. I swear, next time that old witch touches me, I'll give her a Capelli right in her fucking mouth."

We walked a few blocks in silence, until we reached Bath Avenue.

"What are you gonna do?" he said.

"I dunno. What *can* I do?"

"You gonna tell your parents?"

"What for? It's gonna be the same old story—guilty until proven innocent."

When I got home, I heard shouting coming from my parents' bedroom. My father's suit jacket lay over the back of his chair at the dining room table, and a cigarette burned in an ashtray next to a highball glass and an open bottle of Black & White scotch.

"No wonder he's failing in school!" my father was ranting. "He's in front of the goddamn television all night!"

"What do you want from me?" my mother said. "I tell him to turn off the TV, and he doesn't listen to me."

"That's 'cause you protect him, just like you did with the big one!"

"And what about you? What the hell do *you* do? You're never home, and when you are around, half the time you're *ubriaco*—you're *drunk*."

"I pay the goddamn bills is what I do."

"You pay the bills ..." my mother said.

"That's right. I pay the bills!"

"And every month I have to rob from Peter to pay Paul."

"What are you talking about? I bring home *plenty* of money."

"And most of it goes to booze. When are you going to stop drinking?"

Hearing my mother call out my father like that surprised me. She rarely spoke up and often cowered in his presence.

"Aw, get off it, will ya?" he said. "I have a few drinks here and there. Stop making a federal case out of it, for Godsakes. Maybe if you weren't in bed all goddamn day, letting him stay home from school, we wouldn't be getting embarrassing phone calls."

"Yeah, well, maybe if you were a better father and spent more time with your son, he wouldn't be doing so poorly in school."

"What are you saying? I'm not a *good father*? Is *that* what you're telling me?"

"I'm saying I can't do it all."

"That's not what you said. You said, 'if you were a better father.' Are you trying to insult my intelligence?"

"No, no." My mother was trying to sound calm and rational, but I could hear fear creeping into her voice.

"You just said it two seconds ago, right here in front of me. 'Better father'—those were your exact words."

"I said I can't—"

"*Disgraziato!* I should have known you were damaged

goods when I first met you."

Commotion erupted from the bedroom: furniture being knocked around, glass breaking, my mother crying. My father was in there slapping her around. It sounded like he was going at her good. I dropped my book bag and headed toward the bedroom, and my father stepped out of the room. The second we made eye contact I did an about-face and headed for the door.

"C'mere, you." His voice was deep and menacing, and it sent a jolt of fear through me. I turned facing him.

"What?" I said. I was thinking there was still time to bolt out of the house.

"Don't *what* me!" he roared. "You come when I call you!" He pointed to the floor in front of him.

I walked toward him and stopped a few feet away. He wasn't full-blown drunk, but his eyes were red, looking like he'd already put away one or two drinks. I could hear my mother weeping in the bedroom.

"What happened with Mom?" I said, keeping my distance.

"Never mind Mom." He stepped toward me and grabbed the knot of my school tie, drawing my face close to his. "What are you, a clown?" His grip was supertight, and his breath reeked of scotch. He slapped my face. "Answer me!"

"No."

"What are you, a clown in the circus?" He slapped me again, harder. I struggled to breathe.

"No, sir," I gasped. I had never called him "sir" before, but I was so scared, I thought it might appease him and he'd let me go.

He pushed me away. "Your teacher called and told me you're failing in school and you're always clowning around in class. That true?"

A rush of oxygen filled my lungs. "No," I said, my chest heaving.

"She said you have the lowest grades in the class and you don't know the difference between the numerator and the denominator."

"She asked me, and I couldn't remember."

"What do you mean, you couldn't remember? You didn't *know*, or you couldn't *remember?*"

"I ... I couldn't remember."

"Bullshit."

"I couldn't remember."

"Don't lie to me!"

"Okay, so I didn't know."

"That's different than telling me you couldn't remember."

"What about you? Do *you* know the difference?"

"Never mind what I know! I'm not the one in school who has to learn this stuff and ... and ... and pass the exams there."

"You don't know what she did." I burst into tears. "She pushed my head into the blackboard."

"I don't care *what* she did! Your job is to sit in class, keep your big mouth shut, and listen to what the teacher has to say. Not clown around with the other *chooches* you hang out with. Your teacher told me you think everything is a joke."

"I hate school," I said, wiping the tears from my cheeks with my sleeve.

"Me too. I hate a lot of things. Sometimes I hate my job. Does that mean I don't go to work or pay attention to my boss? If I've told you once, I've told you a million times—*English and math, English and math.*" He jabbed my forehead with the tips of his fingers. "Those are the two most important subjects. Without those two under your belt, you can't go anywhere."

Anywhere. Where the fuck was that? Forget anywhere; I didn't understand why I was in school in the first place, let alone see it as a vehicle that would lead me to some rewarding destination. To me it seemed like a cruel ritual that kids were forced to endure, like getting cavities filled or submitting to polio shots.

"Yeah, but—"

"Yeah, but *nothing.* You're grounded for the next two weeks. No television, no hanging out, no nothin'. And if I get another embarrassing phone call from Sister Nemo—"

"It's Sister Nimitz. You don't even know her name."

"Nimitz, Nemo, whatever the hell her name is. I'm coming up to the school there and I'm gonna straighten you out in front of everyone. Now get *crackin'.*"

I couldn't believe Nimitz had had the crust to call my father. Later, when I told Connie what had happened, she thought the old bag made sure to call the house before I got home from school to cover her ass by blaming me first, just in case I'd planned on telling my parents about her smashing my head into the blackboard.

Nimitz could have saved herself a dime—I'd been taking the heat for years before she picked up the phone.

TWENTY

I WAITED FOR Jackie in front of our building. The two of us had planned to head over to Tony's for some of his "Best in Brooklyn" egg creams: a frothy combination of milk and chocolate syrup, topped off with a blast of seltzer. Jackie showed up lugging a phone book under each arm. Every year the phone company delivered a stack of White and Yellow Pages to the lobbies of each building in Bay Haven.

"Where you goin' with those?" I said. "I thought we were goin' to Tony's."

He dropped one of the books at my feet and held the other with both hands. "How much you wanna bet I can rip this book in half?"

"C'mon. Stop pullin' my chain. I'm dying for an egg cream."

"I'm serious. How much you wanna bet?"

"Okay—betcha a thousand dollars."

"No," he said, "how much you wanna bet?"

"Okay—a hundred bucks. I'll betcha a hundred bucks."

"Ya see? You think I'm jokin', right?"

"C'mon, Jackie. Nobody can rip a phone book in half, not even Superman."

"Then bet me."

"Okay, I'll bet you an egg cream."

"Okay, an egg cream."

The deal sounded too good to be true. "No, wait a minute," I said. "I'll bet you *two* egg creams."

"Okay," said Jackie without hesitation. "It's a bet. I rip the book in half—you buy me two egg creams. I don't rip the book in half—I buy *you* two egg creams. Bet?" Jackie held out his hand, pinky extended.

"Bet," I said, curling my pinky, hooking it to his.

I thought for sure that Jackie had lost his mind—the White Pages had to be at least four inches thick. He raised the book high above his head, wrapping both hands around the hard binding. "*By the gods!*" he thundered. In one fluid motion he lifted his leg and slammed the book against the top of his knee, snapping the binding in two. Then he tore each piece in opposite directions, ripping the book in half. "The gods have spoken!" he said, tossing the two bound halves at my feet. I was totally amazed.

"*No way.*" I picked up the two pieces and looked them over. They were torn clean in half. "How the hell'dja do that?"

"It's easy. Once you crack the binding, you just rip it apart. My uncle showed me."

I picked up the other phone book, gripped the binding with two hands, and brought it down hard over my knee. To my surprise it snapped like a wishbone. I then twisted the two pieces in opposite directions, feeling the pages giving way inch by inch until I was finally able to rip the book apart as he had. I felt like Hercules.

"You owe me two egg creams," Jackie said.

"Two? How 'bout six?" My brain was working overtime. I saw a tremendous opportunity to make some fast dough by taking the show on the road.

"Whaddaya mean?"

"You kidding? We can make a *fortune* with this."

Jackie's face lit up.

We scrambled into the lobby and scooped up four telephone books, two for each of us. Instead of testing the market in our neck of the woods, we decided to check out foreign territory. The plan was that I would do the talking and Jackie would do the ripping. We crossed Bay Lane, the street that snaked through the center of Bay Haven, and headed for the public gathering area toward the back end of the complex where a bunch of kids were hanging out on benches. The only guys Jackie and I recognized were the Doyle brothers, two tough Irish kids with pug noses and wavy red hair.

"What're ya, delivering wit' the phone cump'ny or somethin'?" said one of the brothers in his thick Irish accent. He was sitting on the backrest of a bench, his feet on the seat. He looked fresh off the boat from Dublin: baggy corduroy pants, brown high-button shoes, and an ugly tan sweater that could have doubled for a potato sack.

"We already got ours," said the other brother, also sitting on the backrest. He looked a little younger and sported a wrinkled football jersey and faded jeans.

"Are you guys up for a little magic?" I said.

"What kinda magic?" said the older brother. "The kind where you disappear?"

The other kids laughed.

"Very funny," Jackie said. "You should be on *The Ed Sullivan Show*."

"My friend here has the power of Superman," I said,

pointing to Jackie. "He can rip a phone book in half."

"Malarkey," said the older brother. "No man can rip a phone book in half."

"Wanna bet?"

"Yeah," Jackie said, "put your money where your mouth is."

"G'ahead, Jimmy. Bet him," one kid said.

"Yeah, bet him," said another. "He can't rip a book."

"Okay," said the older brother, stepping down off the bench. "I'll betcha two dollars."

I conferred with Jackie to make sure we had enough money to cover the bet, then turned back. "Okay, you're on—two dollars."

"First let's see yer two dollars," the younger brother said.

Jackie and I had pooled together a crumpled dollar bill and a dollar's worth of change. "There," I said, holding the money in my palm. "Two dollars. Now let's see *your* money."

The older brother pulled two one-dollar bills from his pocket and held them up, swishing them back and forth between his fingers.

One of the kids hollered, "Hey, this guy's gonna rip a phone book!" In seconds, a bunch of other kids came running over to see what was going on.

Jackie was a natural at working a crowd. He waited for everyone to quiet down, then closed his eyes and took a deep breath. Once again, he positioned the book over his head, clutching the binding. "*By the gods!*" he thundered. Then he snapped the binding against his knee and tore the book into two pieces. The onlookers were astonished.

"Holy shit!"

"You see *that*?"

"Fuckin' unbelievable!"

Jackie looked cool as a cucumber. He rolled his shoulders and tossed the two ripped pieces in front of the Doyle brothers as if it were just another day at the office.

"There ya go," I said, pointing to the remains. "The gods have spoken. Now cough up." I held out my hand, flapping my fingers.

"No good," the older Doyle said, shaking his head.

"Whaddaya mean, no good?"

"Yeah," Jackie said heatedly. "Whaddaya mean, no good?"

"We're not payin'."

"Why not?"

"Because," the older Doyle said, "he cheated. He ripped the book from the back and not the front. Fer fuck's sake, anyone can do that."

"Fuck that!" Jackie wasn't having any of it.

"Yeah, *fuck that!*" I echoed. "We didn't say anything about front or back; we bet that he could rip the book in half. Now *pay up.*"

The older brother stepped forward. "Lookie here. Why don'cha lads gerrup de yard before you getcha knickers in a twist?"

"What the fuck does *that* mean?" I said. "This is America. Speak fuckin' English."

"It means yer mudder wears size-twelve combat boots, and yer fadder is a cigar-smoking geezer."

"What did you say about my mother?"

"I says your mudder—"

I charged headlong, knocking him back into the

bench, and unleashed a flurry of punches. He tried to get up, but before he could regain his balance, I got him in a headlock and started bashing his face. The younger Doyle nailed me with a couple punches before Jackie smashed his head with a phone book and ripped at his hair. The kid's head jerked back, and Jackie yanked him to the ground, kicking and stomping him.

The older brother's nose was bleeding, but I didn't let up. "Whad'ja say about my mother? Huh? Whad'ja say?" I had that fucker's head trapped good and tight and delighted in making him eat his words.

"Hey, let him go! Let him go!" someone shouted.

Two kids scrambled out of the front entrance of the nearest building and ran toward us. Above them, a third-floor window flew open with a loud clap, and a red-haired man popped his head out. "Hey, you punks, get the fuck odder here!"

"C'mon, let's blow," Jackie said, tugging on my shirt.

I got one last punch in, and then the two of us put it into high gear, heading for our side of Bay Haven.

"Get 'em, Jimmy! Get 'em!" the man hollered from the window.

I glanced over my shoulder. The two brothers and their cronies were chasing us down like hounds. Jackie and I tried to cross Bay Lane but got stalled by a line of passing cars and trucks. When the traffic finally broke, we cut across the street and found ourselves trapped with our backs against a garage door, dodging a barrage of rocks, cans, and bottles. The Doyles were just on the other side of Bay Lane, picking out ammunition from a cluster of curbside garbage cans. I started to panic—there were four of them, and they had us pinned in the driveway of the garage, hurling shit at us from all sides.

To the left of the garage entrance were more garbage cans—big metal jobs filled with charred trash from the building's incinerator rooms. Two of the cans were stuffed with long, white, burnt-out fluorescent bulbs used to light up the underground garages and laundry rooms. I zigzagged to the cans, pulled out one of the bulbs, and chucked it across the street like a javelin. The bulb sailed through the air and landed a couple of feet in front of the Doyles, exploding into a million pieces. A white cloud of phosphor powder rose and hovered over the dark asphalt.

"Look out—it's poison!" one of them yelled. The gang backed away. Before they could regroup, I slipped out another bulb and lobbed it across at the same spot. *Boom!*

Jackie darted over to join me, and together we flung bulbs two at a time, laughing maniacally.

"We'll getcha, ya fuckin' greaseballs!" the older brother said, his sweater spattered with blood.

"*Get this, motherfucker!*" I yelled back, grabbing my crotch.

A sharp whistle blew—one of the Bay Haven uniformed patrolmen. He rushed up the street toward us with a building maintenance man. The Doyle gang scattered like fish. The patrolman cut left, chasing after the brothers, and the maintenance man headed for me and Jackie—a nearly bald middle-aged dude with a basketball-size potbelly pushing out the front of his tan work shirt.

Jackie and I bolted down the middle of Bay Lane. We ran for about twenty yards, and then Jackie cut sharp to his right and onto the sidewalk parallel to the street. From there he shot up a grass embankment and flew like a deer through a row of holly bushes that bordered the center of the complex. The maintenance man chased after him.

I ran another ten yards before slipping over to the sidewalk, where I hunched over, gasping for air, hands resting on my thighs. My lungs were on fire. After a moment or two I headed down the sidewalk, trying to breathe and act normally. I got maybe twenty feet before I heard footsteps behind me—it was the freaking maintenance man. I couldn't believe it. The fat fuck had circled back and was on a mission, chugging after me, but there was no way I was going to let him catch me. I veered into the street, darting in and out of a line of parked cars. Eventually he slowed to a halt, coughing and holding his chest. "Don't let me see you back here again!" He sounded as if he were about to croak.

I wasn't taking any chances on him catching a second wind and following me home. I looped around and ran up Bay Lane to the back of my building. There I climbed a wall onto a huge cement terrace and scuttled four stories up the fire escape that led to Connie's bedroom. I pushed open the window and tumbled into the room, getting tangled in her chiffon curtains. The curtain rod snapped, and I hit the floor with a thud. I heard a loud scream but couldn't see a thing. When I unwound the curtains from my head, I found Connie standing naked in front of her full-length mirror, dripping wet. She had just stepped out of the shower and was drying her hair with a towel. Her body trembled, and she screamed nonstop until she realized it was me.

"What the hell are you doing, you fucking jerk?" she shrieked, covering herself with the towel. "You almost gave me a heart attack!"

"Nothin'," I said.

"Whaddaya mean, *nothin*? Look—you ripped my goddamn curtains!"

My mother rushed into the room. "What happened? What happened?" She looked panic-stricken.

"This moron just climbed up the fire escape and crawled through the window and took down my curtains."

"What? Are you *crazy*?" my mother said. "And look at you. You're all sweaty. What the hell you been doing?"

"Nothin'," I said. "I was outside ... I was just playing with Jackie."

"Ma!" Connie cried. "Get him *out* of here!"

"Get in the bathroom and wash up before I tell your father."

"*Jackass*," Connie said. "And stay the hell out of my room!"

My mother hadn't noticed, but my knuckles were bruised, and my right hand stayed swollen for three days. It was totally crazy, but all I could think about was getting back out on the streets with Jackie and making a killing ripping up phone books.

TWENTY-ONE

FRANK WAS LIVING in a neat one-bedroom apartment on a residential, tree-lined street near Brooklyn College. He occupied the top floor of a two-family home owned by a middle-aged couple. Since his return from the army, he'd been working for Greyson & Jennings, one of the larger advertising firms on Madison Avenue. He frequently talked about the big ad campaigns that G&J produced, always quick to include a dollar amount for each campaign, as if he were one of the firm's founding partners. "We just wrapped up a huge print ad and TV commercial for Skippy peanut butter. You know—Best Foods. That account alone is close to a million bucks. And that's just *one* of our accounts."

Occasionally Frank worked on weekends, and one Saturday he invited me to hang out with him. I was totally pumped. I'd heard so much about his company and was finally going to see where he worked.

Greyson & Jennings occupied the fifteenth floor of a modern, thirty-five-story building with an all-glass facade. The floor was almost the size of a football field, and there wasn't a soul in sight. "Let there be light!" Frank commanded, flipping the master switch just inside G&J's entrance. One by one, a succession of overheard lights flickered and lit up, illuminating a sea of empty desks and drafting tables. "This is the Creative Department." Frank swept his arm in a dramatic arc. "This is where it all happens. C'mon, I'll give you a tour."

I followed my brother around the floor as he eagerly showed me conference rooms, break-out areas, pantries, departments, and subdepartments. Desks were smothered with books, binders, catalogs, knickknacks, and potted plants. Bulletin boards, photos, and posters from old ad campaigns in smart metal frames covered the walls.

Frank led me to the executive offices at the far end of the floor and opened the door to the corner office, an expansive suite dominated by a huge cherrywood desk sitting on a plush gray rug. I felt as if I were visiting the White House and my brother had privileged access to the Oval Office, allowing me a sneak peek.

Two of the walls were floor-to-ceiling windows that converged at the corner and offered a panoramic view of the Manhattan skyline. "This is Todd Greyson's office," Frank said with a hint of reverence in his voice. "He's the man who calls all the shots." He looked around the room with admiration. "One day your brother's gonna have an office just like this."

I smiled, not knowing what to say. Frank had aspirations and a relentless drive that were totally foreign to me. He had his sights set on a corner office, and I was struggling in school, praying to the patron saint of fuck-ups that I wouldn't get held back.

Frank ordered lunch from a nearby deli and had it delivered. We wolfed down tuna heroes and potato chips in a large conference room where Frank sat at the head of the table. As we ate, he occasionally stopped to jot down notes on a legal pad— things he had to do that afternoon.

"Did you hear the one about the guy who took his kid to the circus?" I said, trying to get his attention.

"What?" Frank replied.

"I said, 'Did you hear the one about the guy who took his kid to the circus?'"

"John, I'm tryna write something here."

"C'mon, whaddaya writin', a book? We're having lunch."

"John ..."

"It's a joke," I said. "You don't have time for a freaking joke? What kind of big-time ad man are you?"

"All right." He tossed down his pen. "Whaddaya got, a joke? Let's hear it." He folded his arms across his chest. "This better be good."

"Okay—here goes." I took a quick swig of soda and ran the back of my wrist across my lips. "This guy takes his kid to a three-ring circus. The two of them are sitting in the stands just above the runway leading to the center ring. The guy looks down and sees a line of elephants about to be paraded into the ring. As he's watching, he notices a workman wearing a long rubber glove that goes all the way up his arm. The guy's got his arm halfway up the ass of one of the elephants. He's in there scooping out shit so the elephant doesn't poop in front of the crowd. After a minute or two, the guy in the stands realizes that the guy with the glove is one of his old army buddies. 'Hey, Mac!' he hollers down. 'How ya doin'? It's me—Jimmy!' The guy with the glove looks up and hollers back, 'Jimmy, how ya doin', man? Long time no see!'

"Later the two of them meet outside. 'Whaddaya been up to?' asks the guy workin' with the elephants. 'I'm doing well,' says the man with the kid. 'I'm married, got a son here, plus I own a big construction company.' 'Ya don't say?' says his friend. 'Listen, Mac,' says the man with the kid." I lowered my voice to a gentle, sympathetic tone: "'I, ahh … saw you scoopin' shit out of the elephant's ass back there on the runway. How about you come work for me instead? I got a good job waitin' for ya—pays top dollar.' His friend gets all pissed off. 'And what?' he says. 'Get outta *show business*?'"

Frank gave a short, stingy laugh that sounded like a hiccup. I could tell he liked the joke but wasn't going to allow himself to show it. He was weird like that sometimes. He'd hold back as a matter of principle. *Yes, it was funny, but I'm not expressing full enjoyment because I want you and the world to know that I'm way too hip and adhere to a higher standard.*

After lunch Frank took me into the executive screening area, a dark, soundproof room with half a dozen theater seats facing a white screen. The room even had a small popcorn machine. He set up the projector with a reel of TV commercial bloopers that one of his co-workers had put together. "This thing runs about forty-five minutes," he said. "I have to go do some work now. Help yourself to some popcorn and don't wreck the place. If you need me, I'll be out on the floor."

I had the whole room to myself; I felt like royalty. I sat with my feet up, munching popcorn, watching hilarious blunders from live television commercials. In one clip, a woman was demonstrating a new frost-free refrigerator. "Chipping away at frost and emptying messy drip pans are a thing of the past," she assured viewers. "The new Westinghouse refrigerator always keeps itself frost-free." She attempted to open the door, and the thing wouldn't budge. Frustrated, she yanked the handle a few times, then turned around and looked directly into the camera. "I don't know who it is," she announced, "but somebody's playing games with me."

In another commercial, a stumpy bald guy with a forty-inch neck was selling tires. Halfway through his pitch, the rack of tires behind him gave way and a dozen whitewalls bounced over the floor, knocking over a display of oilcans. After the last tire stopped bouncing and came to a halt, he stepped back onto the set. "*Shit!* Are we still rolling?" He marched toward the camera with an outstretched arm, blocking the lens with his hand. "Turn that fucking thing off!"

After a few more bloopers, I started to feel lonely and wished my brother were sharing the laughter with me. I wandered out of the screening room and spotted Frank at one of the drafting tables. He was working diligently under a fluorescent extension lamp clamped to the edge of the table. I admired his concentration. I looked on for a moment or two, then headed over.

"What's going on?" he said without looking up. "Was there a problem with the projector?"

"No, I just stopped by to say hello."

Frank was measuring and cutting out strips of large type and pictures and pasting them to a white illustration board. "C'mere," he said, motioning me closer. "Learn something."

"Whaddaya workin' on?" I said, stuffing my hands into the back pockets of my jeans.

"This is a storyboard presentation. Before they shoot a

commercial, the Creative Department develops one or two sales concepts to present to the client. A bunch of guys sit in a room trying to come up with different ways of selling soap, breakfast cereal, and other crap to American housewives. This is for Wonder Mist Air Freshener." He pointed to a picture of a woman joyfully spraying mist from an aerosol can. Above the picture were the words *Spray the Magic Back into Your Life.* "I mean, when you think about it, what the hell is air freshener? Some cheap-shit scented water and pressurized air in an eight-ounce can with a plastic nozzle. But we're not selling that. What we're selling is magic. With one press of the button, a housewife can release a sweet-smelling fragrance and clear the room of her deadbeat, stinko marriage. Boom— *all gone.*"

"I never thought of it like that," I said, laughing.

Frank carefully lifted the picture with a single-edge razor blade and readjusted it on the board. "This is what advertising is all about. Nobody really gives a shit if a product is good or bad. The idea is to convince consumers that they need it and that it's gonna make their boring, miserable lives better."

The way Frank emphasized the words "boring, miserable lives" made me think that he viewed the whole world as tedious and dismal, and that by working in advertising he was somehow protecting himself from falling into either of those categories.

"I thought you worked in print production," I said. He had told me about his helping to coordinate the production of subway ads and product brochures between the Art Department and various print shops around Manhattan.

"I still do. But I don't wanna to be there forever. I

wanna be on the creative side. That's where all the money and recognition is." A short silence. "Ya know, this didn't just fall into my lap. For weeks I pestered one of the account execs to let me work on one of his campaigns."

"Do you get paid overtime, you know ... like for weekends?"

Frank turned and looked at me in disbelief. "*Paid?* Are you *kidding?* I'm lucky just to get the opportunity to be *near* this work. Paid ... I'm thankful I don't have to pay *them.* Everybody and their mother wants to work here. There are people out there who would kill to be sitting here doing what I'm doing." Frank was looking increasingly irritated. "There are no shortcuts," he continued. "You gotta make your own opportunities, and you gotta know what the hell you're talking about. This is something the old man doesn't understand 'cause he's too busy trying to fake it. He shows up at work with the suit and the tie and the pressed white shirt, and then two weeks later they pull the plug on him when they realize he doesn't know what the hell he's doing."

Frank turned back to the storyboard, his face gripped with fierce determination. I wanted to tell him how poorly I was doing in school but couldn't bring myself to say it. I was sure he would think of me as a fake, the way he thought of our father—which was exactly how I felt.

After a moment I put my arm around him and rested my head on his shoulder.

Frank looked up. "What are you doing?"

I didn't answer. I was hoping he would stop working for a minute and respond in kind.

"John ..."

"What? I'm just hugging you."

"Yeah, but I'm working now."

"I know. But can't I hug you just a little bit?"

Frank started to say something, and I kissed the side of his head, pressing my cheek against his face, hugging him tighter. His body stiffened like a stray cat in the arms of a stranger. After a second or two he pulled away, checking to see if anyone was watching.

"What?" I said. "There's nobody here."

Frank swallowed hard.

I put my arm around him again. "I love you, Frankie."

"Johnny, you don't understand," he said, struggling to glance at his watch. "I don't have no time for this right now. I … I gotta get this done."

I tried to kiss him again, and he recoiled.

"Are you deaf?" he said, looking at me as if I'd pulled a knife on him.

"I was just—"

"I said I'm working."

Frank looked away, focusing on his work again, and my heart sank. I wanted so much for him to acknowledge me and tell me he loved me. I stood there feeling remarkably self-conscious and aware of the eerie vastness of the room. "I … I'm sorry," I said, barely able to speak.

"Go finish watching the reel," he said. "I'll come get you when I'm done."

As I turned and headed back to the screening room, I could feel my chest deflate like a giant balloon.

TWENTY-TWO

MY MOTHER'S HEALTH was worsening. In addition to her collection of antidepressants, she was taking pills for high blood pressure, water retention, headaches, arthritis, and insomnia. Connie had figured out a routine to pick up the slack: she shopped and cooked, and I did the housecleaning and laundry. Things had been going smoothly for about a week when my mom decided she needed to get out of bed and do more around the house. This might have sounded like a good idea, but just about everything she touched turned into a disaster—like the time she was washing dishes and forced a sponge into a narrow glass, causing it to shatter and cut her thumb pretty badly.

Connie was fit to be tied. "Ma—relax, will ya? Everything's *okay*. Just stay in bed like the doctor told you. We got everything covered. Otherwise you're gonna hurt yourself and make more work for us."

"Nobody loves me," my mother whimpered.

"Whaddaya mean, nobody loves you? We *all* love you. That's why we're breaking our asses here to make sure you're comfortable."

Connie thought our mom would make a great contestant on *Queen for a Day*, a TV game show that awarded prizes (dishwashers, washing machines, etc.) to one of three sobbing women who told the most convincing, personal hard-luck story. The show was taped in front of a live studio audience, and the woman who garnered the loudest round of applause for her tale of woe was crowned and declared the winner.

"I swear, we gotta get her on the show," my sister joked. "She'd clean up *big-time*."

One afternoon Connie came home exhausted, her arms holding two full bags of groceries. "What the hell is that smell?" she said.

"The vacuum cleaner," I said. "Ma was vacuuming the living room and got the cord caught in the roller and burned out the motor. I came home about ten minutes ago and found the machine upside-down on the floor. The freaking thing was still buzzing—she didn't even turn it off."

"*Shit.*" Connie set down the bags on the dining room table, and I followed her into my parents' bedroom, where my mother was lying in bed.

"Ma, what happened?"

"What happened?" my mother repeated, sitting up and blinking. "Where's your father? Is he okay?"

"Daddy's at work," said Connie. "He's fine."

"Are you sure? I forgot to iron his shirts."

"Ma, never mind Daddy's shirts. What happened with the vacuum cleaner?"

"It's in the closet."

"Ma, you were vacuuming the living room," I said. "You got the cord stuck in the roller."

"I did?"

"And you left the machine on," Connie said. "You don't *remember*?"

"I must have forgot. Did you turn it off?"

Connie and I looked at each other, and we knew immediately that something was very wrong.

"Listen, Ma," Connie said, "I told you before. Stay in bed like the doctor told you. We don't want you to hurt yourself."

My mother looked bewildered. Her uncombed, frizzy gray hair drooped down over her forehead, partially covering her face. She shifted her gaze between my sister and me. Then her shoulders slumped and she began to weep.

"What's wrong?" Connie said.

"I don't know anymore." My mother buried her face in her hands. I wasn't sure if she actually didn't know or if she was harboring thoughts and memories too painful to talk about.

"Did you take your pills today?" said Connie, adjusting the pillow behind my mother's back.

My mother didn't respond.

"Where are her special pills?" Connie motioned toward the small end table covered with at least a dozen plastic bottles of prescription drugs. I handed her a single capsule of Miltown and a glass of water.

"Here, take this." Connie placed the pill in my mother's mouth and held the glass to her lips. My mother gulped the water like it was her last drink of liquid, water dribbling down her chin. It was in that moment I had realized that she was no longer the caregiver, and that the responsibility of taking care of the house and our ourselves was now up to my sister and me.

"You'll feel better in a little while," Connie said, running a hand over my mother's head. Try to get some rest."

Moments later Connie was in the kitchen, hastily putting away groceries while sipping a glass of red wine, something I'd never seen her do before, at least not in the apartment. She looked perturbed and totally preoccupied.

"I can't believe she didn't remember screwing up the vacuum," I said.

Connie didn't respond. She removed two cans of tomato sauce from a grocery bag and placed them on the top shelf of the cabinet. "I swear," she said, as if talking to herself. "I didn't sign up for this shit."

I was having a hard time staying focused in class and constantly got busted for talking and horsing around. Sitting in close proximity to Freddy Bufano and Carmine Angelica didn't help—especially Carmine, who was anything but angelic. He had an Adam's apple the size of a doorknob and a mischievous glint in his eyes. He loved to create havoc and took great pleasure in driving Nimitz crazy with outbursts of what she referred to as "hop-headed noises."

Nimitz thought the three of us were sitting too close to each other and split us up. She moved me to a desk next to MaryAnn Quigley, a thin, bookish girl whose curly brown hair rested on her head like a heap of tumbleweeds. MaryAnn was quiet and reserved and Catholic to the bone. She wore a massive silver crucifix around her neck like it was a backstage pass, along with a small ceramic portrait of the Virgin Mary pinned to her navy-blue school jumper.

"Hi." I smiled. "Looks like we're neighbors." MaryAnn eked out a nervous grin and looked away. The general consensus was that she was smart, but most definitely on the weird side. When you spoke to her, she rarely made eye contact.

Once Nimitz tried to get creative. She came up with an "art project" and had each student assemble a "Bankbook of Prayers," a stapled booklet made of white loose-leaf and colored construction paper. The idea was for us to say prayers in our spare time and record the date and number of prayers in our booklets, as if we were recording deposits in our bank accounts. MaryAnn was all over this; she started filling up the pages in her bankbook like she was saving for a split-level home. While the other kids buzzed around the schoolyard, MaryAnn stood off to the side with her rosary beads, saying prayers and diligently making "bankbook" entries.

The whole bankbook thing was totally out there, and I thought MaryAnn's blind compliance was criminal. So did Carmine, who enjoyed rattling MaryAnn's cage. One afternoon she was working her beads at a feverish pace. Carmine stood close behind her and called out across the schoolyard to no one in particular, "Jesus Christ, gimme a fuckin' break, *will ya*?" MaryAnn nearly jumped out of her skin. She made the sign of the cross, acting as if the devil had stuck his head up her skirt and bitten her on the ass.

Nimitz was big on testing. In addition to midterm and final exams, she sprang a test on us at least once a week. Just hearing the word *test* put a knot in my stomach. I'd study as best I could, but I had difficulty retaining the information.

Cheating was forbidden, punishable by flogging, or at least that was how it felt. Still, during exams my eyes wandered, scanning nearby desks for answers. If it was a multiple-choice or true-or-false exam, I had a decent chance of nailing a passing grade. From as far as seven feet away I could scan someone's test paper and glean answers.

During one science exam, my eyes roamed over to MaryAnn's desk. When she noticed me zeroing in on her paper, she started to squirm, clutching her rosary beads.

"Whad'ja get for nine, ten, and fourteen?" I whispered out of the side of my mouth.

MaryAnn looked up and wrinkled her nose as if she smelled smoke and then curled her arm around her test paper.

"C'mon," I said, "nine, ten, and fourteen. Whad'ja get?"

God knows what the hell I was thinking. Forget talking and cheating during an exam; this was someone who got stressed when people passed her in the hall and said hello.

Time was running out. I checked to see if Nimitz was looking and then snatched MaryAnn's test paper from her desk. MaryAnn was totally freaked and started rocking from side to side. Fuck it. For me it wasn't just a race against time, it was a matter of survival. I copied all the answers I needed and slipped the paper back to her as fast as I'd swiped it. The poor girl looked like she was on the verge of a nervous breakdown. After the exam, MaryAnn raised her hand and asked to go to the bathroom. When she got up from her desk to leave the room, I noticed a small wet spot on the back of her school uniform.

I wasn't the only kid in the class embracing the merits of self-help. When it came to cheating, Richard Zimmindorff was Houdini reincarnated. He devised a method for taking exams that opened up the floodgates for me, Carmine, and Freddy. Instead of pulling his pud trying to scrounge answers from the person sitting next to him, Zimmindorff jotted information on three-by-five index cards that Carmine aptly referred to as "Zim's little memory cards." Each card was crammed, front and back, with material written in near-microscopic handwriting. Everything fit onto no more than three index cards that he'd stuff inside his unbuttoned shirt, under the wide portion of his tie. When the class settled down to take the exam, Zim would calmly whip out the cards and go to work. I thought this was the greatest innovation since Reddi-wip.

"Now, ya gotta go easy," Zimmindorff told us, taking a deep drag from his unfiltered cigarette. He was talking to me, Carmine, and Freddy in the schoolyard, nervously checking all sides. Zim was straight-up working-class German. He was tall and bony, and you could see the sharp outlines of his shoulder blades protruding from the back of his shirt like fins on a Cadillac.

"If we all start pulling down nineties and ninety-fives, the old witch is gonna know somethin's up," he went on, twisting his lips and exhaling smoke out of one side of his mouth. "If you look at my average, I'm in the low to mid-eighties. I'm not tryin' to get into fuckin' Harvard, and I don't give a fuck about fuckin' Nimitz slapping a fuckin' gold star on my fuckin' report card. I just wanna fuckin' pass and graduate from this hellhole in one fuckin' piece."

"Good point." I nodded.

"'Good point,'" Carmine mimicked, letting out one of his high-pitched cackles.

"What's so funny?" I said.

"Who the fuck are you, Perry Mason?"

"I got your Perry Mason right here," I fired back, grabbing my crotch.

Carmine faked a jab with his right hand, then tapped my head with his left. I jerked backward, bumping into Freddy, who shoved me into Carmine.

"Awright, you boneheads, knock it off," Zimmindorff said. "This is serious shit. If fuckin' Nimitz gets fuckin' wind of this fuckin' shit, we'll all be fuckin' fucked. Just remember, if you get fuckin' caught, you're on your fuckin' own. I'm not takin' the fuckin' heat for fuckin' anybody."

The following week we had a history exam, and I jotted down a ton of information on the fronts and backs of two cards. Names, dates, locations—I had it all written out. My writing was so small, I think I covered the War of 1812 and the Battle of Gettysburg in four lines. Just like Zim, I stuffed the cards inside my shirt and slipped them out from under my tie when Nimitz wasn't looking. Within weeks, my grades started to improve. They weren't great, but at least my overall average wasn't failing. I wasn't learning dick, but who cared? I was more excited about beating the system. I saw this as an art form, something I could do and do well.

"All right," my father said when I handed him my monthly report card for him to sign. "That's more like it."

I walked away feeling a combination of pride and contempt: pride in the fact that I'd figured out how to pass exams and get my father and Nimitz off my back; contempt for the old man, a self-important drunk who didn't know shit from Shinola.

TWENTY-THREE

WORKING A FEW three-by-five index cards to boost my grades was chickenshit compared to the rush I got from casing out a store and issuing myself a five-finger discount right under the watchful eyes of the owner. Strolling out of a supermarket with a family pack of M&Ms hidden under my sweatshirt, or slipping out of a store with a handful of Magic Markers and a couple of notebooks stuffed in my schoolbag, was like striking gold. It made me feel like a fist-pumping Olympic ski jumper sticking a perfect landing.

In my mind, I wasn't exactly stealing. More like *self-appropriating*. Truth be told, I didn't need three-quarters of the crap I lifted, things like fountain pens, key chains, whistles, a kazoo, hairbrushes, a hockey puck. (A fucking *hockey puck!*) I kept my stash in a cardboard box buried in the back of my closet, behind a pile of old sneakers and winter boots. These were my personal belongings, distinctly different from the things my parents and relatives bought for me. They were objects I went out and got on my own, possessions that filled an intangible void and made me feel I was taking care of myself in a way that others could never understand. They helped me believe that I was my own person.

At least once a week I'd rummage through the box to

admire what I'd amassed. Included in my hoard were four or five pocketknives with shiny blades and plastic handles featuring multicolored Chinese dragons that glittered like Christmas decorations. I loved trying to decide which was my favorite. The collection gave me the same sense of pride that other kids got from mulling over their comic book or stamp collections. The only difference was that my stash was a secret I couldn't share with anyone. Over time it wouldn't grow in value, but it was—as I believed—a clear affirmation of my unrecognized wit, ingenuity, and stealth. It was also a form of self-expression—my way of telling Nimitz, my parents, and every other adult on the planet to bend over, put their heads between their legs, and go *fuck* themselves.

Eighty-Sixth Street was a wide, two-way thoroughfare that cut across southwest Brooklyn from Gravesend to the Narrows. The BMT subway ran along trestles high above the street. Below, sidewalks teemed with shoppers bustling in and out of stores and restaurants ranging from pizza shops to Chinese take-outs and kosher delis. The air was filled with a continual racket of barking street vendors, car horns, and trucks passing through, punctuated with the occasional thundering vibration of the D train barreling to or from Manhattan. "Eighty-Sixth," as it was commonly referred to, lay within walking distance of Bay Haven and Precious Mother. It was where everyone went to buy dungarees, sneakers, 45s, shower curtains, transistor radios, and pop-up toasters. It was also the ideal location for self-appropriating.

I was interested in one establishment in particular:

Richard's, a long, narrow drugstore with a glitzy display window and a glossy sign above the entrance declaring *Richard's* in fancy gold script. Richard's wasn't your typical Brooklyn drugstore, largely because of the owner, whose real name was Riccardo—a slightly effeminate middle-aged man rumored to be from Spain but actually from Cuba.

Riccardo stood about five-ten and had a well-built upper body with a broad chest and competition biceps the size of eggplants. The guy had a flair about him; you couldn't tell if he was a pharmacist or a hairdresser. He wore waist-length, pastel-colored nylon jackets, all short-sleeved and tight-fitting with the initial *R* embroidered on the pocket. He spoke with a faint lisp and a Spanish accent, and he carried himself in a way that was both masculine and feminine. Seeing him move around the store was like watching Mr. Universe sashay around a living room swiping furniture with a dainty feather duster. The cat was as clean as a freaking whistle, always immaculate, with polished nails, spicy cologne, and a full head of black hair with auburn highlights, neatly trimmed and parted on one side. He also had tweezed eyebrows and a perfect, pencil-thin moustache.

Neighborhood women were attracted to Riccardo: married or single, young or old, it didn't make a difference. Just about every time I was in the store, I noticed him chatting up one or two women, talking about new products he'd added. In addition to the usual drugstore crap like thermometers, mouthwash, and heating pads, Riccardo had an artful display of colorful, high-quality soaps, perfumes, scented oils, and hair barrettes that he imported from Europe, the kind of stuff people normally bought in Manhattan.

Riccardo could charm the fangs off a cobra, but underneath his Latin sex appeal and the Liberace twinkle in his eye, he was a shrewd businessman who trusted nobody. The store was fortified with big convex mirrors mounted in all four corners of the shop. Riccardo would schmooze it up with women, showing off his latest perfumes, and all the time he'd be glancing at the mirrors, checking for suspicious activity. Even if you weren't there with the intent to clean him out, one could easily feel like a criminal. The experience may have intimidated some customers, but for me it was a trip to Disneyland. The place was perfect: a neighborhood Fort Knox run by a Cuban tight-ass who was as obsessed with fingering shoplifters as I was with creatively separating merchandise from merchants.

It was midspring, and the Brooklyn air was sweet and warm. Riccardo had installed a new circular kiosk displaying about forty pairs of high-quality sunglasses—French designer jobs. The kiosk rotated in either direction and included two eye-level mirrors. I tried on four or five pairs and then hit the jackpot with some bronze aviator specs, the most expensive glasses on the rack. These babies weren't a kazoo or a lame hockey puck; they were the coolest pair of shades I'd ever seen. The minute I put them on, I knew I had to have them. They made me look older and more mature and, in my mind, more attractive. The only problem was that the damn kiosk was right next to the perfume display, in clear view of the sales counter. I knew there was no way I'd be able to walk those puppies without Riccardo spotting me and squashing my head in his bare hands like a bag of chips. I needed a diversion, something to distract him for a couple of minutes so I could get in, swipe the glasses, and get the hell out of there.

I sat on the idea for a few days and finally concluded that I needed a partner, someone with the balls of a ski jumper who liked to mix things up a bit. I approached Jackie D., and after he heard my proposal, the first words out of his mouth were, "What are you, *drunk?*" But after I laid out my plan and told him I would bag a pair of shades for him as well, my sobriety was no longer in question.

The scheme involved Jackie, me, and a 1943 copper penny. These pennies were worth a fortune, something like twenty-five thousand dollars in 1963, a known fact in most Brooklyn neighborhoods thanks to coverage in the local newspapers. The minting of copper pennies had been halted during World War II because copper was needed for making ammunition. Somehow a few copper-coated bronze planchets had been accidentally minted in '43, making them a wet dream for coin collectors or any poor slob lucky enough to find one.

The plan was that Jackie and I would walk into the store separately and act as if we didn't know each other. Jackie was to buy a pack of gum and some ChapStick and pay for them with a dollar bill. I selected those items because I knew that at least three pennies would be included in his change. As this was going down, I would move closer to where he was standing, casually browsing the display case just underneath the sales counter. Once Jackie received his change, he was to examine the coins and announce that he had found a 1943 copper penny, which would divert Riccardo's attention and give me enough time to fade into the background, score the sunglasses, and get in the wind.

Jackie was as excited about pulling off the job as I was.

I planned it just like a big-time heist: I drew a floor plan of the store and mapped out the aisles, kiosk, counters, and mirrors. I also worked out a few possible scenarios and a backup plan in case things went south.

"This is fuckin' brilliant!" Jackie said.

"Okay, but just remember—after you show me the penny, don't show it to Riccardo or anyone else. You just wanna hold his attention while I take care of business. Then, when you see me leave the store, pull the plug on the whole thing and get the hell outta there."

It was around three p.m., and I walked into Richard's shortly after Jackie and began browsing in an aisle close to the register. Riccardo was looking his usual dapper self, wearing a lavender jacket with the inevitable fancy *R* embroidered on the pocket. He was ringing up a prescription for an elderly couple when Jackie approached the sales counter. I felt self-conscious but didn't dare look up at my reflection in the overhead mirrors. I told myself to relax and stuffed both hands in the back pockets of my dungarees. When I noticed Jackie reach for the gum and ChapStick from the display case, I casually walked over to the counter.

"Do you sell cream for athlete's foot?" I asked.

"About halfway down the aisle," Riccardo said, pointing over my head. "On de second shelf near de sunglasses."

"Thanks."

Jackie handed Riccardo a dollar bill to pay for his stuff, and Riccardo handed Jackie his change before nodding to the customer standing behind Jackie, one of the countermen from the butcher shop. Jackie turned as if to step away, then abruptly stopped, eyeing the change resting in his palm.

"Is something wrong?" Riccardo said.

"No. I mean, yeah … I mean, I don't know."

"Ju give me a dollar, and I give ju back seventy-eight cent," Riccardo said, holding up Jackie's dollar bill.

"Yeah, I know." Jackie raised one of the pennies above his head and examined it with furrowed brows. "But if this is what I think it is …"

"Whaddaya got there, junior?" asked the butcher, a gruff man with a plump, unshaven face. He was wearing a long, bloodstained butcher's coat and holding a bottle of cough medicine.

"Holy smokes!" Jackie said, smacking his hand against his forehead. "When my mother sees this, she's gonna have a *heart attack!*"

"Can I see?" I asked, moving closer. Jackie stuffed the remaining change into his pocket and held out the penny for me to take a quick peek, his other hand ready to cover it up before I could snatch it.

"Holy shit!" I said. "It's a 1943 copper penny!"

"Bullshit," the butcher said. "Lemme see." The guy was a real goon. He held out his hand like he was a privileged member of the rare-coin police.

"No way," Jackie said, stepping back and clutching the coin in his fist.

"May I take a look-see?" Riccardo asked politely, smiling and holding out his hand.

"I'll give ya five bucks," the butcher said. "Just lemme

have a look."

"No way," said Jackie, shaking his head.

Riccardo's eyes darted back and forth between Jackie and the butcher. "I give ju ten," he said, his polite voice and smile vanishing.

While Riccardo and the butcher were facing off like brides-to-be fighting over a wedding gown, I slipped down the aisle to the kiosk and quickly removed two pairs of aviator glasses from the display. I stuffed them down the front of my sweatshirt and made a beeline for the exit. Forget the mirrors —Riccardo was so distracted I could have lifted up the entire kiosk, put it over my shoulder, and strolled out of the store whistling "Dixie."

Just outside the door I collided with Mrs. Cacciola, the administrative assistant at Precious Mother. "Oh, excuse me!" she said, her startled eyes peering down at me through thick, cat-eye-shaped eyeglasses. "Are you okay?"

"Sorry, Mrs. Cacciola." The bottom of my sweatshirt was only partially tucked into my pants, and I could feel the sunglasses slipping down to my waist.

"Goodness, where are you headed in such a hurry?"

"Huh? Nowhere." I adjusted the bulge in my midsection. "I was just on my way home."

Mrs. Cacciola glanced at my waist, and my throat tightened. A portion of the sunglasses peeked out from under my sweatshirt. This was it, I thought. All the planning, all the rehearsing—*gazoom!* Right down the fucking crapper.

"What do you have there?" she asked.

"Medicine," I said, quickly stuffing the shades back under my shirt, hoping she hadn't noticed. "It's ... it's for my mother. She's home sick, and I gotta get this stuff to her right away."

"Oh, I see." Mrs. Cacciola stepped aside. "Well, I hope she feels better."

"Thanks," I said, moving past her. I chugged down Eighty-Sixth with one arm draped across my gut.

About twenty minutes later, Jackie and I met behind the Loew's Oriental, an ornate movie theater near Eighteenth Avenue.

"Whew!" Jackie said. "I thought I'd never get the fuck out of there."

"Man, you were perfect. You almost had *me* distracted."

"I couldn't believe those guys! I had that fruitcake up to twelve bucks. And that slob with the bloody coat—he wanted to see the penny so bad, I thought he was gonna break my arm."

"I almost blew it walking out of the joint."

"What happened?"

"I bumped into Mrs. Cacciola from school and nearly dropped the glasses right in front of her. She wanted to know what I had under my shirt. I told her it was medicine for my mother."

"Sweet. You got the goods?"

I reached under my sweatshirt, pulled out both pairs of glasses, and handed a pair to Jackie. "We did it. We fucking *did it*."

Propped up against the back of the building were two rectangular metal cases with glass doors—decrepit throwaways once used to display jumbo movie posters. Jackie and I stepped over and looked at our reflections. He and I had grown up together, and this was the first time we'd checked each other out since we'd goofed off in front of a distorting fun-house mirror in Coney Island back in the fifth grade. Now here we were pushing thirteen, and I realized how much we'd grown.

"Man, these are boss," Jackie said, admiring his profile from different angles. "We look like movie stars. That was too much fun. We gotta do this again."

The next day Sister Gilhouly made an announcement over the PA system: "Good afternoon, Sister Nimitz. Would you please send Mr. Caruso to my office?" Her voice had that no-nonsense Gilhouly edge, and I knew she had some kind of shit waiting for me. I slunk out of my seat and headed toward the door.

"What's up?" Freddy whispered as I passed his desk.

"Fuck if I know."

Down in Gilhouly's office, my stomach dropped. She was sitting at her desk, arms folded, with Mrs. Cacciola standing beside her. Riccardo sat opposite her, buffed up and wearing one of his pastel jackets. Seated next to him was my father with his back toward me. I hesitated, and he turned around. His jaw muscles were pulsating mad. "Get in here, you," he said.

"Do you know why I asked you to my office?" Gilhouly asked.

"No."

My father got right to the point. "Did you steal some sunglasses from this man's store yesterday?"

"What? *No.*"

"Mr. Morales tells us you were in his drugstore yesterday," Sister Gilhouly said. "He said you asked about some foot cream and then stole a pair of sunglasses."

"Two pair," Riccardo said, holding up two fingers.

"No way," I said. "I mean, I was in his store yesterday, but I didn't take any sunglasses."

"Right after ju left my store jesterday, I notice two pair of de sunglasses missing from de display. I know dis, because jesterday in de morning I took de inventory for to order more sunglasses, and de two aviator was still in de stand. Dis I know for de fact."

"So?" I shrugged. "Why do you think I took them?"

"Because"—he turned, talking at Mrs. Cacciola, as if to implore her endorsement—"when dis lady hear me talking about de missing aviator, she say she saw ju hiding de sunglass under ju shirt."

"Huh?"

"Come on now, John," Mrs. Cacciola said, "tell the truth. We bumped into each other by the door, and I saw the glasses under your shirt. You told me it was medicine for your mother. You said she was sick."

"Is that right?" my father said.

"I don't remember," I said. As the bullshit flew out of my mouth, I could feel my legs turning into Silly Putty.

My father reached into the pocket of his suit jacket and took out the glasses I'd swiped. "What are these?" he said, plopping them onto Gilhouly's desk.

My eyes almost jumped out of my skull.

"Where did those come from?" Gilhouly said.

"My wife found them in one of his drawers," my father said, glaring at me.

"I was gonna return 'em," I said. "I just wanted to wear them outside to see what they were like."

"Where is de other pair?" Riccardo said.

"I don't know. I just took one pair. But I was gonna bring them back."

Riccardo made the sign of the cross. "Ay, Dios mío. I think somebody need to get down on his knees and ask de Lord for forgiveness."

"I'll say," Gilhouly said, scowling at me. "Have you not learned your Ten Commandments?" She turned, drawing everyone's attention to a list of framed commandments hanging on the wall behind her.

"I was gonna return 'em," I insisted.

My father sprang up from his seat. "All right, that's it." He flicked the side of my head with his finger. "I've heard enough out of you, mister. You're grounded for a month."

Getting grounded was a mild punishment that I was sure the old man had dialed up on the spot to show everyone that he was a just and fair-minded parent. He thanked Gilhouly and Mrs. Cacciola for contacting him, then thanked Riccardo for not taking the matter to the police. He even went the distance and offered to pay for the missing pair of glasses.

"I want you to apologize to this man right now," he said to me.

Riccardo sat there with a grin on his face. At first, I thought he was just being his charming old self, but then I realized he was actually enjoying my getting busted.

"I apologize," I said.

"Again, I'm sorry for everyone's time and trouble," my father said. "I promise this won't happen again."

"Das okay," Riccardo said. "I hope maybe ju son learn his lesson."

Riccardo reached for the sunglasses on Gilhouly's desk and lifted them to eye level, examining the lenses for scratches. "Hmmm ..." He smiled. "Turns out de bronze glasses are worth way more dan de copper penny, no?" he said, gloating, then shooting me a sly wink.

In the hall outside Gilhouly's office, my father was noticeably less fair-minded. He punched my shoulder and smacked the back of my head like he was returning a serve at Wimbledon. "You little son of a bitch," he said, pulling me along by the ear. "I've never been so embarrassed in all my life."

"What—I was gonna bring them back—*I swear.*"

"That's okay," he said with unwavering determination. "Wait until I get your ass home."

TWENTY-FOUR

FRANK HAD BEEN dating Sandra Bandino, a petite, soft-spoken woman with a sweet smile. They had met in high school and kept in contact while Frank was in the army. After he returned, they dated steadily for a few months, then got married and moved into a one-bedroom apartment on Ocean Parkway.

Frank was good with his hands and always working on projects in the new apartment. It was a Saturday morning, and he and I were putting the finishing touches on a wall unit.

"Okay, we're going to lift on three," he said, gripping one end of the unit, motioning for me to grip the other. I had helped him build the piece over the course of a few weekends: he did the measuring, cutting, and joining, and I did most of the sanding and staining. After mounting the dark walnut shelving on the wall, Frank placed a level on the middle shelf, checking the gauge. "Look at that fucker," he said, slapping me five. "Right on the money!"

"Looks great," Sandra said, handing us each a mug of hot chocolate. I liked seeing her move around; she was soft and feminine, a demeanor magically highlighted by her funky gray sweatshirt, paint-stained jeans, and red engineer's scarf wrapped around her head.

We sipped our drinks and watched Sandra fill the shelves with books and knickknacks. "Should I put this up?" she asked Frank, holding up their wedding photo. The picture showed the two of them in Central Park, standing in front of a horse-drawn carriage. They were unceremoniously dressed: Frank was sporting one of his work suits, and Sandra was next to him in a smart, no-frills evening gown.

"Please," Frank said. "Don't remind me."

"Jeez, thanks." Sandra placed her hands on her hips.

"Naw, g'ahead." Frank smiled. "I'm joking."

The circumstances around their wedding had caused a bit of a flap. Sandra had also been raised Catholic, but rather than go the traditional route of getting married in a church by a priest, she and Frank had opted for a civil ceremony at the New York Society for Ethical Culture, something my father disapproved of, especially when he learned that my brother had gotten the idea from Gordon Peterson, who was an active member of the society. I didn't know squat about Ethical Culture, but I liked the name because it sounded different. It also—despite my father's virulent criticisms— seemed like a more honest place to tie the knot. I mean, when you thought about it, where did most mobsters consecrate their wedding vows—the New York Society for Ethical Culture or their local Catholic church?

Sandra was a wonderful cook. Later that afternoon she prepared dinner from one of the many recipes she'd clipped from the *New York Times*: broiled salmon with rosemary, scalloped potatoes, and a Greek salad with stuffed grape leaves. While she was busy in the kitchen, Frank and I hung out in the living room playing with Lester, Sandra's fluffy gray-haired cat.

"I love this animal," Frank said, gently grooming Lester with a wire brush. "He's like a dog."

"How so?"

"When you call him, the fucking cat actually comes— right, buddy?" Frank kissed the cat's head and stroked its tail.

Growing up, we weren't allowed to have pets. At one point, Connie and I begged our parents for a dog, but they insisted that if we brought a dog into the house, we would quickly lose interest and they would end up being the caretakers.

It was a simple thing, but I enjoyed watching my brother feed, groom, and pet Lester. My father had beaten Frank so many times, I wouldn't have thought he'd be capable of showing that kind of affection toward an animal.

Sandra attended New York University and was working toward a master's degree in psychology. She had asked me to answer some survey questions she'd put together for school, and I was excited to be a part of her project. My father, however, was jealous of the time I spent with her and my brother. One day I headed over to Frank's place after school without telling him. The old man had no idea where I was, but I didn't care. Either way I knew he was going to give me shit. He called Frank's apartment around five thirty and went ballistic when my brother told him I was there. "Who the hell are you to ask the kid over without telling me?" he demanded. The old man was so irate, all of us could hear his booming tirade blasting from the phone's receiver. He went on and on until Frank finally handed me the phone.

"He wants to talk to you."

"Hello."

"What are you doing over there?"

"I was working with Sandra on one of her projects for school."

"You get your ass home right now."

"But, Dad, Sandra's making dinner."

"Forget dinner. *This* is your home. If you want dinner, you can have dinner right here. We got plenty of food." He hung up.

I considered ignoring him and staying, but Sandra said that would only make things worse. She thought that if I defied the old man, he might forbid me to see Frank at all, in which case I'd be cornered into sneaking visits just to spend time with my own brother.

"Don't worry about it," said Sandra. "Maybe we can work some more on the weekend."

"Fuck!" I shouted at the floor.

George Adamczyk, Connie's boyfriend, lived with his parents in a spacious house stuffed with gaudy, old-world furniture, lamps, and mirrors. Olga, George's mother, was the matriarch-in-residence, a tense, stately woman with heavily styled silver-gray hair, long legs, and tight lips that looked as if they'd been stretched back and pinned to something behind her head. The first time I went there with Connie, she gave me a heads-up. "Behave yourself," she warned me. "Watch your language, and don't joke around. She's not the joking type."

"Oh good," I said with a devilish grin, rubbing my hands together. "This is gonna be fun."

Olga had that "trophy wife" vibe. Whether it was a Saturday night or a rainy Tuesday afternoon, she walked around the house as if she were hosting a cocktail party at the UN. She wore gobs of makeup and heavy jewelry around her neck and wrists that rattled like a string of tin cans dangling off the back bumper of a honeymoon car. Her usual wardrobe was a collection of colorful sundresses, but occasionally she slipped into a festive Chinese outfit. I could never sync up the sunny attire with her dour disposition.

Olga was a tough cookie but spoke in a lethargic drawl, like Katharine Hepburn whacked out on phenobarbital. The old gal smoked unfiltered cigarettes through a long ivory holder and drank continually. She would never get totally shit-faced like my father; instead, she tanked up with style. She'd throw on some Frank Sinatra or smooth Johnny Mathis and nurse a scotch or sweet vermouth on the rocks, taking short sips, two at a time, just enough to keep a mild buzz going while maintaining a coherent conversation.

Whenever Connie was in Olga's presence, her attitude became almost passive, especially when they discussed George. Both she and Olga had strong personalities, but when it came to Olga's son, there was no mistaking who ran the show. It was subtle, but she made my sister feel she wasn't good enough for George, a feeling that prompted Connie to seek Olga's approval for anything George-related—like the time she bought George a couple of Ban-Lon sweaters for his birthday. Ban-Lon, a comfortable and stylish synthetic fabric, was all the craze. I was with Connie when she showed the sweaters to Olga. "Whaddaya think?" she said, excited about the gift. "Aren't they great?"

Olga peered at the garments as if they were a couple of snot rags my sister had scooped up at the five-and-dime. "They're too flimsy," Olga said, rubbing one of them between her thumb and index finger. "My Georgie is not used to cheap material. It makes him too *itchy*."

I hated to see my sister in that position. It made me feel as if our whole family wasn't good enough, something Connie and I both secretly felt but never talked about.

I got the sense that George really liked me. I think he saw me as the kid brother he'd never had, and I was happy to get the attention of any older person who showed a genuine interest in me. I'd sometimes hang out with George and my sister. The three of us would check out a movie, play miniature golf, or jump in George's car and take a drive out of the city to places like Jones Beach or Bear Mountain.

Connie liked the fact that George and I hit it off, but sometimes she would get jealous of our relationship. I think she felt I was moving in on George, vying too much for his attention. Her concerns weren't totally unfounded. I wanted George to like me as much as he did my sister. I felt ashamed and embarrassed by my own loneliness; sometimes I'd lie in bed at night and think: *What's going to happen to me when I get older? Am I always going to be the third wheel?*

Connie had been kicking around the idea of getting an apartment with Ann Gottlieb and a couple of other girlfriends, but moving out of the house wouldn't be as easy for her as it had been for my brother. Frank had joined the army without my father's consent. Once he signed on the dotted line, there was nothing my father could say or do, assuming the old man gave a crap to begin with. With

Connie, it was a different ball game. Even if she'd had a pile of cash to plunk down on an apartment, there was no way my father would let it happen. Under his thick old-world Neapolitan skull, it was plain and simple: Connie was a single woman, and as long as he was still at the helm, my sister wasn't going anywhere.

Connie realized that the only way she could get away from my father was to go the traditional route: get engaged, plan a wedding, get married in a church, book a honeymoon, and then gas up, leaving skid marks in the driveway. So, adding to her collection of diet magazines, she started bringing home magazines like *Modern Bride*, *Mademoiselle*, *Ladies' Home Journal*, and *Glamour*. She had also amassed a collection of glossy honeymoon brochures for country getaways where young newlyweds could eat, drink, sleep, and fuck their brains out.

As far as my parents were concerned, George got a thumbs-up. He wasn't Italian, but at least he was Catholic and a solid citizen who came from—as my father phrased it — a "decent family." No one ever challenged the old man on that topic, but I would have loved to hear him describe a family that was *not* decent.

I think part of the reason my father accepted George was that he wasn't threatening; he was tall and handsome but unassertive, at least around my sister. I once heard Mrs. Pashkin, a neighbor who was friendly with Connie, tell my sister that Jewish and Polish men made the best husbands because they didn't argue. She said you could tell them what to do and they worked like slaves and dropped dead before their wives. The way she sounded, she could just as easily have been talking about a golden retriever or an Irish sheepdog.

Connie had been pushing George to get engaged. I'd hear her on the phone with him yapping away like a used-car salesman trying to move a late-model Buick off the lot. "Honey, just think how great it'll be once we get engaged. And the best part is—there's no rush to get married. There's absolutely *no rush*. We can take our time, but at least we'll have a plan and know where we're going." To me, that was like hearing my sister say, "Listen, I know there's a mudslide heading down the mountain, but hey—there's no rush, just as long as *I can move the fuck out of here before I get smothered to death!*"

From what I gathered, George wasn't jumping up and clicking his heels at the prospect of getting engaged, but I knew the idea of moving out of his mother's mausoleum appealed to him.

When Connie and George announced their engagement, things took a left turn. My father had a hard time wrapping his head around the notion that his daughter was planning a wedding and would be getting married within six months. It wasn't that he suddenly disapproved of George, but he began to realize that with Connie out of the house, he'd be stuck with a feisty thirteen-year-old and a miserable wife in poor health living on a steady diet of antidepressants.

My father began pressuring my sister. At least once a week he'd say stuff like, "I don't know if you know it or not, but marriage is a serious business. I mean, when you stand before the altar of God and the priest says, 'In sickness and in health, for better, for worse, until death do you part'—those aren't just words." Or, "Have you two thought about this? I mean *really thought* about it? Why don't you guys give it

some time, because, you know, once you take those vows—
that's it, sister. There's no turning back."

Sometimes I'd notice my father watching Connie and
George hug and kiss—normal stuff, like hello and goodbye
smooches, which my sister usually initiated. When they first
started dating, my father hadn't seemed concerned by my
sister's open displays of affection. But after Connie
announced her engagement, I could tell the old man felt
uncomfortable seeing his daughter in another man's arms. He
started to reprimand Connie for walking around the
apartment in a bra and slip, something she and my mother
had always done when it was just the family. Occasionally
he'd feed my sister one of his moral platitudes: "It's nice that
you guys are attracted to each other, just as long as you
maintain your boundaries and George respects you."

A few times my father got physical with Connie. He'd
stand behind her, wrap his arms around her waist, and plaster
her neck and cheeks with kisses. "I don't care what anybody
says; you're still my little baby." It would start out looking like
friendly father-daughter affection, but soon my sister would
start to squirm, moving her head away from him. One time
she struggled to avoid his advances, and my father wrapped
his arms around her body, clamping her arms tight against
her sides. "You're my best daughter," he murmured, kissing
her face. "You're my *best, best* daughter."

My sister's eyes bulged as she struggled to escape his
clutches. Finally, he released his grip, and Connie jolted
forward, visibly shaken. "What's the matter?" he said. "You're
so grown up, I can't even show a little affection to my own
daughter?"

"That's not affection!"

"Listen to her. One minute she's complaining that I don't show enough interest in her, the next she doesn't want me to touch her."

"How many times do I have to tell you?" Connie said. "I don't like it when you do that!"

"Aw, go on." He waved a hand. "You don't know what you want."

TWENTY-FIVE

MY MOTHER HAD been complaining of chest pains and heart palpitations. She was admitted to Maimonides Medical Center for a battery of tests, where X-rays revealed that the valve between her aorta and her left ventricle was severely blocked. The doctor told my parents that her chances of surviving another four or five years were slim without open-heart surgery to replace the valve.

Valve-replacement surgery was a relatively new procedure at that time; even if the operation was successful, there was no guarantee that it would add years to my mom's life. It was also expensive. Health insurance would cover most of the hospital expenses, but my parents had almost no savings, which meant they'd have to reach out to relatives to help.

My parents decided to go ahead with the surgery anyway, but not immediately. My father had been working out of town and wanted to wait until his contract ended so that he could be at home full-time when my mother went into the hospital.

Connie thought our mom needed cheering up. She bought her a new bathrobe and matching slippers and planned to cook my mother's favorite meal: stuffed artichokes and rigatoni Bolognese. Frank, Sandra, and George were going to join us for dinner around six.

Connie was in the kitchen cooking up a storm, wearing one of my mother's aprons, her hair tied back in a ponytail. She was in a great mood. The radio was blasting, and she was singing along to Lesley Gore's "It's My Party." I had set the table with my mother's "good" cloth napkins and silverware. I even brought out the red candles that we normally used on holidays.

"Go see if she's up," Connie said. "She's been sleeping all day, God bless her."

I popped my head into my mother's bedroom. The shades were drawn, and she was under the covers, lying on her side. I quietly backed out of the room.

"She's still sleeping," I called back to Connie. "Should I wake her up?"

"Yeah, go ahead and wake her. By the time she washes up and gets dressed, the gang should be here."

"Hey, Ma," I called, stepping into the bedroom. "We're gonna eat soon."

My mother didn't answer. I moved closer to the bed and tapped her foot. "Hey, Ma, it's time to get ready." As I stood there, I smelled a faint acidic odor.

Connie entered the room. "She up?"

"I don't know. She's not answering."

"Hey, lady." Connie shook my mother's leg. "Time to get up. We got a special surprise for you. I made your favorite." She stepped over to the nightstand and turned on the lamp. When the light hit my mother's face, I jerked back. Her cheeks were gaunt, and her skin was grayish white. A line of bile had slithered out of her mouth and down her chin.

"Ma." Connie raised her voice. "*Wake up.*"

"She's not moving," I said.

"Ma!" she said frantically. "Do you hear me? I said *wake up!*" She pulled back the blanket and turned her over onto her back. Her nightgown and bedsheets were soaked with urine. She raised one of my mother's eyelids. Her eyeball was rolled up and motionless, peering off to the side.

"Oh God!" Connie cried, covering her mouth with her hand. The fear in her voice scared me.

"What's wrong with her?"

"I don't know." Connie leaned over and put her face close to my mother's open mouth, then placed an ear flat against her chest. "*Oh, shit.*"

"Is she breathing?"

"I don't think so. I can't hear anything."

"Well, whadda we do?"

"I'm calling an ambulance." Connie rushed out of the room. "Keep an eye on her and holler if she moves."

While Connie was on the phone, I kept watch. My mom's hair was a mess, and her cheeks were contorted in an agonized wince, an expression I'd often seen when she grunted in pain. "Mom, can you hear me?"

From the living room I could hear Connie on the phone, jabbering out details to Coney Island Hospital. "That's right, it's the Bay Haven Apartments," she said, struggling to remain calm. "The number is twenty thirty-four. We're in apartment 4B—*please hurry!*"

She rushed back into the bedroom.

"Are they coming?"

"They're on their way."

"Should we call Frank?"

"Good idea. Tell him to get his ass over here right away."

I dashed into the living room and called my brother at work. That morning he'd told Connie he'd try to leave his job early. Thank God he was at his desk.

"Is she breathing?" he said. Hearing my brother's level-headed voice was comforting.

"Connie checked. It doesn't look like it."

"Did anyone call for an ambulance?"

"Connie did, about five minutes ago."

"Where's Connie now?"

"She's in the bedroom with Mom, trying to get her to breathe. She says for you to get over here right away."

"There's no time for that. Tell Connie I'm leaving work now and I'll meet her at the hospital."

"Is he coming?" Connie hollered.

"He said he'll meet you at the hospital!" I shouted back.

"Tell him to get over here right away!"

"Connie says for you—"

"I heard her," Frank said. "Never mind that. By the time I get there, the ambulance will have come and gone. Now listen to me carefully, this is important. Tell Connie to make sure she goes to the hospital with the ambulance. Tell her she can't leave Mommy alone; she's gotta stay with her all the time. I'm leaving work right now. You got that?"

"Got it," I said. "What about me? Should I go with Connie?"

"No. Stay there and sit tight. I need you to answer the phone. Sandra's at her mother's; she'll come by in about forty-five minutes. I'm leaving for the hospital right now."

"Frankie, what if ..." I paused for a moment. I wanted to ask, what if she's no longer breathing? Or more directly: what if she's *dead*? But suggesting the possibility that our mother was actually deceased was too chilling to articulate.

"What if what?"

"What if, you know ..."

"We can't think about that right now," Frank said quickly. "We won't know what the story is until somebody examines her. For all we know, she may be breathing but in some kind of coma. We just don't know. We're not doctors. Gotta go—talk to you later."

"Ohmygod, ohmygod!" Connie wailed.

I ran back to the bedroom, where my sister was holding one of my mother's plastic pill containers.

"Holy shit!" she cried. "She swallowed a whole fucking bottle of Demerol!"

At first my sister's words didn't register with me. It was like hearing her say, *Holy shit! Tomorrow's called off! That's impossible*, I thought. Nobody swallows a whole bottle of painkillers. Why would anybody do that? Maybe she lost track and took two or three. But not a *whole bottle*.

"Whaddaya mean?"

"Just what I said. She swallowed all the painkillers. I saw her take one last night—I brought her some water. The damn bottle was almost full. *Oh God!*" Connie looked to the heavens, shaking her hands above her head. "Ma, what did *you do*? What did *you do*?"

I felt numb. I couldn't imagine my mother taking her own life. Many times she'd threatened to jump out of a window, but we all thought those were just words—my mother's sorry way of trying to get attention.

"Daddy's gonna kill me," Connie said. "When he finds out, he's gonna blame it all on me—I just know it."

My father's reaction was something I hadn't begun to contemplate. In the moment, I was swept up in my sister's anguish and started thinking he might hold me responsible as well.

"Frank said we won't know anything until the doctors examine her," I told Connie. "He said she may be breathing but in some kind of coma." I wasn't even sure what a coma was, but I recited my brother's words, thinking they might somehow change my sister's perceptions.

"Yeah, right," Connie said in despair.

Twenty minutes later an ambulance crew showed up. Two EMS guys and a police officer went into the bedroom with Connie, while a third crew member propped open the front door with a rubber doorstop that he pulled from his back pocket. "We're gonna need some room here," he told me, pointing to the dining room table. "Can we move some of these chairs?"

One by one, I pulled the chairs away from the table and shuffled them into the living room.

"Okay, Phil, we're ready," said one of the EMS guys, stepping out of the bedroom and motioning to his partner. They carried my mother out on a stretcher and carefully transferred her body to a gurney, an oxygen mask clamped over her nose and mouth.

My sister's eyes were red, and her cheeks were smeared with black eyeliner. She wept as she talked to the police officer, who scribbled notes in a fat, leather-bound notepad.

"We'll need you to come down to the hospital with us

to get her signed in," the officer told her.

"I'll get my bag," Connie said. She untied her apron and headed for her bedroom.

"Is my mother gonna be okay?" I asked the cop.

The guy looked uncomfortable. He turned to one of the crew members, a clean-cut man with friendly eyes, and nodded his head as if to say, *Why don't you take this one?* The man cleared his throat. He glanced at me, then at the cop, and then back at me. "We don't know," he said, measuring his words. "At the moment, things aren't looking so good. We'll know better when we get your mom to the hospital."

My stomach was doing flip-flops. After everyone left, I walked around in circles, wondering what to do with myself. The door to my parents' bedroom was partially open. I wanted to sense my mother's presence and stepped into the room, feeling like a stranger entering hallowed ground. The air was filled with the lingering scent of alcohol. The blanket and top sheet had been pulled all the way back and were lying on the floor at the foot of the bed, along with a syringe wrapper, some white adhesive strips, and a wooden tongue depressor that looked like an oversized Popsicle stick. The room was empty. Yesterday my mother had been home and conscious. Now she was gone.

I sat on the edge of the bed. On my parents' dresser was their wedding photo, adorned with a string of black rosary beads. I stared at her image, thinking about the times she'd cuddled me and kissed my head and neck. I was seized by an unfathomable longing to be near her again, to feel her arms around me once more and have her hug and kiss me. Then suddenly the yearning faded, and I was overcome with rage. How could she just check out like that and leave me and Connie?

"Fuck you! Fuck you!"

I stood up and heard a faint clinking sound by the nightstand. I looked over, thinking that one of the pill bottles had accidentally tipped over, but everything seemed to be upright and in place. I was about to leave the room when I noticed a small white envelope wedged between the bed and the nightstand. I nudged the mattress with my knee, and the envelope fell to the floor with another clink. I reached under the bed and slid it toward me.

"For Janoots" was scribbled on the front of the envelope in my mother's unmistakable, nearly undecipherable handwriting. I tore it open and emptied the contents onto the bed. It was loose change, a total of eighty-six cents: two quarters, two dimes, three nickels, and a penny. I thought she'd made some kind of mistake. Maybe she'd written a note and forgotten to include it with the change. I checked the inside of the envelope three times and then frantically looked all around the nightstand and under the bed—nothing.

What was I going to do with eighty-six cents? Was this her idea of compensation for taking her own life? Her sad and anemic way of saying goodbye?

A hollow, empty feeling swept through me like a draft. I could feel my skin meet the air. I sat back down on the bed and glanced up at her photo again. My stomach shrank, and my chest grew heavy. I tried, but I could no longer hold back the flood of tears. I sat there sobbing into my hands, wishing I were dead.

TWENTY-SIX

MY FATHER HAD been working in Schenectady when Frank called him and gave him the bad news. The next morning, he caught an early flight back to New York and immediately started drinking heavily. "Something is not right here," he said. "I just know it. They botched something up and didn't do enough to save her life."

Before my father talked to a single doctor, he had contacted his attorney to inquire about initiating a malpractice lawsuit. "I swear, I'll take these bums all the way up to the Supreme Court if I have to," I heard him saying on the phone.

"You believe him?" Frank said to Connie and me. "He thinks it was the hospital—the *hospital* fucked up. Meanwhile, Mommy downed over twenty fucking Demerols. The doctor who examined her told me they worked on her for over an hour—pumped her stomach, gave her IVs, the works. We're still waiting for the autopsy report, but he thinks she died at least three hours before the ambulance showed up."

The apartment was crazy. The phone rang constantly, and relatives came and went, cooking and helping with funeral arrangements. My parents' bed was covered with insurance policies and other legal documents my father had dug out from his closet. Uncle Sally Boy, Aunt Rose, Big Joe,

Aunt Lena (my mother's sister) and her husband, Ernie—everyone buzzed around the apartment in their own confused world.

Ernie was the most uptight. He paced around puffing on one of his big-dick cigars. The whole apartment was filled with a thin gray cloud of smoke and smelled like burnt wood. He bumped into me every ten minutes and rattled off haphazard suggestions: "You look hungry. Why don't you grab yourself a snack?" "It's nice outside. Go on downstairs and get some air."

Connie took my mother's death the hardest. She'd seem okay one minute, and the next she'd sob uncontrollably. Seeing my sister cry like that ripped me to pieces. A few times I burst into tears just watching her. We'd hug each other tight and bawl like terrified five-year-olds lost in a train station.

When the house got too crazy for me, I'd grab my transistor radio and head up to the roof, where I'd hang out for a couple of hours. My secret hideout was a few yards past the clothes lines, just behind the small redbrick structure that housed the top of the elevator shaft. I'd sit on the black tar floor with my legs stretched out and my back against the wall, eyes closed, soaking up the warm, radiant sun. The music was my sacred lifeline, harmonious voices and glorious rhythms and melodies, my connection to what I perceived as the real world. My favorite tune was "Our Day Will Come" by Ruby and the Romantics. I don't know what it was, but the moment I heard the celestial sounds of the organ and Ruby's endearing voice blaring out of my nine-volt Motorola, I was magically transported to another universe. The song permeated every cell in my body and somehow made me believe that one day *my* day would come.

Testa's Funeral Home was filled with friends and relatives. My mother's body lay on display in the same viewing room where Grandma Angelina had been placed six years earlier. My mother was laid out in a dark wooden coffin adorned with shiny lavender bunting. The casket rested on a fancy brushed-metal pedestal surrounded by floral wreaths propped up on wire tripods. She was clothed in her favorite blue-and-silver dress with an oversized sash, and a pair of matching blue shoes, the same dress and shoes she'd worn for Frank's wedding, Connie's high school graduation, and my first communion.

Lying in her casket, my mother looked anything but peaceful. Her cheeks and lips were twisted in the same painful expression as when I found her motionless body curled up in bed. It looked as if she were wincing from a sharp, sudden pain. I could almost hear her grunt. The sight of her lying there, her face caked with beige powder and bright red lipstick, made her death more real for me.

My father arrived late to the viewing. Earlier that morning, he had been quiet and kept to himself. "What's going on with Daddy?" I asked Connie.

"I don't know," she said. "I think Mommy's death is just starting to hit him."

When George came to pick us up, my father insisted we go on ahead without him. He said he'd take a taxi to the funeral home and meet us there later. A couple of hours had passed, and I didn't think my father was going to show up.

Then, around noon, I heard a commotion near the entrance of the viewing room. It was my father. He was a wreck. He staggered down the center aisle, headed straight for the casket. "Mary, Mary, Mary!" he wailed, pounding a fist against his chest.

His wailing grew louder and louder, and I felt embarrassed. He stepped up to the casket and wrapped his arms around my mother's body, lifting her torso out of the coffin. "Mary! Mary! My baby! My baby!" My mother's arms unfolded and fell to her sides, and her head dropped back at a severe angle.

Big Joe and Uncle Sally Boy rushed toward my father and grabbed his arms. "C'mon, Bill, relax, will ya?" Uncle Joe pleaded, struggling to pull my father away. "Ya can't do this here ... Ya can't do this."

"Mary, Mary!" my father continued to wail, tears streaming down his cheeks.

Uncle Sally Boy looked as freaked as I was. As he attended to my father, his eyes blinked nervously. He kept glancing over his shoulders to see who might be looking. "It's okay, Bill ... It's okay! Somebody get one of funeral guys," he said, lowering his voice, speaking to a handful of onlookers. "We're all good, Bill. We're all good. Mary knows you love her. Just let go. It's gonna be okay ... It's gonna be okay."

Finally, my uncles were able to pry my father away from my mother, and I watched in near shock as her body slumped back into the coffin. Her head was wrenched to the right, and one of her arms dangled over the side of the casket.

"Mary, Mary!" my father cried. "My baby! My precious baby!"

Big Joe and Sally Boy each wrapped one of his arms

around their shoulders. As they escorted him toward the back of the room, Big Joe bumped into a floral arrangement, knocking it into a stand loaded with sympathy cards and donations. A cascade of orchids, carnations, and small white envelopes tumbled to the floor. Two dark-suited funeral attendants scurried up the center aisle. One picked up the flowers, and the other moved swiftly to reposition my mother's body. Neither man appeared fazed. They worked so efficiently at restoring order, it made me think my father's behavior might be a common occurrence at Italian funerals.

The spectacle had caused a wave of emotion. People were crying profusely. I glanced at Frank. His entire being was devoid of empathy. He looked on, arms folded, his hard, expressionless face clearly repulsed by my father's dramatic performance.

Outside the funeral home I leaned against a car, hunched over, hands on knees. A mild breeze wafted over McDonald Avenue. The cool air felt good on my face and neck.

"Are you okay?" A gentle hand touched the back of my head. I looked up; it was Sandra. What did she want from me? What did anybody want from me? The whole fucking family was crazy.

"How are you feeling?" she asked. Her voice was calm and nurturing.

I shrugged, focusing on a line of black limousines parked along the street. I could feel myself starting to lose control. Sandra placed her hand on my shoulder, and my heart sank, dipping down into my stomach like an ebbing wave. I peered up into her face, and my eyes began to water. She didn't say a word. She just stood there taking me in, her eyes inviting me to confide in her. Her presence and concern felt overwhelming. I opened my mouth to speak, but the words stuck in my throat, and I began to moan and gasp for air as if someone had knocked the wind out of me. My brain raced through a flurry of images, like pictures in an old-time flip-book. I tried to make sense of them, but it was like trying to make sense of a twisted nightmare: *my mother in the kitchen, dishing out plates of hot lasagna ... my father slapping my mother in the foyer ... Frank pinning my arms down with his knees and tickling me senseless ... my mother peeing on the floor, looking helpless ... Connie teaching me to do the Lindy Hop ... my father punching and kicking Frank ... my mother asking me where I had gotten the things I'd stolen ... Riccardo smiling and winking at me ... Connie binge-eating in the dark ... Sister Nimitz's false teeth magnified in a glass of water ... my mother, dressed like the Virgin Mary, kneeling and praying at the foot of the cross ... my father helping the man lying in the street ... my mother's motionless body curled up in bed, her frozen, filmy eyeball gazing into space ...*

Sandra leaned forward and put her arms around me, and I burst into tears.

"I know, I know," she said, resting my head against her shoulder. "It's okay ... It's okay."

The wake went on for two days. Jackie D., Nicky DeMayo, Chicken Head Murphy, and their parents stopped by the funeral home to pay their respects, along with Freddy, Carmine, and a few of my other classmates. Harriet Voriotis and her mother, Samantha, also showed up. Samantha was most generous. She offered me her sympathy along with some heartfelt words of encouragement. It was nice to see everyone, but it felt weird to be in the same room with my friends and my dead mother. I didn't know what to say except "Thanks for coming."

The funeral service was held in the church at Precious Mother. Afterward, family friends and relatives piled into a line of cars and followed a black Cadillac hearse carrying my mother's coffin to Saint John's Cemetery in Queens, where she was buried in the no-frills section, away from all the fancy marble headstones and expensive walk-in mausoleums.

After the burial, people came back to our apartment. Rose and Lena and a few other women had prepared lunch: cold-cut sandwiches, pastries, and coffee. People were stuffing themselves and nervously jabbering with one another, talking about what a good woman my mother had been. "God rest her soul," Aunt Rose said. "Mariooch did *anything* for her kids." The way she said it, it almost sounded as if she were challenging people to disagree with her.

A lot of drinking went on too—Big Joe, Uncle Ernie, and my father were putting away highballs, one after another.

At one point a neighbor stopped by to tell us our mailbox was stuffed. She said that Al, the mailman for our building, thought our family was out of town because our mail hadn't been picked up for days. Connie gave me her keys, and I went down to the lobby and emptied our box. On the elevator back up to the fourth floor, I thumbed through the pile of mail. There were a bunch of sympathy cards, mixed in with utility bills, magazines, and local advertisements. A letter at the bottom of the stack nearly stopped my heart. It was written in my mother's handwriting. The envelope was addressed to my father and postmarked Tuesday, April 16, 1963, the day before she took her life. *This is it*, I thought. *The suicide note.*

In the apartment I dumped the stack of letters in an old wooden salad bowl.

"Got my keys?" Connie said.

I gazed into her eyes, my face frozen and expressionless.

"What's the matter?"

I didn't answer.

"What is it?"

I pulled the envelope from my back pocket and handed it to her. The instant she recognized my mother's handwriting, her face soured. "Oh my God," she said. "I don't know how much more of this I can take."

"It's addressed to Daddy," I said.

Connie stared at the envelope, speechless.

"What do you think she wrote?" I asked.

I didn't say it, but I thought the letter might have contained my mother's true feelings, the only way she could conceive of letting her husband know what a rat bastard he was after twenty-five years of marriage, and that she would rather be dead than live another miserable minute with him.

"I don't know," Connie said, sounding as if she didn't want to know.

"Should we give it to him?"

"Yeah, but not now. It's not even three o'clock, and he already has a load on. He sees this, it'll send him over the top."

"Sees what?" Frank said, stepping out from behind my

sister.

"Nothing," Connie said; she held the envelope down at her side.

"What is it?" Frank peered around my sister. "Whaddaya got there?"

"It's a letter from Mommy," I said.

"You're kidding."

"It's addressed to Daddy."

"Can I see?"

Reluctantly Connie handed him the envelope, and he examined it carefully.

"What do you think?" she asked.

Frank tapped the envelope with his fingers. "I guess this is it, huh?" He smiled.

"What do you mean?" Connie asked.

"It looks like our dear old mom finally mustered up the balls to tell her husband why she decided to check out."

A burst of laughter came from the living room. I could hear Uncle Joe's voice above the rest. He was telling one of his old army stories.

"We don't know that," Connie said.

"Well, let's open it and find out," Frank said.

Connie's face turned dark. "Frank, you're not opening that. It's not addressed to you. You open that letter, and he'll go apeshit," she said, trying to retrieve the letter from Frank's hand.

Frank held the envelope above his head, out of Connie's reach. "Let him. I can think of worse things. Like Mommy swallowing twenty fucking painkillers. If the autopsy report didn't convince the old man that his wife checked out because she couldn't take any more of his shit, maybe he'll believe a letter in her own handwriting. Too bad the phony bastard didn't get this before he put on the big show at the funeral home 'My baby! My precious baby!'"

"Frank, you're not gonna open that letter," Connie rasped.

Frank's face lit up with sadistic glee. "Oh yeah? Watch me."

Before my sister could get another word out, Frank turned and headed for the living room. "Excuse me!" he announced. "May I have your attention, please? I don't mean to interrupt, but something's come up that I'd like to share with everyone."

The room grew quiet. My father was sitting on the couch between Big Joe and Lidia, Uncle Rocco's wife. He was nursing a drink and looked half baked. His forehead and shirt collar were damp with sweat, his eyes bloodshot from three days of crying.

"Whaddaya got for us there, Frankie?" Uncle Sally Boy said.

"Well, we just picked up the mail downstairs and, ahh … it seems we got a letter from Mom. It looks like it was written shortly before she passed away."

Aunt Lena leaned forward. "What?" she said, squinting and looking all around. "What is it? What'd he say?"

"Shush!" said Aunt Rose. "It's a letter from Mary."

"From who?"

"From Mary," Uncle Joe raised his voice. "She wrote a letter."

Sandra and George were near the window, leaning against the radiator cover. George looked uncomfortable and out of place: a tall, shy, clean-cut Polish guy with blond hair in a room full of half-sauced Italians. When Sandra noticed me looking at her, she narrowed her eyes and jutted her chin toward Frank as if to ask, *What the hell is going on?* I shook my head.

"Now, I know all of you loved my mother as we did, especially my father, who's ... been through a lot these past few days. So I'd just like to take this opportunity to share with you some of the love and admiration my parents had for each other."

Frank's voice was somber and respectful, as if he were about to deliver a heartfelt eulogy. I wondered what the hell he was thinking. Was this the cool older brother I had always looked up to? The ambitious hip dresser and fast talker who had ventured out into the world on his own? Listening to Frank unleash his toxic brand of cruelty made me nauseous.

Frank tore the edge of the envelope and blew into the narrow opening. He carefully removed a single sheet of white stationary covered with handwriting. "This is addressed to my father," he said, holding the letter in front of him, a subtle smirk on his face.

"Wait a minute," my father said. "Can I see that?"

"It's okay, Dad. I got this one." My father started to say something else, but Frank cut him off and continued to read. "'Dear Bill, I have so much to tell you ...'" He took a breath, then suddenly stopped. His face was awash with confusion as he read the remainder of the letter in silence.

"Well, what'd she say?" Uncle Joe asked, running a giant hand over the top of his head.

"Yeah, c'mon," said Aunt Lidia. "Ya got us all waiting here, for Chrissakes."

"I can't read this," Frank said with disgust. "Here." He abruptly handed the letter to my father.

"Hold on. Lemme get my glasses." My father tapped his empty shirt pocket. "I can't see a thing." He slipped a hand behind his back, struggling to hoist himself up from the couch, then flopped back into his seat with a grunt.

"Stay, Bill," Aunt Rose said, snatching the letter out of his hand. "I'll read it."

Rose stood in the middle of the living room and cleared her throat. As she read, she fondled the double string of oversized white pearls around her neck:

Dear Bill,

I have so much to tell you, but all I can think of at this time is how much I love you. You mean ever so much to me, since you have been so many people to me wrapped up in one, my sweetheart, my husband, my father and mother, my sister and brother. You gave me all the love and consideration a woman could ask for. I bless the day we met and hope and pray that someday we'll meet again in heaven.

Please forgive me.

Love you with all my heart,

Mary

My father's face was expressionless. At first, I thought he was too inebriated to understand what Rose had read. Then his red eyes began to water, and after a few seconds he lowered his head and wept to himself, his shoulders shaking.

Connie pulled the letter from Rose's hand and read it feverishly, as if Aunt Rose had left out something my mother had written. "Oh my God! She didn't say *anything*!"

"What do you mean?" Aunt Rose asked.

"She didn't say anything," Connie repeated, crying

and walking around in tight circles.

"Anything about what?"

"About *me!*" Connie cried. "There isn't one thing in here about me or *any* of her children! How could she do that? Didn't we matter to her? It—it—it's like we didn't even exist!"

Aunt Rose tried to console my sister, but Connie rushed out of the apartment and into the hall where she exploded, screaming and crying. I followed her and wrapped my arms around her waist from behind, resting the side of my head against her upper back in an attempt to comfort her. Her entire body shuddered, and I could hear and feel the pain in her voice. It was excruciating and echoed through the entire building.

For weeks after the funeral, I grappled with the idea of telling Connie about the eighty-six cents. In the end, though, I decided to keep it a secret. It was nothing—a lousy eighty-six cents. But it was a hell of a lot more than my sister had gotten, and she deserved everything.

TWENTY-SEVEN

IN JUNE OF 1963 I graduated from Precious Mother. It was like busting out of Sing Sing; the whole seven-year stint felt like a blur. On the last day of school, Gilhouly handed out neatly rolled diplomas tied with a red ribbon. After the ceremony, I returned my cap and gown and vowed never to set foot in a church again.

That September I entered Lafayette High School as a freshman. I was eager to go back to public school, attend classes with different teachers, and not have to wear a uniform.

"You're gonna love it," Connie said. "It'll be a lot of fun—new people, new teachers, *girls*. I betcha can't wait." She winked, nudging me with an elbow.

I had this idea of what high school would be like. When Connie went to Lafayette, she'd often spoken about the fun she had being a member of the Speakers' Bureau, a theatrical club that staged plays and comedy skits. I couldn't wait to jump in; I wanted to have the same experiences and make friends with the same kinds of people she'd talked about.

The first week of school, my homeroom teacher pulled me aside and handed me a blue appointment card. She told me that Mr. Friedlander, the dean of boys, wanted to see me in his office. I racked my brain, but for the life of me I couldn't figure out why on earth the dean wanted to see *me*. It was a stretch, but I somehow imagined that Sister Nimitz had contacted the school and supplied him with her book of "troublemakers." Was that witch going to follow me around for life?

"Just go right in," the dean's secretary instructed me. "He'll be with you in a moment."

The dean's office was spacious and had an unexpected homey feel to it. One wall was filled with his personal sports trophies, and another featured at least a dozen photos, a few of him in a US Marine uniform, but mostly framed black-and-white photos taken when he was a student at Lafayette and City College—action shots of him dribbling a basketball, making jump shots, running track, breaking a tape at a finish line, and sliding into home plate in a cloud of dust. Friedlander was tall and muscular, and in just about every photo his face had a tough, hard-assed, *me-first* grimace, like the expression of a GI pulling a pin from a hand grenade with his teeth.

I sat patiently on the couch, and after a few minutes Friedlander walked in, wearing sneakers, khaki pants, and a school sweatshirt. A whistle hung on a chain around his neck. As he neared his desk, he tossed down a jangle of keys, then picked up a manila folder and positioned himself in front of me, leaning against the desk with his long legs stretched out and crossed at the ankles.

"Are you John Caruso?" he said, studying the contents of the folder.

"Yes." I nodded, sitting up attentively.

The dean pulled a three-by-five photo from the folder

and held it up for me to see. It was a snapshot of my cousin Rocco, the older of Uncle Rocco's two sons. Rocco Jr. had graduated from Lafayette the year before. His younger brother, Cosimo, was a sophomore. Our families weren't close, and I didn't know much about either of them. I'd heard from Connie that Rocco Jr. was a rage king and had been issued a JD (juvenile delinquent) card before he was sixteen. In his junior year, he'd flung a lunch tray in the school cafeteria, hitting a teacher in the head. I'd also heard that he'd beaten some kid with a stickball bat in the schoolyard and put him in the hospital. Rocco Jr. had been assigned to the "600," a special program aimed at rehabilitating maladjusted and violent students within a normal school environment. The program was commonly referred to as "600" because the NYC Department of Education paid teachers an extra six hundred bucks (hazardous duty pay) to deal with loose cannons like my cousin.

I leaned forward to get a closer look at the photo. Rocco Jr. was standing against a gymnasium wall, looking just like his old man: stocky, square-faced, and pissed off at the world. If I'd had to write a caption, it would have read: *What the fuck are YOU lookin' at?*

"Are you related to this guy?" asked Friedlander.

"He's my cousin."

Friedlander slipped the photo back into the folder. "Then you also know his brother, Cosimo."

I was starting to get annoyed. "Have I done something wrong?"

"No." Friedlander placed the folder behind him and leaned forward, resting his hands on the desk's edge. "I just wanted to … introduce myself."

I waited, expecting the other shoe to drop.

"Lafayette is a great school, probably the best in Brooklyn, if not the city. It's my alma mater." He smiled. "I graduated in 1952. After high school, I joined the Marines, then came back to New York and went to City College and earned my bachelor's and master's degrees. Had a chance to teach at the college level, but instead I decided to come back here. I'm the school's athletic director and the dean of boys. Have been for the past—oh, what is it—six, going on seven years? What can I tell ya? I love this place. Love my job. These halls, this school—I spend more time here than I do at home. This is my *house*. And I called you in here because I wanted to let you know that when it comes to my house, I don't tolerate any bullshit."

"What bullshit? I just got here. I haven't done anything."

I started to get up, but Friedlander motioned for me to sit back down. "Hold your horses. I'm not finished."

I folded my arms over my chest.

"Son, listen to me. I'm not saying you've done anything. I'm just letting you know up front: if you're anything like your cousin Rocco or his wiseass brother, Cosimo, you and I are gonna lock assholes. And trust me when I tell you, that's not gonna be fun for you. *Capisce?*"

The door to the office swung open, and a kid popped his head in. "Sorry," he said, "I'll come back later." He turned, backing out of the room.

"Hey, *chico!*" Friedlander called out to him.

"You called me?" said the kid.

"What happened yesterday? The detention monitor said you skipped out."

"Yesterday?" the kid repeated, looking confused.

"Yeah, yesterday. *Comprende?* And don't act like you don't know what the hell I'm talking about."

"Oh, yeah, yesterday. Das why I come by to talk to you. Something happen is why I couldn't make it. My moms … you know, she got sick. My father, he was at work, so I had to go and leave school early, so I could, you know, go to the supermarket and stuff."

The kid shot me a nervous glance, as if to test the strength of his alibi. I didn't let on one way or the other, but on a believability scale of one to ten, he came in at minus two hundred.

"Bullshit," Friedlander said.

"No, no—Mr. Freelands, das for real. You can even call my moms."

"Don't stroke me, Mendez," Friedlander said, pointing a hard finger. "I told you before: I don't play that shit. You tried the same crap with me last year."

"I'm not stroking, man."

"All right, that's it. You have an extra hour of detention, starting today."

"C'mon, Mr. Freelands. How you gonna be like dat?"

The kid looked pissed. He made an annoyed sucking sound, then mumbled something in Spanish.

"What's that?" Friedlander challenged, bending his ear forward. "Did I just hear you curse in my house? Did you disrespect me in my own home? Now it's an extra *two* hours of detention."

"Aw, man."

"You got five seconds to get out of my office before I make it *three* hours." The dean glanced at his watch and started counting. "One … two … three …"

The kid stormed out the office in a huff.

"Boy, I'll tell ya," said Friedlander, a self-satisfied smirk on his face. "Life is tough, but it's a helluva lot tougher if ya got nothin' but *cuchifritos* between your ears."

He stood up, and I rose from the couch. I couldn't wait to get the hell out of there.

"Now." He clapped his hands, rubbing them together. "Are we cool? I'm not gonna have any trouble with you, am I?"

"There was never any trouble to begin with," I said.

"Good." He nodded, resting his hand on my shoulder. "That's what I like to hear. Welcome to Lafayette," he added with a wink. "Great school."

TWENTY-EIGHT

IT WAS A FRIDAY afternoon in late November, and I was hanging out with Freddy in the school cafeteria. We had just finished lunch and were about to head to our next class when a kid came running through. "Kennedy's dead! Kennedy's dead!" he shouted. "They shot President Kennedy!"

"Hey, that's not funny, asshole!" someone hollered.

"I'm not joking," the kid said. "I just heard it on the radio."

At first it didn't register with me. It was like hearing someone announce that a spaceship had landed on the White House lawn. Girls were crying, and kids scrambled around like a flock of wild turkeys. The idea the someone had shot and killed the president was unimaginable. Who were "they," and how could anyone do such a thing?

The school principal spoke on the intercom and announced that a tragedy had taken place in Dallas, involving President Kennedy. She instructed all the students to report to their homerooms. Freddy and I headed back to our classroom, and shortly afterward the entire school was sent home early.

For the next few days, Connie and I were glued to the television. Events unfolded one after another. Just about every channel made this announcement: "We interrupt our regular programming to bring you this special news bulletin." During one of the broadcasts, Walter Cronkite stated that Lee Harvey Oswald had been taken into custody and was a lone assassin.

People in the neighborhood threw themselves into the news frenzy. "Didja hear? They got the guy! They got Oswald!" Two days later, everyone was yapping about Jack Ruby. "Didja hear? Ruby shot Oswald! Ruby shot Oswald!" The whole thing felt surreal.

Connie was upset, but she seemed more angry than distressed. In high school she and her girlfriends had participated in a few political rallies and had helped campaign for Kennedy by handing out flyers in Brooklyn neighborhoods. She was convinced that more people than Lee Harvey Oswald had killed Kennedy. A lot of hazy stuff was flying over the airwaves: firsthand accounts, secondhand accounts, the Texas School Book Depository building, the grassy knoll—so many conflicting stories.

One minute Kennedy had been smiling and waving to a crowd, and minutes later he was lying dead in a hospital, his brains blown out. It made me think of my mother and how fragile life was. For days after the assassination, I carried around a gnawing feeling in the pit of my stomach, a disquieting notion that anything could happen to anybody at any time, and that nobody was in control of anything, including me. I hadn't even turned fifteen, and the world felt like a whirlpool of murky bathwater steadily vanishing down a drain.

❧

After the March on Washington in 1963, the civil rights movement had gained momentum and was in full swing by the spring of '64. New York City high school students were pushing the NYC Board of Education to integrate city schools. At Lafayette, there were maybe fifteen Black students. The majority of kids came from all-white, middle-class neighborhoods and had never interacted with Black people. Most of what I knew about Black people came from listening to my brother's jazz records and to popular groups on the radio.

One afternoon there was a demonstration in front of the school's entrance. About two dozen students, mostly upperclassmen, paraded back and forth on the sidewalk chanting, "Two, four, six, eight, we wanna integrate!" They were holding handmade signs that read, "Integrate Now!" "Civil Rights for All!" and "Integration Is an Education!"

I thought there was something special about these kids—they had balls. Out of the entire student body of close to four thousand, they were the only ones out on the street demonstrating for a cause they believed in. I had seen civil rights demonstrations on TV, along with footage of Black people being bitten by attack dogs and bludgeoned by baton-wielding police. I thought it was disgusting, but the images felt distant to me. I'd watch them and think, *What can I do? What can anybody do?* And now, for the first time, I was witnessing fellow students actually doing something.

I stepped forward and joined the line of demonstrators. A girl smiled and handed me a sign that read "Equal Rights Now!" She nodded, encouraging me to chant along with her and the other demonstrators.

Soon the area was mobbed with students who had

gathered to see what was happening. Farther down the sidewalk, a handful of other students, mostly older boys, shouted taunts at us. "Nigger lovers!" "Go home!" "Let 'em move into *your* fuckin' neighborhood!" Two or three police cars showed up, along with a few news crews from local TV stations. The cops had their nightsticks drawn and were shouting at people who had spilled into the street, directing them back onto the sidewalk.

At one point I noticed Gabe Perlman, a popular news reporter from NBC, with a cameraman filming next to him. Microphone in hand, he was interviewing one of the organizers of the demonstration, a smart, composed student wearing glasses, faded jeans, and a button-down shirt.

"Why are you students out here today?" Perlman asked. "What are you hoping to accomplish?"

"We believe the time has come for a change," said the organizer. "We, the Students for Civil Rights and Justice, are asking—no, we're *demanding*—that the New York City Board of Education review its policies and integrate the public school system, making high-quality education available to all New York City residents, not just privileged white communities. We also believe that we're all one people and that integration is an education." He held up his sign, which displayed the same slogan. "It will teach us all how to live and work with each other, prepare us for the future, and make us better citizens and human beings."

"As you can see, a number of counter-protesters are out here today, your fellow classmates and local residents who aren't in favor of school integration," Perlman said, gesturing toward the rowdy crowd of anti-integration protesters. "What would you say to them?"

"I'd simply say there's no room for bigotry or racism in our society. And if our brothers taunting and cursing us want to learn more about what's really at stake beyond the short-term inconvenience of feeling uncomfortable in the presence of people with a different skin color, they're welcome to come and join one of our peaceful, nonviolent meetings."

"Thank you," said Perlman. "And your name?"

"I'm Keith Messing, a senior here at Lafayette High School, and we are SCRJ, Students for Civil Rights and Justice."

The demonstrators applauded, and supportive cheers came from some of the onlookers. As I followed the line and circled around the sidewalk, I noticed Gabe Perlman conferring with his cameraman and pointing at me. Seconds later they headed in my direction.

"Now, here's a civic-minded young man." Perlman smiled admiringly. "May we have a word with you?" Before I could respond, he drew me out of the line, put his arm around my shoulders, and positioned me in front of the camera. "What's your name, if I may ask?"

"Johnny Caruso," I blurted out. "I see you on TV all the time."

"Well, thank you, Johnny." Perlman chuckled. "I appreciate that. You look like you're the youngest protester out here. How old are you?"

"I'm fourteen goin' on fifteen."

"Well, I'll tell ya, Johnny, I've been doing this a while, and I don't believe I've seen too many fourteen-year-olds out on the street, lending their voices to such a controversial issue."

I felt like I was in over my head. For a fleeting moment, I considered dropping my sign and disappearing into the crowd.

Perlman moved closer, holding his microphone inches away from my mouth. "So, Johnny, I'd like to ask you, why are you out here demonstrating this afternoon? I'm sure our viewers would like to know."

My mind was as blank as a fresh sheet of loose-leaf paper. I had no idea what to tell him, and I was afraid of sounding like a complete nincompoop. The other demonstrators watched me closely, listening for my response.

"I'm out here because I'm ... I'm ... I'm all for the Negroes," I offered, hoping he would be satisfied and maybe cut to a commercial or something.

Perlman paused. "Well, that's great," he said, looking slightly puzzled, "but, ah ... is there any other reason why you chose to protest?"

I scrambled for an answer. Then my eye caught the slogan written on Messing's protest sign. "Yes," I said, clutching Perlman's microphone. "*Integration is an education!*" I hollered, pumping my fist in the air. The other demonstrators went wild with cheers.

"Okay, and there you have it!" announced Perlman, looking into the camera. "This is Gabe Perlman, reporting from Lafayette High School in Brooklyn, New York."

That night our telephone jumped off the hook. Perlman's coverage of the demonstration was on the six o'clock news. Part of his report included an edited clip of me proclaiming

"Integration is an education!" with my fist in the air. Jackie, Freddy, Carmine, Sandra, and a handful of neighbors called to say they'd seen me on the news. My face was on the screen for maybe 3.2 seconds, but people were yammering as if I were John Glenn or some other national hero.

Connie was the most excited. She called Ann Gottlieb and jabbered into the phone with her arm around my neck. "Didja see him on the news? That's my fourteen-year-old kid brother. My little *scungilli* was out there with the Students for Civil Rights and Justice. I'm so proud of him! *Mwah! Mwah!*" She smacked her lips against my forehead.

The next day, Keith Messing and Karen Robinson, another organizer from the SCRJ, invited me to their weekly meeting to help plan the group's next protest. Karen was a senior and looked to be about the same age as Messing, seventeen or eighteen.

"We're reaching out to more underclassmen, and we thought you'd be a good fit," said Messing.

"Yeah," said Karen, "you were great yesterday. We want to expand our base, and we're hoping you'd consider checking us out and getting more involved."

These were older students asking *me* if I wanted to help *them*. I felt honored but was also nervous as hell. I told them I was interested but that my joining the street protest had been a spur-of-the-moment thing, and that I really didn't know much about civil rights other than what I'd seen on the news. This didn't seem to faze Messing; his demeanor was mature and calm. Talking to him, I got the feeling he had experience way beyond his age. "That's okay," he said. "What matters most is that you're a willing participant and interested in making the world a better place."

It sounded like a tall order. I was more excited by the opportunity to be part of something bigger than myself, and to be around people who regarded me as an equal, people with a perspective on the world beyond the boundaries of Bay Haven and Precious Mother.

୨

SCRJ met in a student conference room at the far end of the school library. The next day, in the hall outside the library's entrance, I felt a tap on my shoulder from behind. It was my cousin Cosimo.

"Hey, Cosimo, what's up?"

I hadn't seen him in months. He looked like a small-time gangster who had just stepped off the boat from Palermo: black leather sports jacket over a collarless, pastel-blue nylon shirt, and a black, stingy-brim fedora with a red feather in the hatband.

"What are you doin'?" he whispered, his beady eyes checking his sides.

"I'm headed into the library. Something wrong?"

"I saw you protesting with those nigger lovers the other day."

"What?"

"You stick to your own kind," he said, jabbing a finger into my chest.

"Excuse me?" I thought he was joking, and chuckled.

"What the hellaya doin' out on the street, talkin' to the news guy? Now the whole world knows you love jigaboos."

"What's it to you?"

"You're a disgrace to the whole family!"

"Yeah, *I'm* the disgrace."

"This is our fuckin' neighborhood," said Cosimo. "If you want to mix with niggers, why don't you move into *their* neighborhood?"

"Listen, Cosimo, I know you're a tough guy and all, but what I do is *my* business. You don't tell me what the fuck to do or where to go. Not you, not anybody." I turned and opened one of the oak doors to the library and headed for the student conference room.

"Hey," said Cosimo, following close behind. "I'm talking to you!"

Without turning, I raised my hand above my head and flipped him the bird, hoping he'd get the message. Seconds later Cosimo bum-rushed me from behind, shoving me full force into a display of magazines and newspapers. People nearby stopped what they were doing and looked on in stunned silence.

Cosimo stood his ground, staring me down with hateful eyes. "I said, I'm talkin' to you," he shouted.

For a moment, I was gripped with disbelief. Is this *really happening*? Did I just get slammed by my *own cousin*? My jaw tightened, and my temples pulsed with rage. I dropped my books and charged him with clenched fists, arms swinging. We exchanged a flurry of wild punches, two baboons going at it like crazy. The fight seemed to go on forever.

"Hey, break it up! Break it up!" someone hollered.

A teacher and two student librarians rushed over and pulled us apart. We were both sweating, exhausted, and breathing heavily. Cosimo had a bloody nose, and I had a fat bruise near my right eye.

"You're dead," Cosimo said, talking into a bloodstained handkerchief.

"Stay the hell away from me, you fucking *cafone!*"

Determined not to miss the meeting, I headed to the back of the library and joined Messing, Robinson, and six or seven other students from SCRJ.

Karen winced. "God, what happened to *you?*"

"Nothing. I just had a little disagreement with one of my cousins. He thinks I shouldn't be protesting." My face was throbbing, and my eye had swollen badly.

Messing leaned closer to get a better look. "Are you okay?" he said. "You might want go down to the nurse's office and get your eye checked out."

"Naw, I'm fine. Sorry I'm late. Did I miss anything?"

Someone from the library reported my run-in with Cosimo, and the next day my cousin and I were called to the dean's office. Friedlander wasn't playing games. "I've had it with you goombah knuckleheads," he said. "You're both suspended for a week."

In addition to the suspension, I got a week's detention. Cousin Cosimo, who already had a promising high school rap sheet, moved up to the big leagues. He was taken out of the regular curriculum and reassigned to the 600 program, following in the footsteps of his brother.

When my father heard that I'd been suspended, he wigged. "What are you, a fuckin' *stunad?*" he said, jabbing the tips of his fingers into my head. "When you get suspended, that goes on your record, ya big *dummy*."

I explained what had happened, and the old man became more concerned about my joining the SCRJ protest than about my scrap in the library. "Where the hell do you get off marching with a bunch of beatniks who have nothing better to do with their lives?"

"They're not beatniks! You don't know anything."

"And then to top it off, you're on the goddamn television giving interviews! What the hell do *you* know about integration?"

I wasn't sure how to respond, mainly because part of me believed he was right. What the hell did I know about civil rights? Or anything?

"Listen, do me a favor, will ya?" My father was trying to sound less heated and more rational. "In the future, mind your own business. Let other people protest and get their heads cracked open. I got enough troubles. The next thing I know, the FBI will be wanting to investigate me." He walked away, shaking his head. "Integration is an education," he said, then trailed off with some choice words in Italian. "And then people wanna know why I drink."

"I joined the group," I said.

"What's that?"

"Students for Civil Rights and Justice. They asked me to join, and I signed up. We're getting ready for another protest next week." I made it sound like I enlisted in the French Foreign Legion and signed an irreversible contract.

"You're not going to any protest. You're staying right here. You're in enough trouble."

"I don't care—I'm going anyway. And you can't stop

me."

My father's face flared with rage. He lunged at me, and I crouched low, curling both arms over the top of my head. He slapped me twice, and I barreled into him, pushing my hands into his chest, ramming my head into his stomach. "I've had enough of your shit!"

The old man looked shocked. I got the feeling he'd suddenly realized that fucking with me would no longer be a walk in the park. I held my ground, assuming he would unload on me again, but he just stood there, eyeing me curiously. I could tell he was astonished to see that I'd stood up to him, something I'm sure he believed I would never attempt.

"You're not going anywhere," he said. His words sounded vacant and only marginally threatening.

"I am too."

He turned, heading for his bedroom. "Oh *yeah?* We'll see about that."

As I watched him walk away, his once-dominating stature appeared smaller. I had trekked to the top of the forbidden mountain and peered down the other side. The view was liberating.

TWENTY-NINE

CONNIE AND GEORGE planned a June wedding at Saint Fingar, a few blocks from Bay Haven. Connie was constantly on the phone gabbing with her bridesmaids, going over the invitation list or discussing dresses, corsages, food choices, table arrangements, and wedding songs. She went on a crash diet and lost fifteen pounds so she could squeeze into an off-white satin and chiffon dress dotted with white pearls, a picture of which she'd taped to her bedroom mirror. She had also started smoking to help kill her urge for late-night bingeing.

The big day finally arrived. The priest who performed the ceremony was the same priest who had counseled Connie and George in the weeks leading up to the wedding. My sister wasn't thrilled about the premarriage counseling, but it was a requirement for getting hitched in the church. It was included in the three-hundred-dollar "suggested donation," which also covered the church, the priest, altar boys, organist, and maintenance staff. "What's he gonna counsel you on?" asked Frank. "This guy probably never squeezed a pair of tits in his life."

After the ceremony, they held a reception at the Venetian Terrace, a gaudy Brooklyn catering hall where Bensonhurst locals, mostly Italians, hosted proms and celebrated first communions and weddings. The VT was a large, two-story building just off Fourteenth Avenue. Mounted on the roof above the front entrance was a miniature gondola flanked by two large flags, one American and one Italian. The interior was plastered with colorful murals, mostly of Venice: canals, cathedrals, piazze dotted with pigeons.

About a hundred guests had been invited to the reception. My father helped foot the bill with the insurance money he'd received from my mother's passing. Half the guests at the bash were George's relatives, people I'd never seen before. At one table sat ten of George's aunts and uncles, real eye-openers who were a long way from the pretentious sophistication of George's mother, Olga. The women had bleached-blonde or platinum hair, teased to the rafters, and wore gobs of cartoonish blue or green eye shadow. The men had huge necks and beefy hands and sported dark, bulky suits. Collectively, the guys looked like a gaggle of seasoned house movers decked out for a night on the town. As far as I could see, the only thing they had in common with Olga was that they were serious drinkers. They had brought their own bottles of homemade vodka and *nalewka*, a Polish sweet liqueur that they guzzled as if it were cream soda.

The band played American standards mixed with a sprinkling of traditional Italian and Polish music, as well as a few cheeseball versions of Beatles songs and other popular tunes. People were dancing and laughing and seemed to be having a good time, but I couldn't relax. I pretended to enjoy myself, but the whole time I was thinking about my sister and the fact that she and I would never live under the same roof again. As I made small talk with relatives, my eyes periodically wandered in Connie's direction. She looked like a beauty queen, dressed in her white gown and long veil, smiling and chatting with her girlfriends. I couldn't remember the last time I'd seen her so happy. Each smile and gesture filled my stomach with pangs of longing. I wanted to hug and kiss her. I wanted her to tell me that I was still her special kid brother, that I didn't have to worry because things were always going to be the same between us. I wanted her to tell me she loved me.

I was sitting at a round table with Frank and Sandra, Big Joe, Aunt Rose and Uncle Sally Boy, and Aunt Lena and Uncle Ernie and their two sons, Robert and Ernie Jr. Everyone was babbling away and stuffing their faces with *antipasti*.

After dinner Connie and George cut the wedding cake under a barrage of crackling flashbulbs. Minutes later the houselights dimmed and a dapper bandleader, dressed in a blue tuxedo with a pink carnation smartly pinned to his lapel, stepped up to the microphone.

"May I have your attention please?" he said, tapping the mic.

The room quieted down. Frank's face had morphed into a mask of boredom and dread. I knew exactly what he was thinking: *Here we go, more Italian wedding bullshit.* He was focused on the bandleader, who had that polished, *I'm what's happening*, Vegas, rat-pack look—just the type of simonized personality that turned Frank's stomach.

"How's everybody doing this evening?" The bandleader smiled, and the crowd responded with a lukewarm cheer. "What's that? I can't *hear* you," he said, prompting a louder response. "Good, good ..." He nodded. "It's nice to be here this evening and to see so many beautiful people dressed up. You all look so nice. I'd love to take you all home with me." He paused. "Well, maybe just the beautiful women." He winked and slipped a hand under his lapel, sliding it up and down. "Hey, did you hear the one about the couple who just got married? They were on the throughway driving up to Niagara Falls. Halfway there, the man takes his hand off the steering wheel and gently places it on the thigh of his new bride. She turns to him and says, 'Ya know, honey, now that we're married you can go a little further.' Would ya believe?— the son of a gun was so excited he drove all the way to Montreal."

The drummer gave him a chick-a-boom, and people laughed heartily. Frank glanced at his watch, as if he were stuck on a blind date.

"And now, ladies and gentlemen," the bandleader continued in a more reflective tone, "we have arrived at the point in the evening that many of you have been waiting for. It's a time of tradition … a time when we pause to honor the past and embrace the future. It's that special moment in this joyous celebration when we ask Bellisario, the dedicated and loving father of the bride, to dance with the apple of his eye, Concetta Maria, and to give his blessings to his daughter and her new love."

"Dedicated and loving," Frank grumbled. "This guy must be doped up on airplane glue."

In the center of the dance floor, my father and sister danced to Connie's favorite song, Judy Garland singing "Over the Rainbow." They didn't move much; they looked like two deep-sea buoys aimlessly swaying in the ocean. My father had started drinking early in the evening, and I could see by that

all-too-familiar glazed look in his eyes that he was already
half quaffed. Every so often he'd draw my sister close to his
chest, kiss her cheeks, and jabber something in her ear.
Connie had a frozen grin on her face and any boing-boing
with half a noodle could have seen that she wasn't
comfortable. The old man might as well have been feeding
her baseball stats; she just kept nodding in agreement.

Halfway through the song, George stepped onto the
dance floor and tapped my father on the shoulder. This was
part of the tradition, symbolizing a daughter's passing from
father to husband. My father kissed my sister one last time
and stepped away from her, motioning for George to take
over. But the minute George moved closer to Connie, my
father jokingly resumed dancing with her, ignoring his new
son-in-law. This drew a wave of laughter from the audience.
Everyone seemed to think it was funny except Olga, whose
eyes burned with rage. She took a few heated drags from her
cigarette and furiously jammed it into an ashtray.

Big Joe got up from the table and joined the act. He
stepped up to my father and tapped him on the shoulder. But
instead of cutting in and dancing with my sister, Joe began
dancing with the old man, drawing my father's head close to
his chest. My father played along, and this ignited an even
louder wave of laughter. When they finally cleared the floor,
George and Connie embraced and continued the dance to a
round of heartfelt applause. "Let's hear it for the bride and
groom!" the bandleader piped. Connie looked relieved. She
shook her head as if to say, *What a freaking zoo.*

Toward the end of the reception, I looked all over for
Connie. I knew that she and George were headed up to the
Catskills for their honeymoon, and I wanted to say goodbye

and wish her well. I searched everywhere, but she was nowhere to be found. I was pissed when I learned from one of her bridesmaids that they secretly slipped out of the building—some bullshit wedding-night tradition. Why had she cut out on me like that? I wasn't one of her schmo in-laws; I was her kid brother.

Eventually Uncle Sally Boy and Aunt Rose drove my father and me home. Just as Sally Boy pulled up in front of Bay Haven, a light rain began to fall. "Keep an eye on him," Sally Boy said, nodding at my father. "Make sure he doesn't have any more to drink."

The old man was so intoxicated I had to help him keep his balance on the pathway to our building. Up in the apartment he staggered into the bathroom and threw up in the sink; yellow-and-brown vomit splattered everywhere. The stench was horrendous. I gagged and clenched my teeth to keep from puking up my own dinner. I covered the sink with a bath towel and helped my father to his bed, where I loosened his tie and removed his shoes.

In Connie's room I flopped down on her bed and closed my eyes, taking in the sweet scent of her perfume lingering on her pillow. The sky crackled with lightning, and a thunderclap boomed, followed by a heavy downpour. I looked toward the window, listening to raindrops pelt the fire escape. I was physically and mentally exhausted. I closed my eyes again and tried to clear the clatter in my head. After a while I dozed off, and I woke up sometime later, startled by a noise that sounded like moaning coming from an injured animal. I thought I was dreaming. Bleary-eyed, I got out of bed and stumbled into the foyer. The apartment was dark, and after a moment I realized it was my father. He was in his bedroom, crying out for my mother. "Mary! Mary!" The sound of his grief-stricken voice swept through me like an arctic chill. It was the saddest sound I'd ever heard.

THIRTY

CONNIE AND GEORGE lived in Queens. They had moved into a cozy one-bedroom garden apartment near Forest Hills. Initially, they'd considered renting an apartment in Brooklyn, but Connie wanted to live as far away from our father as possible.

I missed her dearly. She and I would talk on the phone, and once or twice a month I'd hop a train out to Queens and visit. Their pad was wonderful: a ground-floor deal with plenty of sunlight. There was a small garden in the back of the house, accessible from their kitchen. Connie had a magic touch and could make any space come alive. The house was filled with plants, art, and tapestries, and a smattering of photos that she'd taken at outdoor folk concerts.

Old Georgie seemed happy and more relaxed. To my surprise, he traded in his clean-cut athletic look for a beard, long hair, and John Lennon sideburns.

My father had been working out of town and came home on weekends. He continued to drink heavily but still managed to do the shopping and cooking. I did the cleaning and laundry. During the week I took care of myself. Occasionally, Mrs. Amato, our next-door neighbor, looked in on me and brought me food, but mostly I cooked my own meals, easy stuff that I'd learned from Connie: bacon and eggs, salads, canned soups and vegetables, burgers and chops. I also ate a lot of cake, cookies, and other crap, and gained about five pounds.

ॐ

After my suspension I continued to meet with SCRJ. I didn't tell my father, and he didn't ask. I think he knew I'd been participating in weekly protests, and I interpreted his silence as tacit approval, just as long as I stayed under the radar and didn't give any more television interviews.

Classes at Lafayette were large, and cheating was a piece of cake. The only problem was, now that I didn't have hatchet-job teachers like Nimitz bashing my brains against a blackboard, I didn't feel motivated to cheat. Kids my age who had come to Lafayette from other public schools were way ahead of me. They talked excitedly about science projects, quoted Shakespeare, knew algebra, and read authors like Dickens and Joyce.

Harriet Voriotis was in my English Lit class. Given the encouragement she got from her educated parents, it wasn't a surprise that she was a straight-A student. Before beginning her freshman year, she had already read everything written by the Bronte sisters. In class she radiated confidence —just listening to her astute comments made me feel as if I'd been living in a hole, and I realized that my cheating had been hurting me. I no longer felt the triumphant exhilaration of sliding through exams. More than anything I was embarrassed and felt stuck.

My father had changed his approach toward my

mediocre grades. Instead of whacking me around and threatening to humiliate me in front of my class, he suggested that my learning problems might be due to "physical disabilities."

"How's your hearing?" he asked. "Are you sure you can hear all right?"

"What do you mean, can I hear all right? I can hear fine."

I was amused by his weak attempt to rationalize my poor grades and annoyed by his stupidity. Could I *hear* all right? I might have been a flop in school, but if the old man had had a freaking brain, he'd be dangerous.

"Naw, I'm serious," he persisted. "How's your eyesight? Can you see okay?"

"Dad, gimme a break, will ya? There's nothing wrong with my eyes and ears."

This type of exchange happened a few times. Once he actually suggested that I might have had a brain injury when I was younger. "Sometimes that kind of thing shows up years later," he said, as if he were an authority on brain injury.

Sandra knew I wasn't doing well in school. When I told her about my father's assessment, she laughed. "Boy, oh boy." She shook her head. "That's just like your father. He'll say anything to avoid responsibility."

Soon she came up with a plan. New York University had a testing and advancement center, and she thought I'd be a perfect candidate for psychological and aptitude testing. "This is a great opportunity," she said. "No more guessing. If you're having trouble in school, this is an invaluable tool that will assess your strengths and weaknesses."

"Are these the kinds of tests they give to crazy

people?" I chuckled, half joking.

"C'mon—you're not crazy." She nudged me. "These are aptitude tests. They help determine your personality type and potential. All kinds of people visit the advancement center. Men, women, young, old. People who are just starting out, people who want to change careers and aren't sure what kinds of skills they have and what type of work they're best suited for."

"I don't know …"

"Think of it this way. Say you have a car, right, and you put the key in the ignition, step on the gas, and the engine rumbles for twenty minutes before it starts. Then you put the car into gear. It putters along, and you hope to God it gets you where you want to go. Now, whaddaya do? Do you take the car to a mechanic to have it looked at, or do you wait until the damn thing drops dead on you in the middle of the Brooklyn-Queens Expressway?"

"Okay, I'll do it. But I can tell you right now, the old man's not gonna go for it."

"Don't worry about your father. I'll talk to him."

Good luck, I thought.

A couple of days later Sandra called me on the phone. "Good news," she said. "I spoke to your father. He agreed to let me schedule you for testing at the advancement center. Isn't that great?"

"You're *shittin'* me. Howdja do it?"

"I used a little reverse psychology. He told me the same thing he told you—that he thought there was something wrong with your hearing and eyesight and that maybe you'd had brain damage when you were a toddler. I told him I thought he might be onto something and that the best way to know for sure was to have you tested."

"That's *great*."

"And just to make sure he didn't weasel out and change his mind at the last minute, I told him that your brother and I would cover any and all costs."

"Oh man—*thanks*." I was lucky to have Sandra on my side, someone who understood me and cared about my well-being.

I was tested in mid-June, shortly after the completion of my freshman year at Lafayette. The NYU testing and advancement center was located on the fifth floor of a gray office building, a block from Washington Square Park. Over a two-week period, I took the train into Manhattan and spent mornings and afternoons at the center, where I underwent a battery of examinations—a total of nineteen tests, covering what seemed like every aptitude and personality assessment known to humankind. I was even given an eye exam and a hearing test. I would arrive at the testing center at 9:00 a.m. and was given an hour for lunch. By 3:30 my brain was fried.

The math and mechanical assessments were murder; half the time I answered any old thing or left questions blank. Some of the other tests, like the drawing and personality assessments, were fun and interesting. I remember one true-or-false question in particular: "My father is a good man. OR (if your father is dead) My father was a good man." I labored over this for a couple of minutes. The answer, I felt, was too complicated to be narrowed down to a true-or-false response. I wound up answering "false" but felt guilty, wishing I could scribble in additional information or explain my answer to someone.

On some afternoons after testing, I walked around Greenwich Village: Bleecker Street, West Fourth Street, MacDougal. I passed all the exciting places that Frank and Connie talked about: The Village Gate, The Bitter End, Cafe Wha?, and Gerdes Folk City, where Bob Dylan played. Seeing these places for myself was like discovering the ancient pyramids. The best was Washington Square Park, an outdoor wonderland with entrances and walkways on all sides that led to a huge circular fountain in the center of the park. On any given day the place teemed with a fascinating mix of people: bearded bohemians in jeans and sandals; artists working on oil paintings; clusters of students strumming guitars and singing folk songs; men hunched over on benches, smoking pipes and playing chess; a Black man blowing sweltering bebop riffs on a saxophone; beat poets, stand-up comedians, and philosophers playing to a captivated audience by the fountain—all surrounded by food carts, panhandlers, and throngs of wide-eyed tourists fresh off the bus from Middle America. I lived thirty minutes over the bridge in Brooklyn, and I was as mesmerized as they were.

On the last day of the testing, I headed straight for Washington Square. It was a late Friday afternoon, and the park was jumping. On the south side a crowd had gathered under a large oak tree, the sound of drums filling the air. I hurried over and burrowed through the throng of onlookers to check out the action. Three guys on folding chairs were cooking up a storm, two playing conga drums and one on bongos. One of the conga players, a shirtless, muscular dude with a light tan and a wild Afro, seemed to be the leader. He was sweating like crazy and played with real passion and technique, his arms flailing and his legs wrapped around the bottom of the drum. Off to the side, two guys were tapping out bell rhythms on empty Coke bottles, using metal bottle openers. They were all brewing a sweet blend of Afro-Cuban rhythms and had a fierce groove going. Then another guy showed up with a flute and joined them; he and the conga players seemed to know one another.

The people in the crowd were bobbing their heads and getting into the groove. After about twenty minutes, one of the guys on the Coke bottles glanced at his watch and motioned to his partner that he had to split. I was standing right behind him. He turned and handed me the bottle and opener as if I were one of the regular park jammers. My first impulse was to hand the bottle off to someone else, but instead, to my own surprise, I jumped right in.

I'd messed around with drumsticks a few years back and had learned how to keep time by playing along with the radio and banging on phone books. I started tapping out straight fours (one-two-three-four), a less complicated pattern than the previous guy had been playing. It was all I knew how to play, but it turned out to be perfect: in seconds it made a notable difference in the dynamic of the rhythm.

The main conga player with the Afro nodded approvingly. "Hol' dat right dare! Hol' dat right dare!" he shouted. I couldn't believe it. It was like getting a thumbs-up from fucking Mongo Santamaría. I had just come to hang out and listen, and now here I was in the middle of the crowd, holding it down with the brothers on a Coke bottle. I could have stayed in that park playing straight fours all day, all night, for the rest of my life.

THIRTY-ONE

THE TESTING AND advancement center sent a four-page typewritten report to Sandra. The report had a dizzying graph of testing percentages and a written assessment of my aptitude and personality traits. At the end was a summary:

"John is quite erratic in his intellectual functioning, but he is a youngster with great academic potential. The marked fluctuation in his intellectual and scholastic performance is primarily due to emotional factors, a severe lack of confidence in himself, a general lack of motivation due to his mother's death, a poor relationship with his father, and immaturity in the development of self-discipline. Not only does he need a supportive school environment in which he could receive individual attention in small classes and much in the way of encouragement and guidance, he also needs remedial training in reading, including phonics and speed-reading, instruction in effective study techniques, and remedial instruction in arithmetic. On the other hand, John is superior in verbal intelligence, the mental ability most fundamental to academic success, exceeding 99 percent of his age group in his ability to reason in abstract and theoretical terms and to reduce complex problems to their basic principles. He would not have difficulty adjusting socially to a boarding school, since he is a highly outgoing and self-assertive individual."

Sandra thought the evaluation was brilliant. "Did you read the part about sensory deficiencies?" she said, holding up the report and grinning with delight. "It says, 'John's scholastic problems are not'—I repeat *not*— 'attributed to sensory deficiencies. The keenness of his hearing and eyesight, as well as his eye-muscle balance, is well within acceptable limits for scholastic work.' Which means that there's nothing wrong with you physically." Sandra smiled. "I'm sure your father will be *overjoyed* to hear it," she added.

My father's reaction was predictable: "These psychologists think they know everything." The truth is he was less surprised to hear that my eyesight and hearing were intact and more embarrassed that the report had identified him as being part of the problem. But it was clear to him that I was performing below my grade level and needed remedial help. Sandra talked about the possibility of sending me to a private boarding school, where I would receive more attention and learn in smaller classes. To my amazement, the old man thought it was a good idea.

Sandra's thesis advisor knew of a small boarding school in western Massachusetts called Bradley Hall. He told her that the school's headmaster, Dr. Warren Farnsworth, accepted and worked with "special cases." I thought that was a curious description. I knew I had some problems, but I didn't think my "case" was any more special than some of the accidents I hung out with on Bay Lane.

Sandra contacted the school and requested a brochure. On the cover, students in white shirts, ties, and dark blazers walked along a narrow path toward a quaint two-story wooden building with window shutters and an inviting A-frame entrance that led to two open doors. Above the photo, "Welcome to Bradley Hall" was written in giant letters. Inside was a photo of Dr. Farnsworth, a heavyset man with a welcoming smile. The text under his picture read, "Nestled in the foothills of the Berkshire Mountains, Bradley Hall for Boys offers a specialized and caring learning environment for students in grades 9–12. Our highly trained teaching staff are dedicated to helping students reveal their character and develop the confidence they need to succeed in high school, college, and beyond."

"I don't know," I said.

"What don't you know?" Sandra asked.

"I mean, it looks okay and all, but I don't know if it's for me. Plus, it's so far away. What about all my friends?"

"What friends?" Frank said. "You mean those half-witted jabonies you run with on Bay Lane? Jerk, *wake up.* This is the opportunity of a lifetime. What would you rather do, go away to a boarding school, where you'll get a good education plus three squares a day and a place to sleep, or live with the old man, watching him drink himself into oblivion?" Frank looked pissed. "When I was your age, I would have given an arm to get the hell out of that house and go away to school. Not only was it not an option, I didn't even know fucking boarding schools *existed!* If you don't jump on this, you're out of your mind."

৯

My father set up an interview with Dr. Farnsworth on a Wednesday afternoon at the Biltmore, an old-world luxury hotel in Manhattan where the headmaster had a rented suite.

My father and I wore suits and ties. I had no idea what to expect, but my old man was more uptight than I was. On our way up in the elevator, his eyes were glued to the floor indicator above the door. "Just be yourself," he said, adjusting his tie. "You got nothing to worry about. Keep your mouth shut and your ears open and let me do the talking. We don't wanna blow this."

Dr. Farnsworth's office was on the twentieth floor, suite 2020. The door was slightly ajar in anticipation of our arrival, and music drifted out. The headmaster was singing along with a record. His voice was deep and operatic and not very good. "'A more humane Mikado never did in Japan exist! To nobody second, I'm certainly reckoned a true philanthropist!'"

My father knocked on the door and waited for a response. The singing continued, and he mumbled some choice words in Italian, the Neapolitan equivalent of *what the fuck?*

"Are you sure this is the right room?" I said.

"I got it right here." He pulled a crumpled piece of paper out of his coat pocket. "The guy said suite 2020." My father knocked on the door again, louder.

"Come in!" hollered Dr. Farnsworth. We heard the sound of the needle scratching across the record.

The living room was spacious and stately. Two high-backed upholstered chairs sat facing an elegant green couch. On the other side of the room, a Victorian-style desk was positioned in front of sliding glass doors that opened onto a small terrace.

"Welcome! Welcome!" Dr. Farnsworth said. He shook our hands, cleared the couch of a heap of newspapers, and motioned for us to sit down. "You'll have to forgive me," he said, stepping over to the desk to retrieve his eyeglasses. "It's been a hectic morning." As he moved around, his huge potbelly hung down over a worn leather belt buckled off to the side.

"Who were you listening to?" my father asked.

Dr. Farnsworth sat in one of the chairs opposite the couch. He struggled to cross his legs, and I noticed a patch of hairless white skin peek out between the cuffs of his gray trousers and brown wool socks. "That was *The Mikado*, by Gilbert and Sullivan," he replied with a belch, covering his mouth with a fist. "We're putting on a little performance up at Bradley next week, and I was rehearsing. The boys have me playing the part of the emperor." Dr. Farnsworth belched again, louder. It sounded like a toilet backing up. "Excuse me!" he said. "Jeez ..." He smiled, exposing a sizeable gap between his two front teeth. "That must be the corned beef sandwich and sauerkraut I ate for lunch. That combination will roll over you like a tank." He shot me a wink. "Are you familiar with Gilbert and Sullivan?"

"A little bit," my father said. "I'm more of an Italian opera fan. I listen to people like wonderful *tenore di grazia* Beniamino Gigli and Tito Schipa, and of course the great Enrico Caruso." I could tell my father was waiting for the headmaster to ask him if he was related to Enrico Caruso. And I was praying that he wouldn't, so I wouldn't have to listen to the old man repeat his bullshit story about how he and *Enrico* were distant cousins.

"Ah, I see," Dr. Farnsworth said. "Another family who loves good music. How about you, John? Do you like music?"

"Oh, he loves music." My father boasted with a smile. "He likes the Beatles, the Beach Boys ... and those other guys with the long hair. Whadda they call themselves?"

I didn't answer or look at him. The old man was getting on my nerves, but I didn't want to make a scene in front of the headmaster.

"C'mon. You know who I'm talkin' about. What's the name? The Rolling somebody."

"The Rolling Stones," I said, still not looking at him.

"Is that right, John?" asked Dr. Farnsworth.

"They're okay." I shrugged. "I like jazz."

"Really? Who do you listen to?"

"A buncha people. Miles Davis, John Coltrane, Charlie Parker." Those were the first names that came to mind, people my brother had turned me on to. I had about twenty albums that Frank had let me keep after he split, albums I played regularly. I wasn't trying to impress the headmaster; I was trying to distance myself from the old man and let the guy know I was my own person, with my own freaking brain.

"Pretty cool stuff there, buddy," Dr. Farnsworth said.

"I never knew you liked jazz," said my father. What a crock. He knew I listened to Frank's albums all the time.

"There are a lot of things you don't know about me," I said.

"You'd probably get along with my oldest son, Jim," Dr. Farnsworth said. "Huge jazz enthusiast. About three weeks ago, he and I drove to Boston to see Dave Brubeck, who was playing at Boston College, my alma mater. Are you familiar with Dave Brubeck?"

"Yeah, he's great," I said. "Joe Morello is my favorite

drummer." *This guy is all right*, I thought. Any father who takes his kid to see a jazz concert has got to be cool.

Dr. Farnsworth put on his glasses and looked over some notes he'd scribbled on a yellow legal pad. The glasses made his round face look more like the headmaster of a boys' prep school, at least in my mind.

"Now, I know you received our brochure, but I want to tell you little bit more about Bradley Hall, and then I'll answer any questions you and John might have."

"That would be great," my father said.

"We're a small school by design. Last year we had a hundred and two students, grades nine through twelve. This year we're up to a hundred and five. We're located in North Edgemont, five miles outside of Kensington. We're a fully accredited institution and licensed by the state of Massachusetts. We have a main campus, where the school building and dining hall are located. As you know, our classes are small and our staff is available for one-on-one tutoring."

"What about the room accommodations?" my father said.

"Good question. There are five dorms, all within walking distance of the school building. The boys sleep two or three to a room. Each dorm is assigned a dorm master, one of our teaching staff who resides in the dorm with the boys. We also have a licensed, full-time nurse on staff and an infirmary that's separate from the dormitories." Dr. Farnsworth paused and glanced down at his notes. "Lemme see ... Do you play any sports?"

"He loves sports," my father said. "He's in the park every day, wearing cut-off jeans and sneakers."

That was it for me. I was about to turn to my old man

and tell him to zip his blow hole, but Dr. Farnsworth quickly intervened. "Excuse me—" he removed his glasses. "If you don't mind, I'd like to hear from John." His tone was firm but respectful.

My father held up his hands in submission, and I felt an instant sense of relief.

"Thank you," said the headmaster. "John ..."

"I love sports," I told him. "I mainly play basketball, softball, and touch football."

"That's great. We just converted a barn into a basketball court and a first-class gymnasium. Bradley is part of a sports conference for prep schools throughout western Mass. We also have a great soccer team. Last year we came in second in our division. We hired a top-notch coach, Vidar Karlsson, who used to play for Norway; he was on their national team. Vidar also heads up our math department."

An uncomfortable silence followed this information. I glanced at my father, and he looked overwhelmed. I knew exactly what he was thinking: this school is out of my league. I tried to come up with something to say that sounded halfway normal, and I remembered a photo in the brochure of couples dancing. "Are there any girls?" I said.

"Well, not at Bradley," Dr. Farnsworth said. "I already have my hands full. But, ah ... since you mentioned it, you'll be interested to know that we have four girls' schools nearby. And we host school dances and socials at least once a month."

"You mean like with Woodward?"

"Ah, I see you've been reading our brochure. Yes, Woodward Academy is one of the schools we partner with. They're over in Willow Falls."

"How's the food?" my father said.

"Well, as you can see, the food is great." Dr. Farnsworth slapped his mammoth gut. "A little *too* good."

I blurted out a laugh. My father smiled, but I could see he was less amused.

"We have a fully equipped kitchen that prepares breakfast, lunch, dinner, and snacks," Dr. Farnsworth said in a more serious tone. "Doris Wallynetz is our wonderful head chef. She plans all the meals; she's also a registered dietitian. The boys love her. They call her Wally, and she treats each and every one of them like they're her own."

The phone rang, and Dr. Farnsworth hoisted himself out of his chair. "Excuse me," he said with a grunt. "I think that's my garage." As he stepped over to the desk, he reached behind his back and tugged out a substantial wad of gray trouser wedged in the crack of his butt.

"What do you think?" my father said in a lower voice.

"I don't know." I shrugged. "It sounds okay. What do you think?"

"I don't know. I gotta see how much this is gonna cost. Dietitians, soccer coaches … I mean, I know you think money grows on trees, but this kind of thing is not cheap."

"C'mon, Dad. Stop jerkin' my bird, will ya? Everybody knows money grows on trees."

The old man eased into a smile. "Ya big chooch." He nudged my head with his fingers. "What the hell am I gonna do with you?"

"I'm sorry, but I had to take that call," Dr. Farnsworth said, shuffling back to his chair. "That was the garage up in Edgemont. One of our buses needs a new clutch, and the mechanic was giving me an estimate. Boy, I'll tell ya." He shook his head. "There's always somethin' that needs to be repaired or replaced up at the school. Heck—these days, even a simple clutch can run ya a small fortune."

"I know what you mean," my father agreed with a nervous chuckle.

"John, do you have any more questions for me?" asked Dr. Farnsworth. "If not, I'd like to have a few words in private with your dad about our selection process."

"Not that I can think of," I said.

"Why don't you go down and wait for me in the lobby?" my father said, resting his hand on my shoulder.

I shook hands with the headmaster and left the suite. On my way down to the lobby, my head felt numb. I was convinced the headmaster had already decided my fate and that the "selection process" was his way of letting my old man know I wouldn't make the cut. Twenty minutes later my father came down to the hotel lobby, where I sat watching manic bellhops run around in red monkey suits and caps, catering to a parade of stuffed shirts and high heels.

"How'd it go?" I asked.

"It went," my father said.

"Whaddaya mean?"

"He wants twenty-one hundred dollars a year."

"I thought it was sixteen hundred."

"Me too. But that's just for day students. The sixteen doesn't include room and board. The guy's gotta be kiddin' me. I told him for twenty-one hundred a year I could clean out the apartment and open my own freaking school."

"Dad, c'mon. You didn't really tell him that, didja?"

"No, but you know ... how about a break? I'm not one of the Rockefellers."

"So how did you leave it?"

"I told him I could do eighteen hundred, eighteen seventy-five tops."

"What'd he say?"

"He said he had to talk it over with the Board of Directors and the Selection Committee and get back to me."

Before we'd arrived at the hotel, I'd felt a tingling of hope, but now everything seemed as if it had slipped down the drain. If I didn't get into Bradley, what would happen? Was I going to be stuck in Bay Haven for the rest of my life?

"You know this isn't the only boarding school in the world," my father said, trying to sound optimistic. "How about a military academy?"

"What?"

"A military academy," he repeated. "It's gotta be cheaper. Plus, you could use a little discipline."

Military academy— I thought for sure the old man had flipped his wig. The last thing I needed was to dress up in a uniform every day and march around saluting teachers like a fucking robot. For a fleeting moment I considered running away from home—stuffing some underwear and socks in a knapsack and hitchhiking across the country to god knows where.

I got up and started to walk away. "Forget it. I'm not goin' to any military academy. I'd rather put a gun in my mouth."

༺

About a week after the interview, my father received a letter from Dr. Farnsworth, written on white stationary with a blue school crest. We were informed that the Board of Directors and the Selection Committee had reviewed my application, and based on a strong recommendation provided by Sandra's thesis advisor at NYU, they were admitting me to Bradley. The school had decided to offer me a special work-study scholarship, which meant that I could attend Bradley as a full-time student with room and board for an annual fee of $1,875, with the provision that I work one or two days a week on a student cleaning crew.

My father didn't have to ask me twice. *Fuck it*, I thought. I can mop floors and empty trash cans standing on my head. Just get me out of here.

THIRTY-TWO

THE FALL SEMESTER would begin in early September of 1964, and Dr. Farnsworth suggested that I come up to school a week early to get settled in along with some other early arrivals, mainly kids who had traveled from abroad.

When Harriet and her mother learned I was shipping out to boarding school, they organized a going-away party. The whole gang was there: Jackie D., Chicken Head Murphy, Big Frenchie, Nicky DeMayo, and Harriet's best friend, Denise Bagliardi. Jackie knew Freddy and Carmine from Lafayette and invited them as well. They all chipped in and got me a present, a brushed-silver name bracelet, with "Johnny C" inscribed on the front. It was the coolest bracelet I'd ever seen.

Connie and George cooked a dinner for me at their apartment and invited Frank and Sandra. Connie also invited our father, who agreed to come but bailed out at the last minute, saying he didn't feel well and couldn't make it. I wasn't surprised. The old man had used the same excuse a number of times in the past when our family had been invited to visit relatives and he was in one of his self-pitying moods. ("I'm gonna sit this one out. Why don't you guys go on without me—I'll be okay.")

"So," Frank said, resting a hand on my shoulder, "you

gonna be all right up there in … where is it?"

"Edgemont, Massachusetts."

"It's in the Berkshires," Sandra said. "A beautiful area."

"I don't know," I said. "I feel like I'm going to Mars."

"Naw, don't worry about it." Frank waved a hand. "You'll be fine. Just act normal. Don't pick your nose in public, keep your hands out of your ass, and when you eat in the dining room, chew with your mouth closed and keep your elbows off the table—you'll fit right in."

It was a Wednesday afternoon around five. My father and I met up with Dr. Farnsworth outside the entrance of the Biltmore where he was moving cardboard boxes from a hand truck into the back of a station wagon. The car looked fairly new, but it was in dire need of a wash and shine: the windows were dusty, and mud had splattered on the hubcaps and the bottom half of the doors.

I had a small suitcase and a steamer trunk jammed with my stuff. Farnsworth helped my father load them into the back of the wagon. "You all set?"

"As set as I'll ever be," I said, eking out a nervous smile.

"C'mon, cheer up," he said, playfully poking my stomach. "Ya look like you're going off to prison, for Godsakes."

"I'm okay."

"Good. I just filled her up. If we hit the road now, we'll beat a lot of the traffic heading out of the city."

Farnsworth shook my father's hand and got in the car, revving up the engine. My father pulled me aside. "I want you to behave yourself up there, mister. No shenanigans. This place is costing me a bundle. You get kicked out of there, you better run under a truck."

"Gee, thanks, Dad. That's just what I need to hear."

I turned to get in the car, and he tugged on my shirt. "Hey, you—" he said, pulling me back. I was sure he was going to hit me with one of his long-winded lectures about keeping my mouth shut and ears open. He put his arm around my neck. "You know I love you, right?" he said, touching his forehead against mine. I hesitated, then nodded. I couldn't help feeling self-conscious. We were practically in the middle of the street, feet away from a parade of slow-moving cars rubbernecking our embrace.

"Huh?" He drew me closer.

I nodded again.

"I'm proud of you, buddy," he said, his voice cracking. "I know you're gonna do well up there."

I couldn't remember my father ever telling me that he was proud of me. I felt like a deaf person suddenly hearing a harmonious symphony for the first time. The sound was foreign and confusing.

"Call me if you need anything," he said, kissing both of my cheeks.

"You 'bout ready?" Farnsworth called out.

"I gotta go," I said.

I opened the door and hopped into the passenger seat. I could feel the weight of my father's anxieties looming over me. I stared straight ahead, but in my peripheral vision I noticed him waving goodbye, his flailing arm begging for my attention. Farnsworth eased into traffic, and I turned and smiled, giving my father a short wave. He smiled back and tilted his head, looking like an abandoned puppy.

"Whaddaya say we shoot over to First Avenue? That way we can get on the FDR Drive up toward Eighty-Seven."

We made our way to the East River Drive and headed north. I didn't have much to say. Farnsworth was a friendly sort, but we had close to three hours of road time ahead of us, and I felt a little uncomfortable being alone in the car with him. We hit a bottleneck up around Harlem where traffic crawled and at one point came to a dead stop. Farnsworth yawned loudly and ran a hand over his plump face and along the side of his head, raking his fingers through a sparse clump of white hair. "You know," he said, slouching in his seat. "I've been in the education business about twenty years." As he spoke, he took his time and peered out the driver-side window, his hand casually draped over the top of the wheel. "I've worked with all types of kids, mostly boys your age and older. Some of them tough, some of them smart, some of them not so smart—all types. And if I've learned one thing, it's usually the kids are not the problem." He paused and then turned, looking directly at me. "It's their parents."

His words caught me by surprise. I could never imagine any adult admitting that, least of all my parents. I was expecting him to say more, but he just continued to look at me, nodding assuredly with raised eyebrows.

We began moving again, and I gazed out at an endless sea of red taillights in front of us. There I was, headed up to a place called Edgemont, Massachusetts, but it felt like I was voyaging to an alien planet located near the far reaches of the universe.

"How about a little music?" said Farnsworth. He turned on the radio and fiddled with the dial for a second or two, settling on a station with a particularly strong signal. I thought I was dreaming. Blaring out of the speaker was Ruby and the Romantics singing "Our Day Will Come." The captivating sound of Ruby's sweet voice filled my ears, and my chest swelled with an overwhelming surge of hope.

"How's that?" he said. "If you want, you're welcome to change it."

"No ... No, it's good," I said. "That's perfect."

ACKNOWLEDGEMENTS

Many thanks to my editors Beverly Ehrman, Philip Elliott, Katie Herman, Paul Hetzler and Ursula DeYoung for their invaluable insights, sensitivity and incredible editing chops.

Thank you to the following literary journals for featuring my writing, and reminding me that—YES, there is light at the end of the tunnel: The Broadkill Review, The Willesden Herald's New Short Stories Series (UK), Adelaide Literary Magazine, and Embark, a journal for novelist.

Also, a big thank you to my buddies Jan Arrigo, Sylvia Parker, Alicia Ralph, and Bill Stein, who graciously plowed through early drafts of my work, and provided me with valuable feedback.

And to Evan *"The Wellerman"* Stein for his great book jacket layout, web design, and tremendous technical support.

About the Author

John grew up in Brooklyn, New York, and lives in Manhattan where he works helping at-risk parolees transition back into the workforce. He's worked as a writer, actor, visual artist, and musician, and has performed in clubs, art galleries, feature films, and Off-Broadway productions. His work is featured in The Broadkill Review, The Willesden Herald's New Short Stories series (UK), Adelaide Literary Magazine, The Writing Disorder, Poetry Super Highway, Across the Margin, and Embark, an international literary journal for novelists.

You can visit John online at: **www.johncalifano.com**

A Conversation with John Califano

After reading Johnny Boy, I was left with a strong sense of what it was like to grow up in working-class Brooklyn in the '50s and '60s. That must have been an incredible experience.

Well, you're probably not going to believe this, but I didn't grow up in Brooklyn. I did a ton of research for this book. I grew up in a small town in rural Pennsylvania, and both of my parents were devout Quakers.

(A short, stunned silence followed by an outburst of laughter.)

Okay, seriously. Brooklyn in the '50s and '60s was a special time and place. People left their front doors unlocked and the streets were filled with kids playing stickball and portable radios blaring rock and roll. There was a real sense of community and many common denominators. Even if you hated your next-door neighbor, you could both agree that the Brooklyn Dodgers and the New York Yankees were the best baseball teams on the planet. Back then, Micky Mantle was a living god who could do everything short of walking on water.

What motivated you to write this novel?

Well, it's a long story, but in a nutshell ... my older sister and I had been estranged for many years. After finally reconnecting and spending some time together, much of our mutual resentment had dissipated.

I had been kicking around an idea for a book, a coming-of-age novel based on my childhood, and my conversations with my sister sparked some new feelings and thoughts. Being able to sit down with her and hash out our differences gave me greater clarity. I had arrived at a place where I was able to see her, and my other family members, as individuals with their own unique perspectives, beliefs, strengths, and limitations. It was truly liberating, both personally and creatively.

Prior to reconnecting with my sister, I'd spent years seeking help and had done a good deal of personal homework. It took me years to fully realize my potential as a human being and as a writer My journey started with a question that gave me pause and opened the floodgates of self-examination: How did I come to act and behave in a manner that was contrary to my personal well-being, and the well-being of others?

Your writing is extremely visual. How did your storytelling style develop and evolve?

As a product of the '50s and '60s, I was fortunate to catch the tail end of live radio broadcasts, which quickly evolved into the golden age of television as the main source of family home entertainment.

When I was around seven and eight, I would lie in bed listening to radio shows like *The Shadow* and *Yours Truly, Johnny Dollar*. These were popular dramas that featured live voice actors and studio sound effects like car horns, creaking doors opening and shutting, footsteps, breaking glass, you name it. The stories were vivid and engaging. But what I enjoyed most was the presentation, which allowed the audience to participate in the narrative. I loved the idea of hearing voices and sounds and being able to interpret and visualize their corresponding images without—as is the case with film—being shown what someone else thinks they should look like. As a kid this had a huge impact on me.

I had a similar experience listening to music and song lyrics. One memorable tune was *Silhouettes*, by The Rays, which was released in 1957 or '58. The story line is moment to moment, and the song has a wonderful melody that is underscored by a steady, suspenseful rhythm. I've listened to that song dozens of times, and in every instance, I was right there on the porch, watching two silhouettes embracing on the window shade. At eight it was breathtaking. It still is.

In my twenties, when I discovered writing, I wanted to do the same thing with words and scenes—not just *show* readers the narrative (as opposed to *telling*), but transport them to another reality via authentic dialogue and vivid characters.

What are some of the books that influenced your writing?

There are many. But at the top of the list, I would have to say, Charles Bukowski's Ham on Rye. After reading his account of growing up in 1930s depression-era Los Angeles, I thought anything was possible. I admired his honesty, and his ability to synthesize and transpose his personal history into a fictionalized narrative that speaks to a greater social commentary about what it's like growing up as a young man in America.

I was also inspired by Salinger's *Catcher in the Rye,* James T. Farrell's *Studs Lonigan,* Richard Yates's *Revolutionary Road,* Harold Brodkey's *First Love and Other Sorrows,* and Richard Wright's unforgettable *Black Boy.*

These are just a few books off the top of my head. The list is too long.

I'm sure you must have heard this question before, but how much of *Johnny Boy* is true to your own life experience?

I love this question.

Why is that?

It's a reader's way of letting me know that my book was perceived as authentic and that the story resonated on a personal level.

Here's the thing. *Johnny Boy* is fiction. Had I intended it to be true to life, I would have written a memoir. I chose not to do that because memoirs are factual accounts. Nothing more, nothing less. Which is totally fine.

My novel is a literary narrative, an amalgam of people, places, and experiences that I've intersected with over the course of my life, past and present. These experiences are uniquely mine. I wouldn't know how to write a story that was detached from my personal life experience. I'm not good at cranking out contrived manipulations, say, a *whodunit,* for example. Some writers are great at that; I'm just not one of them.

What message do you think your book might send to readers?

Messages are not part of my MO. If writers want to

send a message, they should consider using social media where they can shotgun a 280-character Tweet to the world with a tap on their screens.

On the other hand, my hope is that anyone who reads my book is, first and foremost, entertained. I also hope that readers connect with the protagonist on a visceral level, and that the story offers them some meaning as it relates to their own experience, especially young adults.

As a writer, I couldn't ask for more.